CLICK

I0622970

TIMA SMITH

amarok books

CLICK

LILY

CHAPTER ONE

"Well, Anna says, taking a long sip of her peach-mango smoothie, "at least you didn't name *me* after a flower, thank goodness. I guess that's one good thing you did."

Lily looks out the café's big front windows into the too bright sunshine. The glare hurts her eyes, but she doesn't avert them, doesn't even narrow them. It's what she needs right now. A little pain.

"One thing, Anna? I only did *one* thing right?"

Anna shrugs, avoiding her mother's eyes, and takes another long sip.

"Well?" Lily repeats. "Just one?"

She doesn't let these things pass unchallenged the way she used to. All these little pricks Anna sends her way.

"Oh for heaven's sake, Mom, chill will you?" Then she pushes her chair away from the wooden table and stands up. They are negative images of each other. The same delicate bone structure, the same height, the same hair that never stops growing, that can only be controlled by twisting it into a bun or plaiting it into a braid. The first difficult thing Anna ever learned to do. So hard for those small unsure fingers, but she had always been unusually determined. Except Anna's eyes are black-brown to her blue. Anna's hair raven, to her dirty blonde. And Anna's hair is all cut off now, short, spiky, tipped with blue. "Thanks for lunch," Anna says. I gotta go."

Lily nods. "You're welcome. Any plans for the weekend?"

Anna shrugs again. I have a big paper I have to start. And there's some stuff going on ... hanging out. You know."

Lily doesn't worry that the hanging-out will get in the way of the paper. Anna has a well-defined sense of purpose in addition to her determination. Which is probably why this thing between them has lasted so long, become essentially puncture-proof.

She'd thought it was over when Anna announced she'd chosen Mount Holyoke. After all, she could have gone anywhere ... the Sorbonne had been mentioned ... UCLA. Anna is at home in the world after the past four years. But here she is in Western Mass., an hour away from her mother, and Lily had got some crazy idea it was a kind of homecoming.

She sits there for a while after Anna leaves, pushing her napkin back and forth across the trail of moisture from her own largely untouched drink. She should go, too. There's work waiting on her desk. Two recordings to transcribe. And the Bashian project, easily the most boring memoir she's ever encountered. And that's saying something.

But instead of grabbing her bag and going out into that too bright fall sunshine, she sits back and takes a sip of her Peach Bliss, tries to relax a little. And she has to acknowledge that Anna is right about the names. Because she is Lily; her sister, Heather; her mother, Rose; her grandmother, Iris; her great-grandmother, Violet. It did need to end.

Sitting there alone, she discovers that if you avoid the front windows and the too-bright sun a proper set of shades would cure, this is a lovely little café. The plants hanging from the wood ceiling grid are obviously well cared-for, lush and draping. The wooden chair she's sitting in is comfortable with its deep red upholstered seat and back, and the quiet is soothing. Obviously not a place where the student body hangs out. Grad students, yes. She identifies several pecking away at their laptops. And a few professors. A woman about her age in a sheet-metal gray nappy suit and comfortable shoes, a huge lumpy shoulder bag gaping beside her on the floor; two balding men in metal-framed glasses, who get up and walk out together chuckling, each of them with several standard, interdepartmental, grid-printed, manila folders tucked under one arm.

She looks at a man sitting diagonally across the room, his back to the windows, papers spread across the table, eyeglasses sitting low on his nose, good hair that's mostly white, a little too wild and long. Definitely humanities, she thinks.

She looks at the slouch of his shoulders, the way his long legs stretch out beyond the table, ankles crossed, and suddenly the whole place rocks. Her breath goes away and several seconds pass before she can swallow the Peach Bliss in her mouth, before she can carefully lower the glass onto the table before it slides there in a wet heap all by itself.

Christopher.

Gradually, the minor noises around her resume and she is aware of her legs. She pushes her chair back, stands, grabs her bag, and totters, or at least that's what it feels like, out of the place. On the concrete walkway outside, she stops, takes a deep breath, tries to remember if she should go right or go left, if the car is nearby or far. Good god.

A group of students divides itself around her, their voices chattering. There's an eruption of laughter. "Ridiculous," she hears. Yes, isn't it. She hits the unlock on her remote and turns toward the *wick wick*. Her car beckons and she crosses the lot toward it, stands there with her hip against the door, bracing herself. Then she gets in, sits there on the familiar gray fabric with its tiny diamond-shaped pattern, tightens her hands around the familiar circumference of the black, vinyl steering wheel. Christopher.

She looks at the dash clock and watches the digits change: three-thirteen, fourteen, fifteen, sixteen.

Memories roil. Eating peppermint brownies in a rowboat; spilling an entire bag of rice at the Stop & Shop; the time he broke his wrist skating; cracking him up during a Dreiser lecture; the hot fights and the hot making-up; skinny dipping in the lake at night; that way he had of looking at her and turning her insides to jelly.

At three-nineteen, she gets out of the car.

Back in the café, his papers are now in a neat stack and he is scribbling a note on a card. And scribble it is, she knows, remembering how long it took to decipher his writing and how she pointed once to a sentence. "This?" he said, "not legible? Let me see." Adjusting his glasses, because he wore them even back then. "Hmmm ... well ... and then he'd started to laugh. "I have no idea what it says either." Did she love him then? Or did that come later.

She stops beside his table. "Professor?" she says, because the thought of saying his name out loud turns her tongue to wood.

"Yes," he says, without a moment of hesitation, because it's something he's heard a million million times. He looks up at her pleasantly above his glasses, and it's like watching a flower unfold in a four-second time-lapse. Mild curiosity. Recognition. Disbelief. Wonder.

"Lily?" He gets up too fast, hits the table with his thighs. His coffee sloshes and she calms down a bit. So it's rocked him, too.

There are creases now at the corners of his eyes and mouth. But the good looks are still there, and the eyes are still the color of the globe ... topaz and green.

"Lily?" he says again.

He brushes at the wet spots on his pants. She gets napkins. They sop up the coffee on the table, the papers. The flurry of motion helps a little to settle the turbulence in her stomach. "I can't believe it," he says, when they sit down. "I can't believe it's you, Lily..." He looks at her, just looks at her, and suddenly she is feeling senselessly happy. To be alive and to be here and to be with Christopher again.

He shakes his head. "What are you doing here?"

"Well that goes both ways … what are *you* doing here? Last I heard you were in Japan."

"Oh god, Japan was years ago. Ten. Eleven." He leans toward her, almost as though he expects her to suddenly disappear, but if he can keep his eyes on her, then she'll stay. "Lily. Jesus, it's good to see you. Tell me. Tell me everything."

"Twenty years," she says. "You have that much time?"

"Yes," he says, "I do." And she remembers how everything he said sounded like he meant it, because, as she learned, he did.

"It's a little hard to know where to start."

"At the beginning," he says. "From the last time I saw you."

"Ohhh," she says, laughing, "that's a little too daunting. Maybe it's easier to start with now and go backwards a bit." She picks up a brown plastic stirrer straw just to have something to hold onto. "Well," she says, "I have a daughter. She's a freshman. Here. Which is why I'm here today." Is she babbling? Making any sense?

"Here," he repeats, as though what she's said is too much to be believed.

She nods. "We had lunch together just now, and when she left … that's when I saw you." And lying a little … "Of course I had to come over and say hello."

"I can't believe I didn't see *you*. But then, well, you know me …"

"Myopic."

He nods. "Yes. Still myopic. Maybe more so."

He has hardly taken his eyes off her face. That *you are the only person in the world* thing he did, apparently still does. "How is it that I've grown older and you've hardly changed."

"Barely older," she says. "And I *have* changed."

"Very little." He sits back and crosses his arms over his chest, a pose so familiar, it's almost an ache. "A daughter. Any sons?"

She shakes her head. "No. You? Did you finally settle down?"

"Well, I'm settled all right, but not in that way." And then smoothly shifting gears. "Tell me what your work is, Lily. Writing. It *is* writing of course."

She looks down at the stirrer. "I guess you could call it that. I write books for people who can't write them for themselves. It's really more recording than writing."

"But what about *Mackerel Sky*?"

For a second she doesn't know what to say. How long has it been since she's even thought about that book? "You remember it?"

"Remember it? I still have the manuscript. The *half-completed* manuscript. You finished it, didn't you?"

She taps the stirrer on the table, shakes her head. "No, I never did."

There's an uncomfortable silence and she feels a flick of anger. Why should *that*, of all things, matter? How dare he make her feel that *she's* the one who let *him* down.

And so she says the first thing that comes to mind that she knows will sting. "Ancient history," she says. "A very bad novel written by a very young writer who really didn't know what she was doing. About writing or anything else."

For the first time, he moves his eyes away from hers, and she can almost see him weighing it ... whether to take her on or let it pass. But then it was never in his nature to let things pass.

And, sure enough, his eyes lock back onto hers. "A very young writer, yes. But a very good writer. Maybe a potentially exceptional writer. And you're wrong about the book. It was a very good book. And you were so determined, I assumed..." And then he stops and she can see him making a decision to let it go, after all. And of course, why would he not? What can it possibly matter anymore to either of them?

He doesn't say a thing, just looks at her, as though he's trying not just to *see* her, but see *through* her, and she becomes completely unsettled. He takes a deep breath. "Lily, I just want you to know, that I remember our time together as one of the best in my life."

She looks at the window behind him. The sun has moved now, the glare is gone. And so is that inane happiness that had briefly filled her just a minute ago. "What I remember," she says, looking back at him, trying to keep her face neutral, "is that you taught me how to take a punch. And I guess I should thank you for that, because, believe me, it's come in handy."

She senses a small recoil that he recovers from instantly. He glances down at his watch. "I have a quick appointment across campus, Lily. Something I need to sign, and I'm expected in a few minutes. Will you walk with me? We can talk a little. I think we need to do that, don't you?"

Like the glaciers retreating, she feels control slipping away. His walk. His suggestion. But she isn't twenty-three anymore. She can say no. But instead, she reaches into her pocket for her keys. "I can drive you," she says. "My car is right ..."

"No, please ... let's walk. It's a beautiful day. And it won't take long. I promise."

Always the convincer. Almost always his way. *We'll do New Orleans in January...it's the only time I can get away. Let's do the Pattersons, but leave early. Let's have the trout instead of the lobster.* And always, the purist, the skinflint. Why drive when you could walk. Why fly when you could drive. That trip to California. Four days to make it to his orals, and somehow they did. Hardly stopping, sleeping in shifts, buying a bright yellow squirt gun in nowhere Oklahoma. "If I look like I'm falling asleep," he told her, "squirt me in the face." And he had, and she did. And sometimes she did even when he looked perfectly wide awake. "Thanks Annie Oakley," he'd say, letting it drip onto his shirt, "feels good." God it had been so hot. No motels, no showers, no air conditioning. Just driving that endless road with stops for naps and rushed, hot, sticky love in the back seat.

She lets the keys drop back into her pocket.

Outside the café, she feels as though she's experiencing her own personal earthquake. As though those twenty intervening years have vanished and Christopher has just this minute told her, "it's over, Lily. I'm sorry but it's got to be over."

"This is crazy," she says stopping on the sidewalk. "You have things to do. I have things to do. I only wanted to say hello."

He shakes his head. "No. I think you've already said more than that. And maybe it's something we both need. To talk about it."

She sees something she might almost call anguish cross his face.

"I never expected you to simply disappear the way you did," he says. "I waited up all night. You never came home, never got your stuff, never called. And when I talked to your friends all I got was a brush-off. And then I heard you were on the west coast. That you'd taken that job after all."

"Why would I have stayed?" she says, feeling it just as raw and cutting as it had been then. "I mean, really, Chris, you'd already killed us, was there then a reason to dissect us, too?"

"Please, Lily. Let's walk. We may never have this chance again. Please."

As they leave the sidewalk and enter the campus, the trees are still summer green, but here and there, touches of yellow disturb the constancy. The tops of tall complicated roofs break against a slap-in-the-face blue and brilliant sky.

He turns onto a walkway that leads uphill. "I didn't want it to end that way."

"But you wanted it to end," she says. "Exactly what difference did *how* make?"

"No ... it wasn't what I wanted. But at the time, it seemed the only reasonable thing. Before everything and everyone was ... totally compromised."

"Reasonable? How dare you use a word like that to describe what you did? Compromised? What were we, for christ's sake, fucking secret agents?"

He turns to her looking shocked, then bewildered.

And yes, she's stunned, too. That it's all still there. Red-hot and bitter. Locked behind some secret door she'd forgotten even existed. And now the door is open and what she wants to do is exactly what she wanted to do all those years ago. Hit him. Hit him and hit him and hit him until all that terrific festering anger is spent.

"I hated you," she says.

"I can see that."

He is walking surprisingly fast. As fast as he used to, and she finds herself having to skip every once in a while to keep up.

"I even wished you were dead," she says. "Because you weren't feeling even a tenth of what I was feeling."

"How do you know what I was feeling when you never stuck around long enough to find out."

The path goes up and up and all of a sudden she's sure her lungs are going to burst. "Stop," she says, "I can't breathe. Oh, shit …" She puts her hands on her thighs, keeps her head down until the dizziness passes.

"Are you okay?" He puts his hand on her shoulder.

She nods. "I'm very upset. I don't even understand why. And I'm not a speed-walker anymore."

He sighs. "I'm sorry." He points to a small brick building ahead just off the path and leads her to a wood-backed bench. "Wait for me here, okay? I'll only be a few minutes."

She nods and he starts to walk away, stops, turns. "You'll be here? You're not going to disappear?"

She shakes her head. "Unless a handy ambulance comes by."

She doesn't have to look to see his smile. It had been a part of the attraction, the fact she could always make him smile, even in the least funny situations. Always.

She's sweating. Shaking a little. Is it all real or just a bad dream? Or maybe a good dream gone bad. Eventually, her heart stops pounding. She wipes her cheeks and then wipes the sweat onto her capris. She undoes her hair from the elastic and smoothes it back from her face, redoes the pony tail and curls it into a topknot to get it off her neck, fishes in her purse for her wooden hair pin.

"Well, Ollie," she says aloud, "this is a nice mess you've gotten us into."

***

By the time he comes out, she's almost calm. She watches him walk toward her. He would have turned fifty-nine in August. But all the walking seems to have kept him fit, lithe. Not to mention the endless football, basketball, baseball, hockey, though he can't still be doing all that. Still, she can tell nothing hurts. No bad knees or hips. No visible diminishment. Unlike herself, who, apparently, can no longer walk uphill and talk at the same time.

He sits down beside her. "We didn't even manage five good minutes, did we."

"We were never exactly well-mannered," she says. "But we can try for it now. Some amiable chat. I can tell you about my daughter and my cat. You can tell me what you're reading and how Denise is. Then we can say how lovely it was to see each other and go off and try to forget it ever happened."

"Well … I think there is no cat. And as for Denise, there's nothing to talk about. She died a while back."

"She died?"

He nods.

"How?"

"Hit by a car. For some reason she was living in Maine; it was winter. She stepped into the street from behind a snow bank. Driver was in his nineties and had a heart attack right after the police arrived."

"No."

"Yes." He shakes his head. "Leave it to Denise to go out with a peripherally lethal bang, huh?"

For a second, the fact that Denise is dead echoes, and then in her mind she sees an image of Denise trailing all the carnage she caused right up to the end. She chokes back a crazy desire to laugh, which then comes out a snort. "Oh god." She slaps her hand over her mouth. "I am so sorry."

"It's okay," he says, "there were a lot of people who figured she had it coming. Not the old guy, though, that was just sad."

Somewhere far off, she hears the sound of a band. Stopping and starting; playing the same few measures over and over.

"I thought by now," he says, "it wouldn't matter anymore—what happened back then. But I can see it does. And it also matters what you think of me."

"Chris, it's not ..."

"Just be quiet and let me do this, okay?"

As soon as the words are out of his mouth, she is back there. When they spoke to each other from the gut. But it's not the words that make her go silent, as much as the don't-argue-with-me look on his face. This thing they've accidentally fallen into is affecting them equally. She imagines how they must appear, sitting there. Two people trying to avoid each other's eyes. Two strangers who happen to occupy the same bench, and at the same time, know each other to the core.

"Things were very complicated then," he says. "My whole life was imploding. Maybe you remember a phone call and me rushing off that afternoon."

Oh yes, she remembers. Remembers watching him dash off after delivering a death sentence on their future. In a hurry, she imagined, to get away from her. Or perhaps to go off to meet her replacement.

"It was a command performance with the Chancellor, Lily. Not the Dean of the school or the director of the department, though they were involved. My job was hanging by a thread and they were asking me to prove that certain anonymous allegations that had been made against me were untrue.

"Denise," she says.

"Yes. It was something I should have been good at by then. But there was a further complication. The FBI had interviewed me a few days before for an entirely different situation, and the administration knew about that, as well."

She swings her head toward him. "FBI...?"

"Denise." He spits it out. "The academic thing was morals-related, as usual. You knew something similar had happened before..."

She nods. "Yes. But you said it was trivial."

"I hadn't meant to tell you at all, so, yes, I made it sound like nothing. But it hadn't been nothing; it had been a bitch to straighten out. And this time at Yale was worse."

"But the FBI?"

He sighs. "They'd got a tip I was going to kill the President." He glances at her. "Of the United States." He shrugs. "I assumed the Chancellor was going to invite me to leave campus that afternoon. For some reason, he didn't. But he did inform me that my contract would not be picked up the following fall. The thing with the FBI ... well, that ended up being more of a hassle than anything else. But it was before Denise was officially designated a crack-pot, and there was a shit-load of protocol to go through. They didn't take things like that lightly after 1981."

"That's why you were gone so much ..."

He nods.

"Chris, why on earth didn't you *tell* me?"

"Because I made a decision that I wasn't going to take you down with me, that's why. Before I met you I already knew what my life was going to be like. So I'd got in the habit of keeping things light, never getting in too deep. But then *you* came along." He turns and looks at her. "It was my fault, all of it. And I'm telling you this because, better late than never, I want you to know how hard it was for me, too. How much I missed you. And how sorry I am." He leans toward her. "Lily ... I never meant to teach you how to take a punch. Everything I wanted for you was the exact opposite of that."

She sees the look on his face, hears the tone of his voice. Yes. More than anything, he had been the first person to teach her the meaning of cherish. She had been cherished. A rare thing, she would come to learn. Which had made it all the more devastating when she began to sense his going distant. The silences no words filled. Like being at opposite ends of a bridge that had lost its center. No way to cross. No way to get back where she needed to be.

Feeling spent, she leans back against the wooden slats, and after a while, he does, too.

"It's long in the past," he says. "You have a life, and I do, too. It worked out eventually for both of us." He looks at her. "Isn't that right?"

She nods, and they sit not talking while her thoughts tumble. She knows the way he thinks. To him, that unexplained past must have felt like a dissertation that failed to support its conclusion. He's provided the missing information now, so, surely, the thesis conforms to its demands. But that's not how it feels to her. It's still wrong. She just can't get herself to think clearly enough to know why yet.

After a while, he says. "Lily? Are we okay?"

"I guess so," she says, "yes."

Her hand rests on the bench, and he briefly covers it with his. "You sure?"

"Yes," she says, "I'm sure."

"Good." A few minutes pass, and then he says, "So tell me, what does your husband do?"

She has to make herself stop thinking in order to focus on what he's asked. "Financial advisor," she says. "For an international firm."

"And you live in the area?"

"Stockbridge," she says.

"Good town. Your daughter likes it here?"

"So far she seems happy."

"It's a good school, Lily. They take things seriously. And they manage to strike a good balance. The cultural offerings are first-rate."

"I know," she says, "I was glad when she chose it." And now it's her turn to keep this conversation where it belongs. "How about you?" she asks, "you must live nearby?"

"About a twenty-minute walk. And it would surprise you. I have a house. And a car for bad weather. A blue truck. Four-wheel drive." He turns and gives her a 'go figure' look. "The house is small, but roomy by my standards. Got sick of sardine cans, I guess."

She thinks of the apartment over the deli. The two cramped rooms, the low ceilings, the ever-present smells of liverwurst and mortadella, rye bread and garlic. How she'd loved that place. Its warmth and intimacy. The owners, the Picardis, calling out *hello* as she ran up the narrow steps, the apartment door's comforting creak, Christopher's massive hug.

"It's behind a bakery at the south end of town," he says. "Used to be a print shop or a brothel depending on who's doing the telling." Then he takes a deep breath. "Lily … again, I'm sorry. For all of it. It was the best time of my life and I made a complete mess of it at the end. And you didn't deserve it. What you deserved was … something I simply wasn't capable of. And more than anything I'm glad you have that now."

She feels him looking at her, hard, and finally meets the question in his eyes. "Yes," she says, "I do."

For the next half-hour they chat like old acquaintances. About Chris's best friend Steve McNally, who never married Janice, but did marry a girl named Maria and who now lives in Rome. About Christopher's mother, who died just a year ago. About people she remembers and people she does not. About her daughter, who has a penchant for language and math. About 9/11 and where they were and what they felt when it happened.

Then he sits forward, checks his watch. "I have a lecture in fifteen minutes. *Politics in Poetry*, how about that? Today we look at Neruda." He smiles. "Care to sit in?"

"Thanks, but I can't. Maybe some other day?"

He nods. The kind that acknowledges there will undoubtedly be no 'other day.'

Standing, they face each other, and she notices that she feels almost herself again.

"Seeing you is the best thing that's happened in a long time, Lily … I've … well…" He puts out his hand and when she takes it, he pulls her toward him, puts his arms around her, holds her tight.

She closes her eyes and drinks in the feel of him, as familiar as her own skin, drinks it in like a diver surfacing after too long without air.

It lasts not a moment longer than a hug between old friends should, though for a second he keeps his hands on her arms. "Thank you for walking with me. Now I'll be looking for you in all the students who pass by. Does she look like you? Your daughter?"

She shakes her head. "A little. Maybe more like her father."

He nods. "Good bye, Lily."

She watches him walk off, waits for the inevitable turn-around, and they wave. Old friends who have touched each other one final time.

CHAPTER TWO

She heads back the way they came, opposite from the direction Christopher took, back toward her car and her life before this day went completely opposite to all intentions. She takes a deep breath. Now ... where *was* she? There had been Anna, lunch, the usual discomfort. And what had she planned for the rest of the day? Well that was easy ... home, desk, work. The structure of her derring-do life. Except the thought of going back to it after everything that's just gone on feels like a thick gray cloud in her soul.

To shake it, she veers right, onto a path that appears to stretch to a distant sparkle of water. A lake or pond to sit by would be nice.

As she makes her way toward it, she sees him back then, in that gargantuan pool with his arms spread out on top of the water, his face dripping, his wet hair stuck to his forehead.

"But that's crazy," he says. "Everybody knows how to swim."

She looks down at him. "Well. I. Don't."

"Then I'll teach you. C'mon." He holds his arms up to her.

House sitting, somebody's house, she can't remember whose or where. A dilapidated little house, but with a pool out back that was positively Olympic. And a heat wave, she remembers that, too, a hundred degrees for days and days.

Chris had pulled in under the car port, unlocked a door that opened directly into a kitchen. Also dilapidated. "Last man in is a girl," he said, before they'd even carried in their bags, and she watched him hop out of his shorts half-way through the living room, fling his underwear into a plant, charge out the back door and cannonball into that flat sparkling incredibly huge blue surface.

"Jesus," he said, rising out of the water like Poseidon, "even the goddamn water's hot." Then he put his arms out. "But good and wet. Join me."

"I can't." She shook her head. "I can't swim." And then the usual back and forth took place. Except Christopher wouldn't give up.

"I know I can teach you," he said.

"No." She shook her head. You don't understand. It doesn't work. Don't you think I've tried? I'm not a swimmer, Chris, I'm a sinker."

He cocked his head. "That's cuz you're too skinny. No buoyancy. But also no problem." He held his hands out to her, palms up. "I'll hold you. I won't *let* you sink."

She remembers looking into that bottomless blue void and already feeling the pressure of it against her chest, remembers the sun beating down, the heat reflecting up from the cement in waves. Sweat dripping off her chin and down her back, and Chris waiting. *C'mon, you can do it, Lily*. She sees herself eying the perimeter of the surrounding fence—no houses to the left, no houses to the right—pulling her tee shirt over her head, stepping out of her shorts and underwear, leaving her flip-flops on until just before she leaped, feeling scared and giddy and reckless.

She remembers his hands around her, holding her up, their lips touching just under the surface, "like the fish do it," he said.

He'd sung something in her ear while he floated on his back, her settled on top of him like a baby manatee on its mother's stomach. *You must have been a beautiful baby ... you must have been a wonderful child ... when you were only startin' to go to kindergarten ...*

She finds herself smiling, almost still able to feel the touch of their bodies beneath the water, when a girl on roller skates whizzes by, and inside Lily's purse, her phone trills and her real life falls into place. Four o'clock, and Paul is phoning as he always does mid-Friday-afternoon to see if she's running on time or should he pick her up a half-hour later. Paul lives his life by minutes and seconds. But he understands that she loses track when she's concentrating.

She leaves the phone where it is, and after six trills, it stops.

A whole summer they sat that dilapidated little house, swam in the pool, ate watermelon, drank piña coladas, ate a pint of vanilla ice cream on the pool deck every night until the mosquitoes drove them inside.

They painted the dilapidated kitchen sunny yellow once the heat wave broke and Chris fixed all the leaky faucets, laying with his head inside a cabinet while he instructed her to hand him *the red wrench; no, the blue one, oh for christ's sake, just give me a hammer.* He made his famous fettuccini the last night they were there, and they argued over mushrooms versus olives. *It'll ruin it for me if you put those olives in, I swear, Chris, I won't eat one bite. Oh for Pete's sake, Lily, you have the sophisticated palate of a twelve-year-old.* But the olives stayed in the jar.

True to his word, he had not let her sink. And, somehow, he'd taught her how to float.

***

She passes a glass building that looks familiar now. School of Physical Science. The last time she passed it, the glass panes reflected a high yellow sun, and now the sun is low and turning red. Time, she decides, to give up on this walk-about. Besides, her feet hurt in these silly sandals.

She stops to get her bearings and a fallish chill in the air makes her shiver. She's used up three hours of her life walking, sitting by a pond, thinking about things she never thought she'd think about again. But at least she's remembered to send Paul a text saying she's staying with Anna and won't be home until very late. An excuse he cannot complain about.

She makes her way back to the car and realizes she's famished. But she can't go back inside the café, not when she's just starting to come to terms with it all.

For one thing, she's discovered the flaw in Chris' dissertation. Yes, he's supplied his reasons for ending their relationship, but he's left her out of the equation entirely. As though her presence was only under his control; her will, unimportant. Which, in turn, has helped her make several decisions. One of them being that she is an adult. And that everything that happened today is just an illusion. As it was back then.

She was young and pretty and he was hungry for that, for her energy, for this precocious young girl who was essentially a blank slate. And she was hungry, too. For all *he* offered, and willing to take it even over the protests of her best friend, her sister, her mother, even Chris' best friend, who had the balls and the wisdom to come out and tell her it was not in her best interest, and not in Christopher's either. Though she didn't listen to a word.

Chris must have heard his share. Probably more than his share. And some of it he must have told himself. But the two of them were cocky enough to think they'd duck fate, and at least for a while they had.

And then, of course, there was the most obvious thing ... that it hadn't lasted long enough to tarnish; the reason its glow is still intact. Though meaningless. So if today has done nothing else, it has at least released her from a delusion.

She remembers his now-dead mother ... Vera? Valerie? Terminally embittered that her amazing magnificent handsome brilliant son had turned his back on three years of medical school to take up with Dostoyevsky. And who vehemently disliked the young woman to whom she usually referred as *that girl*. That horrible girl who had bewitched her son despite his protestations, his tears, his attempts to flee.

Although once or twice the feisty Mrs. *Valerie* Cheykin, that was it, had actually used her name, called her Lily. But said it as though it were certainly no flower, but a particularly toxic weed. "Don't pay any attention to her," Chris would say. "She doesn't like anybody." But Lily wanted to be liked.

And she remembers the night the rock came through the window above the deli. The shock of it. The splintered glass on the floor. Then a second. And a third. Chris running down the stairs and outside. She remembers snapping on the outside flood when the rocks finally stopped and seeing him there, holding a woman from behind, a woman with long dark wild hair, his arms wrapped hard around her, a woman who screamed and flailed and kept saying over and over, *you fucking son-of-a-bitch bastard you fucking son of a bitch* ...

"9-1-1," he yelled up to her.

She'd never seen anyone taken away in a straight jacket.

And after it was over, she'd never sat with someone who was so obviously suffering.

They'd cleaned up the glass. And then he'd apologized to her and sketched out the facts. Denise: the ex-wife. Condition: manic-depression complicated by other undiagnosed personality disorders. Future: certain to never change.

She'd asked questions: *Where does she live?* He didn't know. *Is she dangerous?* Not really. *How did she get here?* The cops are towing away a car with Arizona plates that might be stolen. *Should you go with her? I mean, to make sure she's okay?* No. Absolutely not.

He didn't want to talk about it; that was obvious. So they'd sat leaning against each other well into the next morning, saying nothing, both of them falling asleep that way on the couch. He'd never talked about it again.

***

She drives around until she finds a diner. EATS flashes red and orange on the roof. Inside, the green and white floor tiles are shiny; every booth has its own table-top jukebox. She orders mac and cheese, a salad, a vanilla frappe. The waitress brings two warm rolls crusty on the outside, soft on the inside, and watching the butter melt as she spreads it makes her mouth water. She doesn't usually eat this way. She hasn't had mac and cheese since Anna was a child. And she can't remember the last time she had a vanilla frappe. Normally, she eats fruit and oatmeal and makes soup. And sometimes she forgets to eat at all.

When everything the waitress sets before her is gone, she sits there, too full to move, looks out the window at a little clothing shop with a sign made of stitched letters, *By Hand*, and eventually she pays for her dinner and crosses the street and goes inside. The hippie-looking girl arranging knit slippers smiles and says hello, and Lily smiles back, takes her time walking up and down the single aisle, picking things up, admiring the materials, the handiwork. Saris and long pleated cotton skirts hang on the walls; colorful dyed scarves, woolen mittens, and socks overflow baskets. Hand-knit sweaters are piled on a table, and that's where she lingers until she chooses a beige, Merino wool pull-over with a zippered high neck and sleeves that come well below her wrists so she can curl her fingers up around the edges or even pull her hands up inside. It costs a hundred and seventy-five dollars and she tells the girl she doesn't need a bag, that she'll wear it out of the store. She's always wanted a sweater like this, and now she has one.

She stops to get gas and asks if there's a bakery nearby. "Yes, Ma'am. Quarter-mile down the road," the polite teenage boy with a nose ring and bright orange hair says, "south," and points. "But it's closed now, ma'am."

She looks toward the indicated direction, but when she leaves, she heads north, toward home, and decides to take the long way. She presses *SEEK* until she finds jazz and turns the volume down so she doesn't have to hear it if she doesn't want to.

She never met Denise, was never closer to her than seeing her in Christopher's arms that night. She hated her then. And now she realizes she hates her all over again. Which makes no sense for many reasons. For one thing, because she's dead. And for another, how can you hate someone you never knew? Especially someone not even responsible for what she did.

But now, Lily knows a little more about what Denise did to Chris. And, in turn, to her. And so for the introduction of chaos into her life? For teaching her doubt, uncertainty, exposing her to the existence of random disaster, hopeless frustration, and tragedy? Yes, maybe for those things she is allowed to hate her.

It used to drive Anna's father mad. What's wrong? I don't get it. Why can't you just enjoy things like other people? Why?" Though in the beginning, before it began to drive him mad, it may have been what attracted him. A mystery he needed to solve. The inscrutable angst of Lily Shea.

And anyway, she *did* enjoy things. She enjoyed Anna all out of proportion. Laughed with her, played, sang and ran. Shared secrets and stories and played make-believe. Taught her how to pump on a swing and ride a bike, how to write her name and tie a bow. Even how to knit. And god knows she certainly loved her. Loves her. Though Anna makes it hard to *like* her now.

Sometimes, in fact, she wonders if she loved Anna too much. Can you love someone too much?

She turns the jazz up. All this thinking is giving her a headache, so she concentrates on driving. But she can't help thinking one more thing before she stops thinking at all. Why are these long-ago moments with Chris still so vivid? So easy to recall. When she has no memory of even one night with David, with her own daughter's father? They had a child together, for heaven's sake, but if she had to swear under oath that he was present for that, could she? And then she tells herself, *enough*!

South Hadley becomes Amherst, which becomes Northampton, which is about to become Florence, when she pulls into an empty parking lot and sits there flicking the key ring hanging from the ignition.

She never saw any hatred in Christopher. Sadness, yes. And she'd been so foolishly certain she could make that go away. Is that what David had tried to do for her?

On the edge of the parking lot, a digital sign rains a shower of brilliant fall leaves, and then a message appears, *DON'T FORGET TO WINTERIZE YOUR CAR.*

Watching the leaves fall to the bottom of the sign, two things in her mind fall into place.

The night someone followed her across campus. A late-night discussion group, everyone going off in one direction, she in another, their voices fading into the night. That edge of the campus always deserted, her own footsteps sounding in the quiet air as she walked in and out of the pools of light from the tall wrought iron lamp posts.

She only sensed that there was someone behind her at first. Fought it. Told herself it was simply imagination. But how many miles had she trooped those walkways without a hint of apprehension, and now the hair on the back of her neck was up, her armpits prickled, her mouth was dry. And then she heard it. Someone else beside herself.

At one point, she felt a rise of anger that made her stop and turn around. To do what, she wonders? Confront whoever it was and vanquish him with her hair pin? And she *had* fished it out of her purse, her trusty wooden poker, the thing that held eight ounces of her hair on the top of her head. But looking behind her, able to see essentially nothing beyond eight feet, a tsunami of fear had overwhelmed her, and she took off running.

She ran until she submerged herself inside the darkness of the deli's side door, taken what felt like an eternity to insert her key and get inside. Then she'd run up the steep steps to the apartment and fallen half-way up.

She remembers a sharp pain in her shin, the door above opening, Chris saying her name, coming down, picking her up and carrying her inside. "Someone was following me," she gasped, as he wiped the blood from her knee and leg. "I've never been so scared in my life."

And then there was the dress. The amethyst polished cotton with the corset bodice and the handkerchief skirt she'd found at the consignment shop for four dollars. It was summer, a weekend concert, and the dress was perfect. She'd washed it in the sink with Woolite, hung it on a hanger from a tree branch behind the deli. She remembers going out to get it that evening and yelling up to Chris, "It's gone! My dress is gone!" But not really gone. Just ripped to shreds ... dozens of amethyst scraps tossed around like confetti.

He'd been quiet, gathering up the pieces, a quiet she'd taken as indifference.

"What could have done this?" she'd asked.

"Raccoons," he'd answered.

Such a pretty dress. And maybe she understands a little better now what he was feeling once her knee was bandaged and she'd calmed down. Once the dress scraps were in the trash.

Of course it had been Denise.

She takes a deep breath, lets it out. Today, her journal, if she kept one, would read *From shock to happiness, from happiness to anger, from anger to reason, from reason to complete uncertainty.* Oh god, Lily, she moans half out loud, you're such a jerk.

The towns reverse themselves, twenty thirty forty-five minutes until she's back in South Hadley. She passes the bakery three times before she pulls into the tight little street beside it and parks across from his house. There are no streetlights, but there is a moon, and it reflects off the pick-up parked there. The house is very small. Painted white, with a peaked roof, and there are lights on downstairs. There are no curtains and the windows are open, and she sees him once, passing from one room to another.

Stalker, weirdo, peeping Tom, idiot. But she needs to do this. See him one last time with clear eyes. It was not, she tells herself, the best two years of her life. It was just two years of her life. He is not the best person she'd ever known. He is just a person, and certainly no knight on a white horse. And he did not love her so well that it has ruined her ability to love anyone else. That's only the way she has chosen to remember it. An excuse for everything that came after.

The downstairs light goes out. Then a minute later, an upstairs light comes on. Eleven o'clock. He doesn't stay up until two anymore. She watches the lit window, and then that light goes dark, too, and she lets out her breath. Isn't it time to go home now?

But she hesitates, and the image of that moment they were caught in the spotlight comes back. Denise and Christopher in the back alley of the deli. An image that has never faded, never grown distorted or fuzzy or hard to recall. It's as clear as if she had just seen it moments ago. And yes, she was frightened and everything was deeper, more richly etched, dimensionalized in a special way. But there was something else beside the fear and the shock. It was the way he held her, crazy out-of-control Denise. Without anger or fear. Without resentment or malice. He held her hard, but he held her gently. And she fought him helplessly. And Lily knew there was still love there. As broken and distorted and catastrophic as it was.

What she did not know was that after that night she would never feel completely happy again.

She reaches for the key in the ignition, hits the windshield wiper instead, and then his front door opens and he's standing there, his white hair moonlit, his face unseeable. He crosses his arms, his legs slightly spread, waiting for whatever's going to happen, and she feels that old heat spread through her, that leap of elation still so inexplicably alive. And just like that, all her fine figuring crumbles.

Nothing makes sense. Except this one thing that stays true, that she can count on ... this feeling pulsing inside her.

She gets out of the car and he meets her half-way. "Lily," he says. Just that. But the way he says it takes her back. To her struggle with the graduate program and her decision to quit. To the time she took her tuition check and bought two tickets to Antigua. To that way he had of stepping out of the role of lover into the role of *magister*.

She holds up one hand. "Before you even *think* of lecturing me," she says, "you need to know a few things. First, I'm not sure why this is happening, but I think it needs to. Second, I don't have a husband. He died about the same time Denise did. Well, he didn't really *die*, but he might as well have. Third, I'm not a child anymore." At this he tips his head down and looks at her over the top of his glasses. "Which," she says, "leads to number four and why I'm here. It's because right now it's where I want to be. And Christopher, don't you dare try to send me away." She wags her finger at him. "You never get to do that again."

Then she steps against him, feels the expulsion of his breath on her hair.

For a second, he does nothing. And then he folds his arms around her and she closes her eyes. There's that fit. The feel and the smell of him. "Let's go inside," he says. "That is, if you're finished with your list."

They walk toward the door wrong-footed, bumping with every other step. He rubs his hand up and down her arm. "Nice sweater," he says.

"I bought it so I'd have something new to wear when I saw you again."

He smiles. He's wearing a tee-shirt. Always hot, while she's always cold.

CHAPTER THREE

"You had a job offer, Lily. A good one. Which you were about to turn down. You were twenty-three, for christ's sake. *Twenty-three*. And instead of moving forward, you were resisting a life that was just getting started in order to tie yourself to mine. To me." He aims a thumb toward his chest. "A guy with this insidious problem that was *never* going away. And if I went down because of it, which was becoming clearer all the time, I was going to take you with me."

He's been pacing for the last five minutes while she sits on the couch, head in her hands. Back and forth from the door to the table he goes, exasperated with her or himself, she can't tell which. He stops pacing and looks at her. "Why would I have wanted that for you. Half my life a fucking nightmare. Is that what you offer someone you love? A fucking nightmare?"

"We could have weathered it."

"Maybe." He looks at her. "And maybe not. I had sixteen years on you, and my sad experience told me it wasn't worth the risk. So for once in my life, I did what I needed to do instead of what I wanted to do."

"But you had no right," she says. "It was not just *my* life and *your* life; it was *our* life. Twenty-three, yes, it's young. But I was old enough to take to bed, wasn't I. Old enough to become part of your life. But you gave me no chance to make a decision about my place in it. You just went and blew us up!"

He starts pacing again, stops. "And what decision would you have made? Truthfully. If I'd given you that chance, what would you have done?"

She looks beyond him at the one piece of furniture she remembers. The bookcase he'd made for her two decades ago. "I'd have stayed," she says.

He nods emphatically. "That's right. You'd have elected to stay. I lost that job, Lily. And three more after that. And each job got shittier and shittier."

"Schools were soliciting you!"

"At first. Yes. But with Denise's help I acquired a reputation. Sure, there weren't a lot of Russian Lit scholars out there, and, yes, I was top in the field. But there *were* always other candidates. And even if they weren't as good and hadn't published as much, at least they didn't have a crazy ex-wife who showed up ranting in the middle of classes or called the Dean to warn him one of his graduate professors was a pedophile or some other kind of deviant. Every damn school that hired me, she was there!" He runs his hands through his hair. "No, that's not true. Japan. That was the only place she never ventured."

"So what I'm hearing is that she fucked you whether I was there or not."

He lifts his arms and lets them fall to his side, turns away, then back to her. "Yes!" he almost shouts. "Yes. She fucked me until the day she died, but she never had the chance to fuck YOU!"

She is suddenly exhausted. They've been doing this for more than two hours. With the exception of the first half hour, which consisted of civilized conversation, of inhaling the atmosphere of the place, of getting comfortable.

But then it came out, in the middle of a sentence that had something to do with the Japanese block print on the wall, the question she's been carrying around all these years, that seemed to spill out of its own accord. *How could you, Chris? How could you do that to me?*

He rubs a hand across his face, glances at the clock on the wall. "Christ, it's after two."

She sighs. "I get it. I do. You wanted to protect me. The thing is, I didn't need protecting. What I needed was for you to trust me." Her voice breaks.

He comes and kneels on the rug beside her, puts his forehead against hers, *Oh baby,* he whispers, *if we could do it all over ...*

She wipes her eyes with her hand. "We could have had little Japanese babies."

"Japanese babies?"

She shakes her head.

"Do we stop this now?" he asks. "Can we say it's over?"

She nods, and they stay there for a while, forehead to forehead.

Then his stomach growls and they both laugh.

"All this getting worked up," he says, "has made me terrifically hungry. How about some eggs? I could scramble us some eggs." Which means he wants eggs but doesn't want to eat them alone.

"Okay," she says. "Bathroom?"

"Upstairs. Second door on the left."

She walks the length of the hall upstairs. First on the right, a tiny room filled with books and boxes in piles on the floor. Then his bedroom, with a bed, a chair, a bureau, some art posters on the wall—a Klimt and a Magritte she thinks—and books and boxes in piles on the floor. She uses the bathroom, and when she looks in the mirror wishes she'd kept the light off. She lets her hair down, tries to runs his comb through it, puts some toothpaste on her finger and pushes it around inside her mouth. Her eyes are red-rimmed, her face pale except for a raw-looking crimson circle on each cheek. She gathers her hair into a pony tail, tries to wrap it into a bun, pulls out the elastic and combs it again. If she's lucky, he won't put his glasses back on until after she's left.

Downstairs, the eggs smell wonderful. And there's an English muffin to split ... *sorry I only had one* ... and orange juice ... *I tasted it to make sure it was still okay* ... and the eggs have a Mexican flair ... *for some reason I had some fresh cilantro*.

She remembers the thanksgiving dinner he cooked for them. The leftover turkey they finally threw away because after four days neither of them could stomach another dried-out turkey sandwich. The apple pie he made from scratch that was so good they ate the whole thing right out of the pie plate in one sitting. The rolls he burned black, and the sweet potatoes he forgot to bring to the table. "Remind me to never do this again," he'd muttered, trying to get the lumps out of the gravy.

"What are you smiling at?" he asks.

"Nothing," she says.

They eat without talking. He finishes first. Two people, she thinks, awash in old and new feelings. She glances at him. He smiles, and she can almost see it, bright-blue and flying, that old electricity zipping back and forth across the table.

He looks at his watch. "Three o'clock, Lily. Too late for you to drive an hour home. Almost too late to even bother going to bed at all."

She feels a rush of heat. "I was just thinking the same thing ... I mean, that it's so late." She has to make herself meet his eyes, although he seems to be having no such trouble, his gaze direct, watchful. Is he waiting for a cue? "But shouldn't we clean up the dishes first?" she says.

"Isn't it our habit to do that in the morning?" He looks at her. "I could always take the couch."

She smiles. "Take it where?"

He shakes his head, stands up, holds out his hand, and they walk toward the stairs.

"You go up and wait for me," she says, "give me two minutes, okay? Just two minutes."

Then she grabs her purse and shakes things out onto a chair. All she has is a tube of hand cream, but that will have to do.

Upstairs in the bathroom, she does the best she can with a washcloth, then sticks one foot into the sink, the other, uses the hand cream on her arms and legs, takes his deodorant out of the cabinet and swipes herself. She tries to tame her hair with her fingers. Butterflies ... when was the last time she had butterflies?

He's in bed when she's finally done. She starts to say, "Sorry, a little longer than..." but stops. His breathing is deep, even. He can't be asleep ... but he is, and she climbs onto the bed, sits there on her knees, looking at him. At the high forehead and cheekbones, the square chin. Still handsome, though in a different way. She touches the thick white hair. He'd already had a sprinkling back then. "It runs in the family," he'd said. "We go gray early. But it never falls out."

She looks at the rugged contours of his face. Still as familiar as her own, touches his cheek, leans down and kisses his shoulder. Then she lays down beside him, pulls the blanket over her.

She looks at the moon-lit Magritte. *The Mysteries of the Horizon*. Three men in bowler hats, each facing a different direction, each with his own crescent moon above his head. Nothing is as it seems. The Klimt is *Nuda Veritas*, but she can see no detail there ... the moonlight doesn't reach.

She listens to his breathing, puts her leg against his gently, draws in his heat and wonders how many times in one's life this kind of sheer contentment is allowed.

***

She wakes to his hand on her stomach. The moon has shifted away from the window. She doesn't move when his hand slides up to her breasts then down, but her breath catches.

"For a second," he says, "I thought it was all a dream." He moves himself toward her, over her, looks down into her face. "Are you a dream, Lily?"

"No," she says, feeling him go hard against her hip. "I'm real. I'm here."

He kisses her, their tongues connect, his hands cup her breasts, his knee pushes her legs apart, and she pushes up against him. Then everything dissolves ... time, thought, self. They are only bodies with hands lips tongues. There is nothing sweet or slow or tender. It's more a battle of desire, a selfish scrabble of sensation and wanting, hunger and satisfaction, a kind of desperation, as though they were both starved and have finally found food. And under the intensity of how they come together, how they try to get inside each other, there's something else, something that almost feels like sorrow. And she does cry.

When it's done, when his weight is pressing against her and she's spent, when the emptiness is met and the terrible longing is over, he whispers *Lily* in her ear, lifts his head, looks down at her. She puts her arms around his neck, and neither of them moves their eyes off the other's, stretching the connection, the re-connection, healing from what they've just done to each other, recovering what had been lost, unwilling to withdraw and become two separate people again.

Finally he rolls to the side and she turns to face him, and he reaches down, pulls the blanket up, covers her, not himself, tucks it around her back and shoulders, because he knows that without his body on hers, she's already cold.

She burrows against him, warm in back, warm in front. "Speak it," she whispers. And without hesitation he growls something rough and guttural into her ear. "What?" she asks.

"What did it sound like?"

"Something obscene and sexy."

"I said, *the dog barks in the field.*"

She giggles. "Say something else."

This time she catches a word she thinks she knows. *Zadnitsa.*

"What," she says.

"I said, *may I feel your beautiful ass.*"

"Yes," she says, "you may." And he does. And then he follows it with a rush of words, and another wave of wanting washes through her. "More," she says, pushing herself against him and they're off again, but this time it's all for her, gentle and slow and he knows the right spots, he remembers. He remembers the right combination of hard and soft, fast and slow, so she comes and then comes again, tiny little spasms that hardly end before another starts. And just when it feels that it must be over, he comes, too, hard inside her, everything in synch—breath, heartbeat, contraction and release, until they are perfectly quiet, perfectly filled with each other.

She lies in his arms holding onto this … this *wonder*, as long as she can. And then he whispers something.

"What," she whispers back.

"I said *Young woman, no more Russian, please. I can't do this again. I may not live through it.*"

She smiles, kisses his cheeks. "Go to sleep." And in seconds, he does. But she waits, fights to keep her eyes open, because this is a time she wants to etch hard inside her, etch so deep into her core that what she feels now, she'll be able to feel again whenever she wills it.

CHAPTER FOUR

When she wakes up, sunshine floods the room and the air is filled with the smell of newly-baked bread. Chris is gone, though she hears him whistling downstairs ... *when my life is throoough ... and the angels ask me to recall ... the thrill of it all ... then I will tell them I remember ...*

She smiles, stretches, turns over and looks at the clock. Eleven? She blinks and looks again. Eleven!

He's left his bathrobe on the bed and she puts it on, takes a tee shirt out of a drawer, along with a pair of pajama bottoms. In the bathroom, she rinses out her underwear and hangs them on the windowsill in the sun. Then she steps into the shower. Her skin feels overly sensitive, too alive even to her own touch, and if she closes her eyes, she can still feel him inside her.

When she gets to the bottom of the stairs, he's pouring circles of batter onto a griddle, still whistling, but something else now ... *it had to be yooou ... it had to be yooou ...*

"Hey, beautiful, I thought you were going to sleep all day."

She lifts her arms toward the ceiling, stretches. "I think I could have. But I missed you." She comes up behind him, puts her arms around him, rests her head between his shoulder blades.

"Me, I've been up since eight. Stared at this woman in my bed for at least an hour, went out and got some syrup, some fruit. And some croissants at the bakery." He flips the pancakes over, then slides them off the griddle onto a plate. He turns around inside her embrace, puts his arms around her, rubs her nose with his. "Good morning."

"Good morning."

She has two pancakes; he has five. He has coffee; she has tea. They split a croissant filled with cream. She peels a tangerine.

"What do you do on Saturdays?" she asks.

He seems to ponder. "Nothing on the calendar I can think of. You know me. Minute to minute." He looks at her. "And you?"

"I keep busy," she says, "but at the moment I can't think how."

"Good," he says. "Then we spend this day together?"

She nods, and puts her hand on his arm. "It was amazing."

He glances at her, his eyebrows rise a bit. "Only because of you." And then he finishes his last pancake. "So," he says, "tell me about your career. Exactly what you do."

"What I do ... well, I get paid to write the stories of people's lives. Their careers, their discoveries. Their ordeals. Or ..." she shrugs. "to be more precise ... how they would like others to see their lives, careers, discoveries and ordeals."

Then she tells him about some of the books, the people. "I used to try to ensure that I had an accurate picture. You know, so the tale would be as it had actually happened. But pretty soon I found out that's not what most people really want. They want to be the heroes and heroines of their lives. So I guess, in a way, I'm still writing fiction." She smiles at him. "Only now I get paid for it."

"You find it satisfactory?"

She thinks about it for a second. "Satisfactory, as in satisfying?"

"No," he says, "they're two different things. Satisfactory is adequate, sufficient, passable. Satisfying is pleasurable, fulfilling. I doubt you find it satisfying ... but you may find it satisfactory."

She folds her hands on the table and leans toward him. I find you terrifically satisfying."

"And I find you evasive."

"Okay. No. The work I do is not satisfying. And most of the time it's not even satisfactory. Though I've encountered a few legitimately interesting lives and I've learned how to write my way into adequate solvency. Would you call *that* satisfactory?"

"I would call it necessary," he says. "And smart."

"I hated that job in San Francisco, by the way. The only thing it had going for it was the three thousand miles it put between us. I hated the editing. I hated the people. I hated the building. I hated the city. I especially hated the trolleys ding-dinging up and down the hills. I even hated the bridge; and, by association, Tony Bennett. But that was mostly *your* fault because you turned me into a bitter, nasty woman."

"As I remember you were already passably nasty when I met you."

She ignores him. "But then I did get over it. Mostly."

"By marrying an MBA?"

"Don't be snide." She nods. "Yes. His name is David. And he was the opposite of *you*. Which I guess was the point."

"But didn't work."

"Not in the least."

"Did you leave him or did he ..."

"You can't leave someone you were never really with," she says. "We just sort of slowly oozed away from each other."

He sits there watching her.

"You know, for a long time," she says, "I thought I'd left most of myself behind with you." She looks around. "You didn't find any of me, did you?"

"You were everywhere," he says. Then, "so you and David oozed away from each other but he left you a daughter."

She nods.

"Tell me about her."

"Anna is terrific," she says. "She's been beautiful and bright from the second she was born. Trouble is, Anna hates me. Don't frown. I'm not being dramatic. It's true. She used to love me and now she hates me and I don't know why and I really don't want to talk about it."

"Okay," he says. "What *do* you want."

"I want us to spend today together. No, the whole weekend."
She leans toward him. "Can you do that? Do you want to?"

"Okay. Yes."

And I want it to slip along. Can we just slip along the way we
used to?"

He covers both of her hands with his. "In any direction you
point."

"Let's start with a walk."

"You do know you're wearing my pajamas."

"I'll put on my capris."

He stands up. "Can I watch you put on your capris?"

She stands up and gives him a push toward the kitchen. "You
have to do the dishes."

Upstairs, she puts on her underwear, still damp on one side;
her wrinkled capris. She finds one sandal, has to get down on her
knees and look under the bed for the other. The sandal is there,
along with a black bobby pin, which she picks up, carries into the
bathroom, and leaves on the sink, where he'll see it. Then through
the window, his voice floats up from below ... clearly, then not
clearly, turning away from the window, then turning back.

... sorry ... something's come up ... thanks ... yes ... call you ...

She puts her hair into a ponytail, plaits it into a braid.

"Ready?" he asks, when she comes downstairs. He's holding a
football, asks the question 'should he bring it' with his eyebrows
and she nods.

"Ready. Yes."

They head away from the college, step off the main road onto
a path to what he calls 'the pines.'

"Everything okay?" he says, after a while.

"Yes. Why?"

"You've gone quiet."

"I guess it's all starting to dawn on me."

"As on a May morning or a November fog?"

She doesn't say anything. And then she can sense him figuring it out.

"I had a thing tomorrow for dinner. I canceled it. Should I not have done that?"

She still doesn't say anything.

"She's an adjunct. I've known her for a while. She's a friend."

Lily nods. "It isn't any of my business. And I shouldn't be able to waltz in and disrupt your life. And, dammit, it shouldn't bother me."

"Lily." He grabs her arm. "For christ's sake, will you slow down?"

"It's all crazy," she says. "I mean, this time yesterday we were completely unaware of one another, last night we're like dogs in heat, and now you're canceling your life, and I'm pissed about something I have no right to be pissed about. What in hell are we doing?"

"We're dealing, Lily. With what happened. With what's happening. Isn't that why you came?"

"Yes. I just didn't realize it would include a ticket on a rollercoaster."

"Well you don't just snap your fingers and have everything miraculously fall into place. We have decisions to make. We can do this. Or we can let it go. We can walk around joined at the elbow for the rest of our lives. Or we can fit each other in now and then. Or we can do a dozen things in-between. And twenty-four hours into it probably isn't the time to decide."

"I hate it when you're like this," she says, walking on ahead of him. "You and your goddamn rationality."

"You want me to be *ir*rational??"

"I don't want to be the only one acting out, Chris. I don't *do* that anymore. I've been a completely sensible person for twenty years, and now I don't even recognize myself. Look at me! I'm furious over something you have every right to do and I have no right to even complain about. I'm going off half-cocked for the first time in ages, and I seem to be the only one doing it!"

"Look," he says, grabbing her hand and making her face him. "Historically, and I use that word with intention because I'm moving painfully close to a century, and that plays into this, too, you know ... *historically*, giving in to what I *feel* like doing has not always worked well. And I don't want this to turn into just another fuck-up."

"And you think I do?"

"Is that what I said?"

"Oh, I suppose I've just committed a ... a qualification fallacy or something."

"Quantification," he says, "and it's actually syllogistic."

She looks up at the sky and lets out a yell.

"You need to calm down," he says.

"Yes, I do need to calm down."

They walk without talking, and after a while he takes hold of her hand and she lets him.

They are surrounded as far as she can see by pine trees. Some reach into the sky, while a nursery ranging from seedlings to six-foot juveniles creates a solid mass of green on both sides of the trail. Every once in a while the smell of Christmas saturates the air.

"This is lovely," she says.

"I'm sorry," he says. "What I did back there. It's just. Christ, it's like you go direct to my spine."

"Tell me what she looks like."

"Who?"

"The person you have a date with tomorrow."

"*Had*," he says. And it wasn't a *date*. I think I'm a little past *dating*."

"Okay. Assignation. Tryst. Rendezvous. Whatever ..." She stops, looks at him. "Say it in Russian, *date*."

"Not a *svidaniye*," he says. "We were having dinner."

"*Svidaniye,*" she repeats, letting it roll slowly off her tongue. "My mother called you a playboy."

He laughs. "That's a word I haven't heard in a long time."

"She may have said gigolo."

"She believed you were *supporting* me?"

"She wasn't into definition. She just thought you were a run-of-the-mill womanizer."

"Me?" he says. "A rake?"

"You *were* kind of a wolf."

He lifts his face to the sky and howls. "Stop," she says, pushing at him, laughing, and then he points straight up and they stand there watching one, two, three hawks wheeling above the pines.

He takes her hand again and they walk.

"Where is your mother?" he asks.

"In Florida. She married a nice man who collects bird nests. We don't see each other very often. I think motherhood wasn't really her calling, and once Heather and I were more or less on our own, she pretty much gave up on it."

"And Heather?"

"Heather lives in Haiti. She runs a clinic there."

"So she did it, became a doctor. Good for Heather. I liked her. She was authentic. Though I think she thought somewhat less of me."

"She thought there was a good chance I'd get hurt," Lily says. "But she also understood. She told me once if she had the guts and the opportunity, she'd have done the same thing, because even though you were risky, you were worth it."

"They both misunderstood," he says. "They thought *I* was the risk, but the risks were in the circumstances. In reality, I was completely risk-averse when it came to you."

"You don't have to convince me," she says, squeezing his hand. "What other people thought didn't matter then and doesn't matter now. But you haven't answered my question."

"Question," he says, tossing the football up and catching it a few times. "Oh, right … what does she look like. Well, I'm ashamed to admit she's pretty much of a hag. Eighty-five if she's a day, bunch of missing teeth, and her nose goes in several different directions." His hand zigzags in the air. "Does that make you happy?"

"It would if it were true."

He sighs. "She's an average-looking woman who will be sooner than later receiving a monthly check from SSA."

"Age-appropriate then."

"Very. Unlike you. And speaking of you … you're a part-time nun, I hear?"

"Essentially," she says, "most of the time."

"Well," he says, "considering the nunishness and then considering last night, you've certainly managed to keep your game intact."

She looks straight ahead. "Do you speak Russian to her?"

"I've only spoken Russian-when-horizontal to one person in my life. This pain-in-the-ass woman I love named Lily." Then he stops, and she stops, and he pulls on her braid until she's looking up at him. "That's the thing. I love you. Always have. Always will. We were apart for a very long time. We both had lives. Work and play. But for me, the play?…" he shakes his head, "just encounters, Lily. Just passing time with someone beside myself." He looks at her for a second. "That playboy your mother talked about? He was really a one-woman man. And that woman has always been you. You, and only you." He lowers his face until their foreheads touch. "Do you believe that?"

"I think, down deep, I've always believed that."

They get to a clearing in the pines and he starts to pop the football up in the air again. "Long one?" he says.

"I haven't caught a football in ages."

"Me neither. We'll practice and get good again."

He stays where he is and she walks out into the field, glances back at him, knowing he must be thinking of it, too, the first time.

"Hey," he'd said, tossing the football in the living room and just missing the ceiling every time. "Want to learn how to throw?"

"I think I know how to throw a ball," she said.

He held it up, wagged it back and forth at her. "Not a football, I bet."

He took her outside and showed her how to hold it, where to place her fingers, how to hold her wrist, her elbow, how to follow-through. She loved his seriousness, his concentration. "It'll be hard at first, but you'll get it."

He tossed the first one to her from ten feet away, a high, slow ball that she caught easily in both hands.

"Good catch," he said, "now throw it back."

And she did, soft and easy and straight as an arrow, and he only just managed to catch it, too surprised to react quick enough.

"You know how," he said, accusing her, laughing, running backwards to open more space between them. Back and forth they went, high loopy throws, straight hard throws, sometimes both of them laughing too much to make a proper catch, until his last throw, intentionally too high for her, over her head and hard, as though he didn't think she could fall back and jump. Which she could.

"Okay," she said, "that's the last one. I'm not dislocating my shoulders for you and your male athlete ego thing." And she'd hugged the ball to her chest.

"C'mon, couple more."

"No. I said no and I mean it."

And then he'd started at her. A run. And she'd yelled "Don't you dare ... don't you dare tackle me," and tossed the ball away and took off running, too. But his stride was two of hers, and the small back yard held them in circles, and he was fast, and when he grabbed her she went down, still yelling *Don't!*, like a sack of rocks.

"You FUCK!" she'd yelled, as soon as she got her breath back. And he'd rolled her over. "What did you say?"

"I said, you FUCK!"

His face was six inches from hers and he'd stared at her for a split-second before kissing her so hard and so long that her lips had felt bruised the rest of the day.

She called them his *cave-man moments.* They didn't come often, but often enough to be named. And she could feel them form and grow like lightning. Something in him that was still sixteen-years-old and out of control. *You can do this*, it whispered to him, *because you're bigger than she is, stronger, faster. And you need to show her and show yourself.*

He never hurt her, and it was always in the guise of a game. *I can hold you down and tickle you til you cry. I can pick you up and carry you there whether you want to go or not.* And she was always the one who started it by not giving in or by refusing to cooperate. Usually, he just shrugged and let it go. But every once in a while, he didn't, and fell straight into the stone age.

"You didn't have to break the guy's hand," she remembers half-yelling at him, turning to face him as they crossed the quad toward home. So mad she shoved him, made him lose his balance and almost fall. And then she walked away.

Hey," he said, catching up and putting himself in front of her so she had to stop. "I was getting you out of a situation. That guy had his hands all over you and you're mad at *me*??"

"I was handling it," she said, walking past him. "I wasn't yelling for help. And then you charge in and break his hand! Who the hell do you think you are?? Rambo?"

A party, getting late, everybody feeling a little too high, and this drunk lecturer, who'd gotten more stupid and more bold as the night went on, had cornered her when she came out of the bathroom and backed her against a wall. Leaned in to her, breathing his whiskey breath all over.

"Leave me alone," she said.

"Oh I like a girl who protests."

"I'm going to count to three."

He laughed. He put his hand on the front of her dress. And just as she was getting ready to knee him good and hard, Chris was there, throwing the guy against the opposite wall, grabbing his hand, forcing him down to his knees.

"You could have let him go," she said over her shoulder, as she walked away. "You didn't have to break his hand. You ... you ... Neanderthal!!"

They'd made up. They always made up. And they'd spotted the lecturer a few weeks later with his wrist still in a cast. She knew Chris wasn't feeling guilty or accountable or even a shade of sorry about it. Was, instead, quite convinced his actions had been entirely what the situation required. As far as he was concerned, he'd done what he needed to do and saved his woman. His cave-woman.

But today, walking out into the field, Lily knows he won't tackle her, won't throw a ball he thinks she can't catch. She's pretty sure that's out of him now, now that he's finally a grown-up. Though if he thought she were in trouble? He might still do something stupid. And, she supposed, slightly magnificent.

The two of them are rusty at first and have to chase the ball too much, but after a while they fall into a rhythm of easy throws, solid catches.

"Anna knows how to throw a football," she calls to him.

"I bet," he calls back.

"And a baseball."

"Why wouldn't she with a mother like you."

And then after a while, she says, "My hands hurt."

And he stops mid-throw. "Mine, too,"

The rest of the way, he tosses the ball up and catches it and whistles. First, *Walkin' My Baby Back Home,* and she sings along when she knows the words ... *arm in arm over meadow and farm ... we stop for a while, she gives me a smile ....* Then when he gets to the end, he starts *They Can't Take That Away From Me*, and she knows it almost all the way through because she's watched *Shall We Dance* at least a hundred times. *...the way you wear your hat, the way you sip your tea, the memory of all that, no no they can't take that away from me....*

CHAPTER FIVE

They skip lunch, decide to drive to her place for dinner, stop in Lenox on the way and visit the Edith Wharton house, where the gardens are still in full fall color and the Wharton library is once again intact.

"Lily Bart," he says. "Not a bad heroine to share a name with."

"If I remember," Lily says, "the poor naive thing committed suicide. She believed in love and paid the price."

"True. Okay then, how about Lily Briscoe?"

"Remind me."

"Woolf. *To the Lighthouse*. Artist. Alive and well at book's end. Having discovered that her art is her passion."

She lifts an imaginary toast. "To Lily Briscoe."

"No," he says. "To Lily Shea."

***

When they reach her driveway, she stops and grabs her mail from the box, and when she parks in front of the house they sit and look at it, which makes her see all its problems in high definition. The roof that needs replacing, the peeling paint, the sagging gutters.

"The realtor advertised it as a *get-away cabin*," she says. "Which of course means that everyone wanted to get away from it."

He looks at her, then back at the house. "It was affordable?"

"Very."

"Then you're on you own. I mean, no help from Anna's father."

"He's offered. I'd rather take care of myself. And anyway, we had something bigger and nicer, Anna and I, while she was growing up. But then she left and I couldn't stand echoing around there all by myself. So I found this."

"She left?"

"I'll tell you," she says, glancing over at him, "just not right now." She looks back at the house. "It's nicer inside, you'll see. And some day ..." She smiles. "Want to hear about my dream house?"

He nods.

"It's a perfect little Stickley Craftsman," she says, using her hands to help paint the picture, "with a full, open, front porch supported by tapered columns on stone bases, and maybe a gable, but definitely a central second-floor dormer ... three windows wide ... with stained glass in the upper panes. And inside, the first floor is completely open, the wood trim is all unpainted gum wood, and the ceilings have exposed rafters and beams. Oh," she adds, "and a fireplace," she smiles, "have to have a fireplace."

When she glances at him, he's looking at her with a smile she can't quite define. "Silly," she says, "I know. Anything to keep the rain off should do."

"And this," he cocks his head toward the house, "does that?"

She laughs. "Most of the time."

For a while, they sit there not talking, and then Chris says, "Lily?"

She looks at him.

"There's something you need to know, need to think about. Before we go any further." And then he stops.

He's not a person who's ever at a loss for words. Doesn't have trouble addressing things. She reaches for his hand, thinking *Is it too much to ask? A little stretch of uncomplicated time to make up for all the time we didn't have.* She steels herself. "What?" she says.

"It's been a long time since back then," he says. "I guess it's occurred to you that not everything might be the same. I mean me. Not the same me." He clears his throat. "I'm not..." his hand moves in a *how do I say this* half circle. "I'm not, you know, that *thing* you used to call me..." He makes a face that shouts discomfort.

She struggles to know what he's saying, what he's *not* saying … what she's not understanding … *what she used to call him what she used to call him*. And then she gets it. And along with it, a flooding sense of relief. "Every-night-Chris?" she says. "Is that what you're talking about?"

He frowns. "Yeah. That. I'm not that anymore." He shrugs. "I mean, last night. That was pretty exceptional."

For a second, she almost wants to laugh. Such a small thing in comparison to what she was expecting. "Is *that* the reason you think I loved you?" she says. "Is that what you really think?"

He shrugs. "It probably helped.

"Maybe. A little." She pulls his hand up to her lips, kisses his fingers. Strong fingers, long and perfectly-shaped. She holds his hand against her cheek for a second. "Is it something like … every-year-Chris, now?"

He smiles, turns toward her and puts his hands on either side of her face. "A little better than that, I think."

"Oh good. Because I really was considering throwing you back."

He smiles. "Lily, oh Lily," he says, "how have I managed without you all this time."

***

While Chris, yawning, stretches out on the sofa, she changes her clothes, sees what's available for dinner, all the while feeling about as light as she's felt in a long time. The sun coming through the windows is brighter. The colors of the fruit in the basket on the kitchen table seem to pulse. And when she glances at herself in the mirror, the woman looking back seems to have a perpetual smile on her face. Pretty soon she can hear him snoring.

She pulls a bag of frozen spinach out of the freezer, opens a can of artichoke hearts and two cans of tomatoes. There's sour cream in the fridge, fresh parsley, green onions, garlic, ginger. She lines up the bottles she'll need … soy sauce, rice vinegar, hot chili oil. She'll start with a roux and make a creamy vegetable hot and sour soup. And while it's cooking, she'll put together a salad and make biscuits—he always looked ridiculously happy when she made biscuits. And for dessert? She finds a jar of pears, drains them, arranges them in a baking dish, pours on some brandy. Ice cream would be nice, but there is none, so a sprinkle of brown sugar under the broiler will have to do.

She takes down some of her good plates, sets the table with candles, wine glasses, cloth napkins, doing it all to the comforting, regular sounds of his sleep from the couch.

She opens a bottle of red wine and sets it on the table. Two hours, done.

She kneels beside the couch and watches him sleep, then presses his arm. "Chris."

He opens his eyes. "Don't tell me I did it again." Then he lifts his head off the cushion and kisses her on the mouth. "Something smells fantastic."

"Hungry?" she asks.

"Starving. But I should go soak my head and wake up first."

"You only have time for a two-minute soak. Dinner's ready."

He swings his legs off the couch, kisses her on top of the head. "Be right back."

They eat in almost total silence, except for when he says, "You've learned how to cook. Aced it, I'd say!"

The silence has an agreed-upon feel to it. So many words already exchanged. Time for getting used to each other again, to the way he holds his knife and pours the wine; the way they look at each other across the candle flame; the way his being there shrinks the table. All of it familiar and strange. And the way she has to keep saying to herself, *he's here, he's really here*.

He eats an enormous amount of food. Offers the last pear to her and then eats it himself when she shakes her head *no*.

"There's a little screened porch out back," she says. "It's nice sitting there at night. The sounds of the tree frogs and the crickets."

They clear off the dishes and leave them in the sink. She gets a comforter, offers him half on the porch, and when he declines, settles it around herself.

"Remember that Christmas in Lubec?" he asks.

"With no heat, no electricity, no water, no bathroom? Oh yes, I remember. Though most of the houses you picked lacked at least some of those things."

"My shoes were frozen to the floor in the morning."

"And the outhouse door was frozen shut so I had to pee in the snow."

"You were cute peeing in the snow."

"And then you made that enormous snow man," she says, laughing. "I bet it was still there in July."

He puts his hand over hers. "We had fun, didn't we."

"Even when it wasn't fun, it was fun."

For a while, they're quiet.

"Do you ever play the trumpet?" she asks.

"Not in a long time."

"I don't have a piano anymore. No room."

"I don't usually fall asleep during the day like that."

"Well, you didn't get much sleep last night, did you."

"The nap was unintended."

"We've been under a strain." And then she yawns and giggles. "I don't usually giggle."

He puts his arm around her, reaches under the comforter and feels around in an exaggerated way until he finds her hand. Which makes her giggle again.

"You can keep your dinner-date tomorrow," she says. "If you want. I don't mind. Really. Earlier, well, that was a kind of momentary madness."

"Why would I want to have dinner with someone else when I can have dinner with you." He leans his head against hers.

"Chris ... we should take it one day at a time, right?"

"Probably. In case my attraction suddenly pales."

"Meaning your attraction to me or mine to you?"

"My attraction to you will end when time does. Maybe not even then."

Not so far away, an owl hoots.

She presses herself against him. "How could we have done it, Chris. How could we have wasted all those years."

"We're here, baby. Let's just focus on that."

When they go to her room, they undress in the dark, he on one side of the bed, she on the other. It takes her longer, and when she turns around, he's standing there watching her. "Hey," he says.

"Hey."

In bed, he brushes his lips against hers, that light-as-a-butterfly kiss he always starts with.

"What happened to not-every-night-anymore-Chris," she says.

"He seems to have found some kind of steroid named Lily."

"Do you know what I want tonight?" she says, feeling about as satisfied as she can imagine.

"Tell me."

"I just want you to hold me."

So that's what he does.

***

The next morning, they both seem to open their eyes at the same moment. Early. After the best night's sleep Lily can remember in a long time.

"Hi," he says.

"Hi."

"I like your wall."

"It's Anna growing up."

"You're there, too," he says. "Where's her father?"

"I really didn't want him in my bedroom," she says. "Besides, he wasn't around all that much." He pushes her hair off her cheek. "Anna loves him. They talk. More than she talks to me."

"You said she left."

She moves away to the edge of the bed, ignoring the *you can't keep putting this off* look he gives her. "I have to pee."

When she comes back, he's already up and gone. "Coffee?" he calls from the kitchen. "In the freezer," she says. She pulls a tee shirt on and joins him. "It's hard to talk about," she says, taking a box of coffee filters out of a cupboard and setting it near the coffee maker. "And I want this weekend to end on a high note, okay? Not with my sad failure as a mother."

"Can't imagine you a sad failure at anything. But whatever you say."

"Right now I want to show you something, so bring your coffee into the living room when it's ready."

She opens a drawer and lifts out albums and manila envelopes full of photos until she finds what she's looking for at the bottom.

She sits on the couch, opens the small white album, and when he comes in with his mug, says, "Come. Sit."

"It's us," he says, turning the pages. "We were quite the couple, weren't we."

"P-Town," she says, pointing to him climbing a rocky ledge. Then to one of her in a polka-dot bikini."

"I remember that," he says, leaning against her. "That was one dangerous bathing suit. As I recall it tied on in five minutes and untied in five seconds."

She laughs, turns the page.

"Niven's party for that visiting jackass?" he says.

"He had no idea we were a couple."

"Maybe not the first time. What about the second?" He turns the page. "Guy was a prick. Probably still is."

"I hated those parties," she says. "No one was nice."

"That's because the men were jealous and the women knew it."

And so they go through the pages. Chris in the Olympic pool. Lily sitting on the edge of the Olympic pool. Chris hamming for the camera outside the deli. Chris and Lily in front of the Lincoln Monument. Lily at her desk studying, chin on hands, hair in a long braid down her back. Chris playing basketball, playing football, playing hockey, running the bases. Chris and Lily all dressed up for something. Chris eating an ice cream cone. Lily perched on a fence. Lily standing on the seat of a motorcycle, arms in the air. Lily and Chris together on the motorcycle, her arms tight around him. Chris retreating from the camera on the motorcycle.

When they get to the end, he closes it. The back cover is blackened, the vinyl melted at the center. He rubs the scar with his fingers. "I threw it into a fireplace," she says. "When I got to San Francisco and was unpacking. But then I changed my mind and grabbed it out. Burned my fingers, too." She holds up one hand, points to a white mark on her thumb. "See that? That's your fault."

He takes her hand, kisses her thumb. "Can I try to make it up to you? *Vse dlya vas?*"

He puts his hand on her thigh and slides it slowly up. This time she doesn't have to ask *what?* She remembers what it means. *Everything for you.*

The first time he'd said it, she'd tried to say it back. No, he'd said. *Vas* is *you*. If *you* say it back, then it has to be *da, vse dlya menya*. *Yes, everything for me.*

"But I want it to be everything for you, too," she said.

"But that's not the idea. Besides, I thought of it first."

So she'd tried to say it … da, *vse dlya menya* … but all it had done was make him laugh.

What," she'd said, "why are you laughing."

"Because I think you just said something in a completely different language."

But, oh yes, she remembers *Vse dlya vas* … although it hardly ever ended that way. Like the other night. And just thinking about it, she suddenly gets very wet.

***

In the kitchen, he makes himself a fresh pot of coffee, throws the cold cupful he never finished down the drain. She puts cereal bowls on the table, spoons, milk, cuts up an apple and stirs the oatmeal.

Their bowls are still half-full when there's a knock on the kitchen door. They look at each other. "Company?" he says.

She looks down at her tee shirt, which is inside out and too short, runs into the bathroom and grabs her robe, comes back, opens the door a crack. "Paul!"

"Lily, good lord! I've called a hundred times since yesterday morning. Why didn't you answer? I even tried to call Anna, but the school wouldn't give me her number."

Her phone. Dead, of course. The last thing on her mind these forty-eight hours.

"Are you okay?" He steps inside. "Are you…" He stops when he sees Christopher sitting there in his tee shirt and boxer shorts. And she figures they might as well be wearing signs, she and Chris, WE JUST HAD WILD INCREDIBLE SEX ON THE COUCH.

For a second no one says anything, and then Chris holds up his mug. "Coffee?" he says to Paul.

What follows is three minutes of exquisite discomfort.

"Paul, this is Chris. Chris, Paul."

Chris sticks out his hand. "Excuse me if I don't get up," he says. "Usually I try not to meet people in my underwear." Then he folds his arms and sits back, as though it's a play and he's just bought a ticket.

"Chris is an old friend," she explains. "We ran into each other. Yesterday. Unexpectedly."

"Old old friend," Chris says. "And now we're having breakfast. How about some oatmeal? Juice?"

Paul backs toward the door. "Thanks, no. I ...I was on my way ... somewhere ... else."

"Paul," she says, "I'm sorry. I should have ... it was really sweet of you ... I ... bye," and she closes the door very gently, as though that will somehow help. She stands there looking at Chris.

"He your Father Superior?" Chris says.

"Oh shut up. That was horrible. And *you* were horrible. He's a nice person and he didn't deserve that."

"Maybe not, but he walked right into it. What were we supposed to do? I guess you could have introduced me as your father. I'd have gone along."

"Stop it, Chris. It's not funny. He *never* comes here without calling first. He never does *anything* without calling first."

"As he said, he *did* call. About a hundred times. I'd have done the same thing. And considering he said he's been trying to get you since yesterday morning, I think he showed a good degree of discipline." He shrugs. "Or maybe a lack of sufficient concern. I would have been here after two hours. Maybe one."

She goes into the living room and comes back with her purse, takes out her phone and plugs it in near the stove. She taps her bare foot on the floor until it comes on, then checks for messages, groans.

"He did call a hundred times." She shakes her head. "Literally. But none from Anna, thank god."

"Lily ... he's a grown-up. You'll talk to him. He'll get over it."

"Would *you* get over it?"

"Absolutely not. I'd lay odds you'll never see the guy again."

"You shit," she says. "You *do* think it's funny."

"I am not a shit. It's simply a matter of perspective dependent upon one's relationship to it. Paul will probably never see anything funny about it. You will, but it will take a while. Me? Okay, yes, funny. And convenient. Because it saves me from having to punch the son-of-a-bitch in the nose."

"Chris!"

He stands up. "Lily, twenty years ago I was a complete asshole. I may still be an asshole, but no longer a complete one. I made a big mistake. And you were right, I should have trusted you. So as of this moment I'm hereby reclaiming my position in your life. No waiting to see how things work out, no testing the waters, no slow disentanglement from other entanglements. Standing here in your kitchen in my underwear, I hereby pledge thee my troth. And I'm talking about that in an according-to-Hoyle manner." He takes a step toward her. "Lily Shea ... will you marry me?"

CHAPTER SIX

Driving back to his house, she tells him about Anna, because he has insisted she invite Anna to dinner at his place on Thursday so he can meet her and she can meet him.

Lily is terrified to even think of it.

"She won't come," she tells him. "And even if she does, she'll either act as though she couldn't care less, which I would prefer, or she'll stalk out and never speak to me again."

"I think she'll come," he says, "and I think she'll be civil. Because unless you've developed a habit of introducing her to a new guy every week, she'll at least be curious. And I assume you taught her manners."

"She has excellent manners. And the only man she's met in a decade is Paul. But she didn't seem to much like him. She's terrifically judgmental."

"Bet this will be different."

"Oh yes," she says, "you and your melting manner."

"It's always worked on you."

"You have no idea. She won't be charmed and she probably won't be charming. So I hope she does come. Because it will serve you right."

"Don't you think it's time to tell me," he says, "because I'd like to know exactly what happened to those two smiling faces in all the photos on your wall."

For a second, she tries to gird herself, then ends up plunging in. "David and I split up when Anna was three," she says. "We agreed he'd see her at least twice a week and have her every other weekend. But she was very young and she was her mother's girl and she wasn't happy going off with a father she hadn't seen all that much even when we were together. So for a month it was once a week, for very short outings, a couple of hours at a playground or lunch with her grandmother. But he'd always traveled a lot on business and she had to be worked into his schedule and she wasn't always in a mood to go off. So it quickly became once a month, and from the time she was five to about fourteen, they saw each other twice a year."

"Twice a year," Chris repeats.

"He wasn't happy about it. It's just the way things worked out. And he was generous. To both of us. Anna never lacked for anything. And then right after she turned fourteen, he stayed in the states for six months, made a real effort. They got to know each other. If she didn't exactly love him, she liked him a lot."

"And that was good."

"Yes. She seemed happy. He seemed happy. And then he wanted to see me one day. He said he had to go back to Paris for an extended period and could she come with him. For as short or as long as she liked. He was hoping for the school year, but if she got homesick in twenty-four hours, he'd turn around and bring her back. She'd have wonderful experiences, see a little of the world, become fluent in French. And also he thought he deserved it. *You've had her all to yourself for ten years*, he said, *can I please have her for nine months?*

"And you said yes."

"At first, no, I didn't. I couldn't possibly imagine sending her off for such a long time. She'd gone to summer camp for a week the summer before and I'd had a hard time with *that*. And the thing is, *she* didn't want to go. I actually talked her into it while I was trying to talk myself into it."

"So she went."

"Yes. And when she got to Paris, we talked on the phone every day, sometimes several times a day, and at first she was not happy. After she told me she wanted to come home for the third time, I talked to David and he begged me for another week, and then a week more. And she did stop asking to come home. She began to like school. She made friends. Her father took her skiing in

Switzerland and boating on the Mediterranean. And even though I kept calling every day, after a while she didn't seem to have much time to talk. Then the school year was over and I said I would come and bring her home. That's when she said she wanted to stay. I flew there anyway, but I barely saw her; and when I did, it was as if she'd become a stranger. Distant. Cool." Her voice wavers ever so slightly.

Chris puts his hand on her shoulder, waits before he says … "When did she come back?"

Lily shakes her head. "She didn't. I've seen her eight times in the last four years. My turn to see her twice a year. And I'll tell you, it was completely devastating." She takes a deep breath, wipes at her eyes.

"Why don't you pull over. I'll drive."

"No, it's okay. I'm okay." She takes another deep breath. "So when she said she was coming here for college, I thought, well, maybe it's over. Now we can pick up where we left off. But it's as if she hates me. We can hardly have a decent conversation."

"And what does her father say about it?"

"He says he tries to talk to her, but she just shuts him down. I keep in touch. I invite her to lunch or to go shopping, and sometimes she says 'yes' and sometimes she says 'no.'"

"And when you bring it up —this problem between you— then what?"

"She refuses to talk about it. And then says 'no' to my seeing her at all for a while."

They drive a good two miles in silence.

"Let's go ahead and do dinner on Thursday," he says, "see how things go."

"Meaning if they go badly we won't tell her about us, or there won't *be* an us."

He turns toward her. "Lily, there's nothing that's going to cancel us. Nothing. And I think Anna did come home. But four years is a long time at that age. Maybe it's just going to take a while to set it all straight."

She nods, stares at the road ahead. God knows, she wants to believe it, that Anna's come home. But aside from the fact that she's physically an hour away, there's precious little proof that it's true.

After a while Chris says, "Remember Josh and Maryann Mayo?"

She thinks for a second. "The couple who were pregnant?"

"Yeah," he says. "It became a habit with them. Six kids. In six, seven years."

"Six little Mayos, one right after the other? Poor Maryann."

"No, she did fine. And they were cute as hell. But with a maximum sell date of about ten minutes, at least when they were all under ten. But, of course, they did grow up and eventually they had six teenagers. I hadn't seen Josh in a while—they were out west, I was down south—and then one day he was at my door. Seems he'd run away from home."

"Josh?"

"Josh. The three oldest were girls, pretty like their mother, and he couldn't stand the fact they'd gone from thinking he was Prince Charming and Superman rolled into one, to barely acknowledging his existence. Once he started talking about it, he kept asking why they seemed to hate him."

"They really hated him?"

"No. But they'd stopped laughing at his dumb jokes and didn't want to go everywhere with him the way they always had. He kept asking, *How did I turn into someone who's a complete embarrassment to my own kids?*"

"And you were wise and counseled him and sent him home with a new way of looking at things, of course."

"Hell no. I didn't have a clue. I took him to a bar, we got drunk, he stayed overnight and went home the next day. But he did call me a couple of years later, and when I asked him how things were going with the kids, he said he'd learned not to take it personally."

"So you're telling me I should try not to take Anna's attitude personally."

"Well, if you suddenly started to hate me, I wouldn't take it personally."

She laughs. "You're ludicrous."

"It's my sworn duty."

"To be ludicrous?"

"To try to make you laugh when things aren't all that funny."

"Yes," she says, "that's true. It is your duty."

She exits off the highway, thinks about this day that's almost over now, that easily feels like two days, so much has happened. She thinks about their making love on the couch, which would have set the day off in italics all by itself; thinks about the photo album, the two of them so confident in each other and in the life they would create together. Thinks about Chris standing there in her kitchen, barefoot and earnest, saying ...*will you marry me, Lily Shea, will you marry me,* and a little of the feeling from that moment comes back—all bubbles and glitter. And then she remembers Paul, and cringes. Oh god, poor Paul.

After a while, she says, "October twentieth. That's our date, right?"

He nods. "That's the one we settled on."

"It's not even two weeks away, Chris. Just thinking about it gives me the he-be-gee-bees."

"Does that imply second thoughts?"

"No. Never. It's just that I have so much to do."

He hesitates, says, "As in?"

"Well, I have to buy a dress and I'll need shoes. Actually, what I need is a whole trousseau. And then it takes time to pick out a silver pattern, you know ... china, cookware. I have to register it all. And there's the invitations—we haven't even talked about who we're inviting, but I can think of twenty-five people right off the bat. And a caterer to arrange. Flowers. Music..." She falls silent, knowing that at the moment he's fairly certain she's not serious.

"How do you feel about a single cello?" she says. "Just quiet in the background. Wouldn't that be lovely? Don't you think it would?"

He makes a noise, half-grunt, half-agreement, and now he doesn't know quite what to think, does he.

She lets him wallow for almost a quarter-mile, admiring the way he's taking it. Not a word. Not even a sigh. And then decides to let him off the hook. "That," she says, "is for asking Paul if he wanted oatmeal, and for unnecessarily pointing out that you were in your underwear. But mostly it's for enjoying it all so damn much."

He lets out a sigh. "You little snake," he says.

***

The next morning she leaves just after dawn. He's already up reading student papers he should have finished over the weekend. She bends down and puts her arms around his neck. "I'll see you Thursday," she says.

"I won't be home until after five, but if you want to get the marriage license, I'm free from twelve to two. And the door here, it's always unlocked."

"I don't even know your schedule."

"If I'm not with you, I'm in class. If I'm not in class, I'm with you."

She laughs. "I'll come early on Thursday and start dinner. I mean, even if Anna won't come, *I'll* be here."

She gives him a kiss; he rubs her leg.

Before she closes the door, he says, "Lily?"

She looks back at him from across the room.

"I liked hearing you upstairs this morning. Getting up, getting ready."

She smiles, blows him a kiss.

***

Just before she gets into Stockbridge, she calls Anna. Seven-thirty, she'll be up and showered. An early bird since she was a toddler.

"How was your weekend?" she asks.

"Okay."

"Anna ... after we had lunch on Friday, I ran into an old friend. He teaches in the Graduate program there."

Silence.

"He'd like to meet you and since he lives practically on campus, I thought I'd make dinner for the three of us on Thursday at his place. Anna? Can you come?"

"And why do I want to meet him?"

"Well, he and I knew each other a long time ago. We were actually together for a while, and we've re-connected. I'd like you two to know each other, Anna. Besides, it wouldn't hurt to have a good faculty contact, would it?" She can hear Anna tapping on her computer. "Anna?"

"How am I supposed to get there? Wherever it is."

"I'll pick you up at your dorm. Five-thirty?"

"I guess."

"Okay. Great. See you then." She hangs up, exhausted by the three-minute ordeal. But there's a difference now. Because no matter what happens or fails to happen, she has this new buoyancy in her life. This thing that wasn't, and now is.

λ

She spends the next three days catching up on laundry, working on the Bashian memoir, trying to finish two other smaller projects, sending e-mails, answering e-mails, wondering if she should phone Paul and then deciding not to, because what is there to say? She spends too much time mooning, runs every day to try and get herself focused, but it doesn't work, and she doesn't sleep well, either, keeps waking up and then can't stop thinking.

By Wednesday night, she can't stand it. Her work isn't flowing, and when she reads what she's written, it's just awful. She spends half-an-hour arguing with herself; wins, then loses and tosses some clothes into a bag, along with her lap top, and starts for South Hadley around eleven.

By the time she gets there, it's after midnight and the house is dark. She lets herself in, deposits her stuff on the floor at the bottom of the stairs and goes up barefoot, feeling like a kid waking up on Christmas morning.

He's asleep, a motionless mound under the sheet, and she drapes her clothes over a chair and slides in beside him as quietly as she can. She lays there, not moving, ridiculously happy. And then he rolls toward her, throws his arm over her, says in her ear, "Are you absolutely determined to never let me catch up on my sleep?"

"No," she whispers. "I want you to sleep. I just missed you, that's all. Go back to sleep."

"No Russian?"

"No. No Russian." And pretty soon his breathing is deep and regular again.

She is warm. His arm protects her. *Daragoj*, she says under her breath, *moya daragoj*. That one she remembers. *My darling*.

CHAPTER SEVEN

Something wakes her very early, too early to get up, she thinks, but then she opens her eyes, and Chris is there in the thin gray light from the window, up on one elbow, watching her.

"Sorry," he says, "I wasn't trying to wake you."

She closes her eyes. "What are you doing?"

"Just looking at you. Go back to sleep."

"Can I ask a question?"

"Sure."

"Who are you?"

He doesn't say anything for a second. "Just a guy who wandered in."

"Is that a habit you have?" she murmurs. "Getting into a strange woman's bed and watching her?"

"Only if she's very watchable."

"And that's all you do?"

"Sometimes. Other times I do this." He kisses her neck. "Or this." He kisses her lips. "Or this." He pulls back the blanket, kisses both her breasts, makes her shiver.

"I have a fiancée, you know," she says, "and he'll be back in just a few minutes."

"Great. Because a few minutes is all I need." He rubs his lips across her nipples, takes one in his mouth, then the other, and, beneath the blanket, sides his hand between her legs.

"Are you going to ravish me?" she whispers.

"Oh yes," he says, pressing with his fingers until she moans.

"Do it," she says, "oh Chris, please please do it."

***

When she wakes up again, he's gone, the sun is bright along the wall, and for one glorious moment, she feels a sense of compete bliss. She tries to hold onto it, knowing it will fade slowly away, but also knowing the cause of it was no dream. It was real. It was Chris. And she knows she can have that feeling now whenever she wants.

She stretches, and her arm touches a sheet of paper on his pillow. She squints at the words. *Quite fine, was it not? Repeat performance at your command. See you at twelve. Our place.*

She reads it again, smiling, tucks it under her pillow, and then remembers that it's Thursday, and tonight Anna comes for dinner.

Almost instantly, ninety-nine percent of her fragile bliss evaporates. But she tells herself that even if everything that happens in the next twelve hours is less than what she wants, at least she's had this rather extraordinary feeling that still lingers just a bit.

She showers, dresses, then sends Anna a text that she'll be waiting outside the dorm at five-thirty, and after a half-hour, when she hears nothing back, assumes dinner is on and goes to the grocery store. She'll make stuffed mushrooms for an appetizer, then a tomato and goat cheese frittata served with a salad and garlic sweet potatoes. And for dessert, Anna's favorite, blueberry pie á la mode. She buys a good bottle of wine, paper napkins, and a bright yellow mum for the table.

At twelve o'clock, she picks Chris up at their café. "You sure you don't want something for lunch?" he asks, getting into the car with a brown paper bag in one hand and a coffee in the other.

"No," she says, "thanks."

"You look in a bit of a twist." He puts his coffee in the holder.

"I think that describes how I'm feeling rather perfectly."

"Not about where we're going..."

"No." She puts her hand on his leg. "Not that. Tonight. About tonight."

He takes his sandwich out and unwraps it. Holds half out to her. "Hummus … your favorite. One bite?"

She shakes her head.

"I predict it will be fine. She wouldn't be coming at all if things were hopeless between you." He takes a bite. "You've developed a slant toward pessimism, Lily. Try seeing tonight as a potential success instead of a potential disaster."

"I'm afraid to. This whole thing with Anna so blind-sided me. I'm afraid to count on anything anymore." Then she looks at him, smiles. "Except you. I'll count on you."

"I would hope."

"Go ahead. Eat your lunch."

As she drives, she thinks about what he said. Pessimism. Yes, he may be right, and wonders when it became a habit.

He chews, points ahead. "That brick building up there on the left." Then he says, "Maybe Anna feels exactly the same way."

Lily pulls in and parks. She looks at him. "She got blind-sided, too?"

He takes a sip of coffee, pops the last piece of sandwich in his mouth, then opens his door and gets out first. They look at each other over the top of the car. He doesn't say anything, just gives her a look that says *think about it*.

The town clerk slides the marriage license form across the counter and Lily fills out her portion and signs it, then slides it to Chris, who starts to fill out his side, stops, turns it toward Lily and taps her side. "What's that?" he asks.

She looks. "That's my name."

"Your name is *Cranfield*?"

"Yes. David's name. And Anna's name. And my name."

"You're Lily *Cranfield*?"

The clerk, Lily notices, has taken on a sense of heightened attention. "Yes," Lily says.

"How did I not know that?"

"I guess we never got around to it," Lily says.

"And now you want to be Lily Cheykin?"

"Isn't that the idea?"

"Well, yes, but you want to take my name?"

"Would you rather I didn't?"

"No."

"Would you rather I kept David's?"

"No."

She gives him a look that gets him back to filling out his side of the form.

When he's finished, he passes it across the counter to the clerk, who gives him a pleasant smile. "Are you Professor Cheykin at the college?" she asks, and when Chris says he is, she tells him that her daughter was in his class a couple of years ago and just loved it. "She still thinks you were one of the best professors she had," she says.

Chris thanks her and tells her to give her daughter his best. "Now everybody in town," he says, once they're outside, "is going to know that Professor Cheykin is marrying a woman whose name he doesn't even know." Which sends them on a laughing jag that lasts until he's given her his last wave goodbye as he starts up the hill to his office.

***

Lily's fine until about four o'clock, but by the time Chris comes home at five-fifteen, she's a complete wreck.

"You want me to pick her up?" he asks.

"How will you know her?" she says, slamming the refrigerator door. "You've never seen her and she's never seen you."

"Her face is exactly like yours," he says, "And her hair. I'll know her."

"She's a dark brunette with blue tips like half the girls on campus and her hair is very short now. She cut it all off in France. You'll pick up the wrong girl."

"Like I do that all the…"

"*Please*, Chris. I'll do it. It's *fine*." And then, on her way out of the kitchen, she tries to kiss him on the chin to say *sorry for the sharp tone* but misses and gets his shirt instead. She runs out the door, gets in the car, and then has to run back inside for the keys. Chris looks at her but doesn't say a word.

***

She and Anna are half-way up the walk, when he comes out the door to greet them. It was a short and mostly silent ride, except for the abrupt stop Lily made when they pulled in next to his truck that made them both lurch forward, as though putting on the brake was a new and strange experience for her. "Jeeze," Anna said, as Lily mumbled *sorry*.

He comes down the steps, holds out his hand. "Anna, it's very good to meet you. I'm Chris." Anna shakes hands and says, "Hi."

So far so good, Lily thinks.

"C'mon in," Chris says, and as they follow him up the steps Anna looks at her and lip synchs the word *old* with a look that gives it an exclamation point.

They go inside, and Lily's mouth is so dry she knows not a word will come out. But then Chris takes over. He seats Anna, asks her if she wants a ginger ale, which Lily has stocked up on, and keeps the conversation going, asking questions about school, classes, professors, which cafeteria she eats at.

Lily, perched on the edge of the couch and wishing she could relax even a little, says, "Well, I guess I'll go finish up dinner," which neither of them seems to hear, and then flees into the kitchen.

After five minutes or so, Chris comes in. "Everything okay?"

"Great," she says, and hands him a plate of stuffed mushrooms, which he takes back into the living room. She hears him say, "I'll get some napkins." He comes back to the kitchen, and while he's opening the napkin drawer, he calls into the living room, "So, Anna, is your dorm haunted?"

Haunted? Lily thinks.

"Haunted?" Anna says.

Lily looks at Chris.

"You're in what dorm?" he calls out.

"Howland," Anna says, sounding a little hesitant.

"On, no problem then." He marches back to the living room as Lily watches, wondering what in hell he's doing.

"Howland," he says, "was haunted a couple of years ago. So it wouldn't be haunted again this quick. It'll be a different one. Maybe Benson or Clarke."

"I don't get it," Anna says. "Why are the dorms haunted? Haunted by *ghosts*?"

"Just one dorm. And yeah, as much as anything can be haunted by ghosts. I mean, there's no such thing, right?"

Lily hears her hesitate again. "Right."

"But it still happens every year. Then the frats put together a ghost-busters team and do an extermination."

"It's all a joke," Anna says.

"Of course. But a good reason for a very big party on Halloween."

"I hope Howland *is* haunted," she says.

"Well, it only takes one person to say she saw a ghost."

And they both laugh.

The conversation in the living room keeps going, so Lily concentrates on the frittata, the potatoes, the salad; and when everything's ready she starts to carry things to the table. "Dinner," she calls, and they stroll over.

"I can't believe you did that," Anna says, looking at Lily.

"Did what?" Lily says.

"Sit here, Anna," Chris says. "I was just telling Anna about the first time I saw you at Yale."

"The first time?" Lily says, "and that would be...?"

"The *very* first time."

"Oh," she says, "*that* time," and she goes back to the counter for the salad but brings only the salad forks and leaves the bowl on the counter.

"So," Chris says, "we got something like four feet of snow by morning, which closed down the whole campus —no classes, no nothing— and I got my skis, cross country, and went out that afternoon and saw something going on near one of the grad dorms. I'm skiing along, trying to figure out what it is and then I see bodies jumping out of a second-floor window. When I get closer, I see one in particular. Skinny girl, bare naked like all the rest, with this amazing long braid..." he points up to the ceiling, "that stands straight up in the air as she jumps and falls into the snow."

"Oh my god," Anna says, and snaps her head from Chris to Lily. "Mom, I can't believe you did that! How come you never told me?"

Lily shakes her head. "I can't imagine," she says, looking at Chris in a way that just might make him die.

"So," he continues, "they were going into the showers, getting all heated up, and then leaping into the snow." He smiles at Lily. "Very Swedish."

"I only did it once," Lily says.

"Good thing. Because the more kids that jumped, the more the snow got packed down and froze into ice. One of the last jumpers broke his leg."

Lily glances at Anna, who is looking at her as though she's not really sure it's Lily sitting there.

"And the second time I noticed her was in a lecture when she reproached me for having indecipherable handwriting."

"She *told* you that?" Anna says, and Chris nods.

"All I did," Lily says, was tell you I couldn't read one word. One."

"Right. 'I can't read one word,' is what you said."

"Chris! What I said was *one* word, just *one*."

"Okay, Anna ... if someone says to you that she can't read one word you've written, what does that mean to you?" and Anna laughs. And then Lily has to laugh, too.

"Course I didn't recognize her from the blizzard. Since in the lecture she always wore clothes. The braid, though, I recognized that when she turned around and walked away."

"We shouldn't let our frittatas get cold," Lily says.

He puts a forkful in his mouth. "Mine's nice and hot."

Anna nods. "Mine, too."

"This tastes great, Lily," he says, and Anna murmurs agreement, while Lily notices that she seems to have lost all sense of taste. "When I first knew her," he says, "your mother could make three things. Macaroni with butter and salt, oatmeal, and really good biscuits."

"I grew up on those," Anna says. "Especially the oatmeal. Every single morning of my life."

"Hardly," Lily says. "I seem to remember pancakes and eggs and even an occasional omelet."

"I don't," Anna says. "Just oatmeal."

Chris gets up and retrieves the salad from the counter, fills the salad bowls. "It's pretty good oatmeal, though, isn't it? I just had some the other morning."

"So ... are you still liking your classes?" Lily asks.

Anna shrugs. "They're okay," then says to Chris, "it's the cinnamon. She uses a lot."

And so it goes, through dinner, a bottle of wine, dessert and after. Anna talks about Paris, more than Lily's ever heard. And she and Chris discover they both learned to enter the Louvre via the less crowded *rue de Rivoli* entrance and often ate at *La Frégate* across the street.

"Anna's thinking of majoring in languages," Lily says.

"Fluent in French ... any other?" Chris asks.

"Not fluent in Spanish, but I get by, and I'm taking Mandarin Chinese, if I can hack it."

"Chris speaks Russian," Lily says, and then can't let herself look at him.

"I grew up in a multi-lingual home," he says. "Russian was almost exclusive within the family."

"I know *bol'shoye spasibo*," Anna says.

"Nice pronunciation, and *dobro pazhalovta, you're welcome.*"

They smile at each other, and Lily can only wonder how he's done it. How he's won Anna over in less than an hour, when she herself can't even begin to.

Chris tells Anna about the time they went to the Jersey shore and stayed in a summer house a friend had offered.

"You mean, summer *shack*," Lily says. She tells Anna, "Chris was famous for never paying for anything, so the only way we went anywhere was if the *anywhere* was free. And at the Jersey shore, *free* meant holes in the walls instead of windows and no indoor plumbing." She looks at him. "Why is it almost everywhere we went had no indoor plumbing?"

"There were no mosquitoes," he says. "The holes in the wall let in fresh air." He smiles at Lily. "And all the water in the world was just…"

She smiles back, "…a block away," they say in unison.

"And if it hadn't been for the fire," Chris says, "it would have been a pretty decent week."

Anna's eyes go wide. "Fire?"

Lily says, "Well, if it hadn't been for the fact there was no electricity, we wouldn't have needed candles in the first place." She looks at Anna. "That's what started the fire. But it was just a little fire. Hardly any damage."

"Yeah," Chris says, "my stuff got burned. Her stuff was fine. That's why she calls it *little*."

"And then there was the cabin in Maine," Lily says, "again no plumbing, an entire population of mice, mosquitoes with teeth…"

"Those were black flies," Chris says, "not mosquitoes."

"…a porcupine as big as a bear…"

"Which was a heck of a lot more scared of you than you were of it." He looks at Anna and laughs, "though she *was* pretty scared of it." He looks back at Lily. "There was also that lake. With a full moon shining across it every night. And the loons."

"Yes." Lily nods. "Those things did make up for everything else."

"You were always a good sport," he says. "I could always count on you making the best of a bad situation." Then he looks at Anna. "But I guess you know that about your mother better than anyone."

Anna frowns a little, like she's searching for an answer, then one seems to hit her and she nods. "Yeah, I guess she is. Like the time I was supposed to go to a sleepover, but my friend who was giving it had to cancel at the last minute. So Mom said we could have it at our house instead." She looks at Lily. "And you let us make chocolate chip cookies even though it was almost midnight."

"I was cleaning flour off everything for a week."

"But you didn't yell at us. All the other mothers always started yelling at a certain point."

"Did you have French sleepovers?" Chris asks.

Anna shakes her head. "No. Our place was too small."

Lily gets up to take the ice cream to the freezer before it completely melts, and when she comes back, she finds Anna watching her again, a look on her face impossible to decipher.

"And we used to go to Nova Scotia every summer," Anna says, "remember, Mom?"

"I certainly do."

"We went to a place called Lunenburg," Anna tells Chris, "and we always stayed in a house that was painted the color of a fire engine."

"Mrs. Fabaret," Lily says. "She was the owner and she was always baking things for us."

"Dirt cake," Anna says. "It was the best cake in the world." She looks at Chris. "Lots of ground-up Oreos." She laughs. "And she had a ton of cats."

Chris says. "I guess you liked it there. In Lunenburg."

"We loved it," Anna says. "And we saw the northern lights once. Mom and I put up a tent on the beach, because they said on the news the lights might be visible that night." She looks at Lily. "And I fell asleep, but you woke me up so I didn't miss it."

"Gaff Point," Lily says, looking at Chris, who doesn't say anything. Then she says to Anna, "we always came home with thirty pounds of beach stones, thanks to you. We used to put them in the garden, remember?" Anna nods. "Maybe," Lily says, "we should go back sometime. To Gaff Point."

Anna shrugs. "Maybe."

Chris has coffee. Lily and Anna have tea. Chris tells Anna how to avoid Professor Harrison's customary first-semester 'C' (speak up in class and know at least one fact about Diderot), and Anna tells them that she's getting a ski pass at Berkshire East and can't wait until it snows, which makes both Lily and Chris groan. Then, suddenly, it's nine o'clock and Anna says she has to go. But Lily had never expected it to last even this long.

"I'll drive Anna back to the dorm," Chris says. "I need to pick something up anyway," and he leans down and gives Lily a no-argument kiss on the cheek. "Be right back."

Lily looks at Anna. "See you soon?"

Anna nods, and for a second nobody moves. "Give your mother a hug and let's get going," Chris says, moving toward the door.

And miracle of miracles, Anna does.

CHAPTER EIGHT

Lily has everything cleaned up by the time Chris comes back.

"That took a while," she says.

He holds up a brown paper bag. "I stopped at the Packy's. Thought you could use a highball to calm yourself down." He takes out a bottle of Jim Beam, pours a nip into two glasses and adds a little water. Then he hands her one glass, takes her hand, and leads her to the table. "She's a great girl," he says, sitting down.

She nods, sits across from him. "Tonight was very good," she holds her glass up to him, "mostly thanks to you."

"It wasn't hard." He drains his glass in one swallow. "I was right. She has come home. It's just that it's been four years, a long time, and neither of you knows how to bridge it."

"She told you that? About coming home?"

"She didn't need to, Lily. It's obvious. You're afraid and guilty, and Anna's angry because you let her go in the first place."

"She told you that?"

"I said she didn't tell me anything. It's in your faces, your body language, the way you speak to each other. You walked in that door looking like some up-tight, apprehensive, guilt-ridden shadow of yourself, and Anna walked in with a chip on her shoulder and no idea what to make of you. It's like she doesn't know you anymore."

"I didn't *make* her go," Lily says. "I didn't *want* this to happen."

"I know. And maybe at some level she knows that, too. But the fact that she gained a father doesn't quite make up for the fact that she feels she lost her mother."

"But she didn't lose me."

"She probably thought she had. I sent you away for what I thought were valid reasons, and you were twenty-three and kept a grudge for twenty years. She was fourteen. Why would you expect more from her than you would from yourself?"

She doesn't know what to say.

He stands up, leans across the table and kisses her above her nose, right between her eyebrows. "Talk to her. Give it time. And relax. You're really two peas in a pod, you know. Stubborn, outspoken, curious." He looks at her. "And now you've got those same worry lines you used to get." He kisses the spot again, stands up.

"And a tension headache to go with them." She rubs her forehead.

"Well, sweetheart," he says, "you handed *me* one hell of a surprise tonight. Because to tell you the truth, I didn't know you had it in you."

"Had what in me?"

"Mothering. All that ... *mothering.*"

She sips some of her whiskey. "What are you talking about?"

He goes back into the kitchen. "You don't know you do it?"

"Do what? Chris ... what do I do?"

"*Is the frittata okay, Anna? Is it too hot? Can I blow on it for you? Oh no, now is it too cold? Here, I'll heat it up. Are the mushrooms the way you like them? Maybe they need more cheese? If the ginger ale glass is too heavy I could hold it for you...*"

"Chris!" She gets up and follows him into the kitchen. "I never said any of those things!"

"*Can I cut your frittata for you? Does it need salt? Are you sure it's not too salty now?*"

He glances sideways at her, teasing, smiling.

"Christopher!" She puts her hands on her hips. "Remember the other day? When you said you weren't a *complete* asshole anymore...?"

"Okay, so maybe you didn't actually *say* the words, but it's in everything you do, every look you give her. And actually, it's kind of nice. A part of you I never got to see. I'm glad I got to see it." He starts up the stairs, looks back at her. *Can I chew your potatoes for you, Anna?*

She grabs a towel and goes after him, flicking it at his legs.

"Ow. Jesus, Lily, that hurts."

"Good," she says, "because you deserve it. And what about that thing *you* actually *did* say ... *just had your mother's oatmeal the other morning.* And that story ... who tells a daughter their mother jumped *naked* into a snow drift???"

He stops half-way up the stairs, looks down at her over his shoulder. "Someone who's trying to get her to see the Lily you really are. Feisty and fearless and fun." Then he grins. *"Can I carry you back to the dorm, Anna?"*

"You shit." She chases him up the stairs and down the hall, laughing now, but he's fast and gets into the bedroom, half-closes the door on her and holds it there. She pushes as hard as she can, both of them laughing, but he won't let the door budge. "Lose the towel," he tells her, "and then maybe I'll let you in."

"You're a horrible awful dreadful maddening person," she says.

"And you don't have a headache anymore, do you."

No. She doesn't.

She tosses the towel. He opens the door.

"I don't want to go back to Stockbridge anymore," she says.

"Good. Because I don't want you to. We'll get your stuff this weekend."

She nods, and they put their arms around each other.

"Bit of advice?" he says.

"Do I have an option?"

"No." He says it quietly, against her ear, holding her, rocking her a little in his arms. "Try to do things as though the last four years never happened. Just be the mother you were when she was fourteen. That mother came through tonight and she was fantastic."

Lily is suddenly very tired, and she lets herself relax against him, lets him hold her up. It's something she'll have to work on, in addition to everything else, letting him take over when she's too tired to hold the world up all by herself.

"You took her to Gaff Point," he says.

"Every summer."

"Did you ever think of us?"

"Every summer."

After a while, he starts to hum softly, the two of them swaying ever so slightly, and she feels herself swimming into sleep, knowing he'll get her to the bed, cover her, that he'll always take care of her when she needs taking care of.

...it had to be you, it had to be you ... I wandered around and finally found somebody who...

CHAPTER NINE

The first thing she does Monday morning is text Anna and ask to meet her for lunch at one —at the café, the infamous café— and Anna texts back *OK*.

Lily gets there early and chooses a table against the wall. If she faints during the telling, she hopes it will help hold her up. She orders a peach-mango smoothie for Anna, an iced tea for herself, and an avocado rollup to share. Anna's always late, and she wants to get right down to business as soon as she can.

It's one-fifteen when Anna arrives, and the food and drinks are on the table.

"I told everybody the dorm is haunted," Anna says, as soon as she sits down, "but I guess Thurston is haunted, too. And that's never happened before —two haunted dorms. So now there's this big *thing* about where the party's gonna be or should there be two parties, and it's all anybody's talking about. Tell Chris, okay?"

Lily nods. "Sure. I will." She puts her napkin on her lap. "Thursday was great. I'm so glad you came. And Chris really liked you. I hope you liked him, too, because I..." She stops.

The look on Anna's face is hard to read. "Because *you* like him, Mom ... you don't really need to say it. It's a little obvious? I mean, you're completely ... gooney."

Gooney. She's *gooney*? And when was the last time Anna used *that* word? *Their* word when she was a little girl. Everything silly was gooney, and just hearing Lily say the word would send Anna into uncontrollable giggles. And, yes, maybe she is completely gooney. "I didn't know it showed," she says.

"Oh please." Anna bites into her rollup, chews. "I mean, it's kind of nice the way he looks at you; but it's kind of embarrassing the way you look at him."

Lily tries very hard not to take it personally, and then her announcement just blurts out. "We're getting married." And she imagines the same look of shock on both their faces, because she practiced lead-ins all the way to the café, and now it's just burst out like that.

Anna's look of shock changes to consternation. "Married? Didn't you just meet each other last week?"

"Well yes. But we've really known each for twenty years."

"You mean you *haven't* known each other for twenty years."

"You're right. And I guess it's hard to understand. Even for me. But it's real, Anna. And we're both certain about that. So ... why wait?"

"He's kind of old, you know."

"Not so old. It didn't make any difference before."

"He wasn't old then."

"He was still older than I was."

Anna shrugs. "He was hot then, right?"

Lily can't help smiling. "Yeah, he was hot."

"I knew from the pictures."

"What pictures?"

"The white album in the drawer."

"You've looked at that?"

"I used to look at it all the time. I used to think it was Dad until I got older."

"Oh," Lily says, at a loss for words.

"I kind of recognized him, even with the white hair. I kind of felt like I already knew him from the pictures." She takes a sip from her cup. "And he said you were hot, too."

"Chris? When did he say that?

Anna shrugs. "We talked a little when he dropped me off."

"What else did he say?"

Anna shrugs. "Not much. Oh, something about how very important you are to him." She shrugs again. "As if I couldn't tell."

Lily doesn't say anything.

Anna takes another bite of her sandwich. "I guess he doesn't really *act* old."

Lily shakes her head. "No, he doesn't."

"So like..." Anna frowns. "...when are you doing this?"

"A week from Friday."

"Whoa." Then she laughs a little. "Are you afraid he's going to die if you wait too long?"

"Anna!"

"Whatever." She takes a long sip on her smoothie, finishes her half of the rollup.

"I want you to be there. We both do. Will you come?"

"Like a quickie thing at the town hall?"

"Yes. You'll be a witness, too. Will you do that and come?"

She chews, thinking about it.

"And then afterwards the three of us will go out to dinner. Someplace nice. We'll schedule it for when your classes are over for the day."

"I guess," Anna says.

They sit in silence for a while. Lily eats half her rollup. "I'm going to buy a new dress. Maybe you could come help me pick something out?"

"What am *I* supposed to wear?"

"You can get something new, too."

"This is very weird," Anna says.

"Half the time I can't believe it either."

"I can go shopping on Saturday. That way, if we don't find something, we still have Sunday. Am I supposed to throw something at you?"

"Throw something at me?"

"At both of you. After it's over. Like rice or silly string."

"No. I think we won't do that."

"Good, because I can't believe what people do at these things."

"At wedding ceremonies."

"Yeah. Bubbles. Rose petals. Balloons. Doves! I mean, why would you want to throw birds?" She frowns. "I'm never getting married."

"You might change your mind."

Anna shakes her head. "I don't think so. Look at you."

"What do you mean?"

"Well it didn't work out so great, did it?"

Lily folds her napkin and places it beside her plate, thinks about what Chris said and tries to channel the mother she was when it was easy and automatic. "Yeah, honey, actually it did," she says. "I got you."

Anna slides her eyes off Lily's; she finishes her smoothie. "So you'll pick me up Saturday? Noon?"

Lily nods, and then Anna checks her cell phone, which means their conversation is over. But it's more of a conversation than they've had in a very long time.

CHAPTER TEN

"Should we write our own vows?" she asks Chris. "Just to personalize the thing?"

"The thing?" he says.

"The ceremony. Tomorrow. Our marriage ceremony."

"Right," he says. "Personalize it?"

"Well, it is *ours*. Maybe we should say something meaningful instead of what some stranger reads."

"That's a bunch of crap," he says, sounding downright testy. "We say meaningful things to each other when we're with each other and no stranger is present." Then he hesitates. "Don't we?"

"Yes. Of course we do. I guess it's just getting to me. It's strangely unsettling."

"The idea of...?"

"The *ceremony*. For heaven's sake, Chris, what's wrong with you?"

"Nothing. Nothing's wrong with me. That's why we should have done it that day. The day I asked you. No time to think about it then."

"Right," she says. "That day. With you in your underwear and me in my old ratty bathrobe. There was a three-day wait for the license, Chris. And there was Anna."

"I'd have put on a pair of pants," he says.

She narrows her eyes at him. "You need your hair trimmed."

"My hair's fine."

"I'll do it right now. Just a trim."

He sits backwards on a wooden chair and she tucks a towel around his neck. "Samson and Delilah, redux," he says. And when she's done, she folds the towel upward to keep the hair inside and carries it into the kitchen. When she comes back into the living room, he's standing at the window looking out, hands in his pockets.

"What?" she says. "You hate the trim?"

"The trim's fine."

"Then what's wrong? You're staring out the window. The only time you stare out a window is when you're thinking about a problem."

He doesn't say anything for a while, and then, "Has it occurred to you, Lily, that you're getting the short end of this bargain. Because it's occurred to me. And I think you need to be very sure of this before we go any further."

"What I think," she says, "is that you're wondering if *you're* sure about it."

He turns around. "Okay, yeah. Maybe I'm not so sure."

She swallows.

"Lily... It's not 1988 anymore. We've been acting like it is. *I've* been acting like it is. I haven't been jealous in twenty years, but that day, the day your friend showed up, I really did want to hit him. I feel like the calendar's flipped backwards. I'm obsessed with you. I can barely think of anything else. But it's not going to stay this way. Nothing this fine can stay. And I'm going to disappoint you. Maybe sooner than either of us wants to think."

He turns back toward the window, shoves his hands deeper into his pockets. "Let's not kid ourselves. What we had back then ... it was eighty percent lust. I couldn't keep my hands off you. But really ... I'm not the man I used to be." He laughs a little. "I saw it in your daughter's eyes when she came to the house. W*ow, an old guy.*"

"Everybody over the age of twenty-five is old to Anna."

"I realize that, but it's a fact we have to face. What's it going to be like for you when eighty percent of our relationship goes pfffttt. Pills? Maybe. For a while. And then what? You with some old geezer in a chair with wheels, a blanket over his knees? I don't want that for you."

"Look at me," she says. "Chris … look at me." And when he turns around, "is your brain truly still attached to your penis?" He blinks. "Eighty percent? *Eighty*? So we were horizontal, or partially horizontal, nineteen hours a day? However did you manage to squeeze lectures and classes and papers and office hours and sleep, not to mention your Ph.D. orals into the five hours left. And however did I manage to escape being prone long enough to get my MFA."

She knows he wants to look away, but she won't let him. "Is that what you really remember?"

"Lily….

"Still my turn," she says. "So the only thing we had going for us was sex. With a little food thrown in, I imagine. Maybe a word, or was it just a grunt here and there between the fucking and the eating??"

"That's not what I meant…"

"But that's exactly what you said. And what you remember is not what I remember at all. I remember loving your brain, your eyes, your heart, your soul. The sound of your voice and the way you smiled and the way you looked at me. And I saw that you loved me back in exactly the same way. Completely. Yes, you loved my body, but that's not all you loved. And that's got to be true now more than ever." She touches the spot between her eyebrows. "Those worry lines you kissed away the other night are going to become permanent any day now. And my orgasms don't last half as long as they used to. Care to throw me back?"

"Okay, you can stop, I…"

"We love each other, Chris. Not just the parts that make us feel good. You asked me to marry you, I said yes, and dammit we're doing it tomorrow. Whatever comes after that we'll deal with. You're not the only one who's going to break, you know."

He takes a step toward her and wraps her in his arms. "Me," he says, "cool, practical me gets an attack of nerves at the last minute." They hold each other tight and then he laughs. "I mean, when you get down to it, the only thing this should have anything to do with is sheer practicality."

"Practicality?"

"Do you realize," he says, "where I am on the Actuarial Life Table?"

She pushes away. "Didn't we just settle this?"

"No, no ... this is a completely different consideration. I'm fifty-nine, Lily. Do you have any idea how many more years I'm expected to hang around?"

"Don't," she says. "I mean it, Chris, don't." She puts her hands over her ears. "I won't hear it. I am not listening..."

He lowers his head so they're face to face. "Read my lips then." He raises his voice. "...twenty. I looked it up." He flashes ten fingers at her, than flashes them again. "And that's if nothing goes wrong. You, on the other hand have double that." He points at her and flashes ten plus ten plus ten plus ten. Then he says, "stop that," and pulls her hands away from her ears. "Plus, the way you eat, it's probably more like triple. And I plan to provide for as many of those years as I can."

"You don't even have any money," she says. "You've never had any money. And I can take care of myself."

"*Now*, you can take care of yourself. But what if you ... run out of memoirs? And you're wrong. I do have money. I have everything I didn't spend on vacations, hotels, and five-star restaurants for the last thirty years."

"Which means you still won't?"

"Still won't what?"

"Go on vacation and stay at hotels and eat at nice restaurants?"

"What's that got to do with this?"

"Nothing," she says, "it has nothing to do with this. But you're serious, aren't you."

"Yes," he says, "I'm serious."

So she has to add these new things into the Christopher equation – brilliant, funny, a great whistler, sexy, powerless to resist her, and now, doubtful, rich, and mortal.

"And while we're still being serious," he says, "I want you to promise me one thing." He looks at her. She looks back. "That chair with the wheels?" He makes circles in the air with his hands. "If that comes to pass, you have to promise you'll wheel me to the top of a very high hill and give it a push. The chair. With me in it. A good big push. Promise me."

She nods.

"Say it."

"I promise." For a second she almost thinks she could cry, but that's no easy way out of whatever this is. So instead, she cocks her head at him. "You mean you're really loaded?"

He frowns, she moves up against him, puts her arms around his neck. "I suspected, but now that you've confirmed it…. I mean, did you really think I was after anything else?" She nuzzles his chest, slides one hand down his back and inside his belt.

For a second he says nothing, then, "And do you really think you should be telling me this now? Not wait until tomorrow, after it's a done deal?"

She reaches up and bites at his lower lip, presses herself against him. "Why? Does it make a difference?"

"Not a bit," he says, lowering his hands to her rear end. I always suspected you were nothing less than a seductress. A temptress. A brazen hussy." He whispers into her ear, "You Jezebel."

"Strumpet," she whispers back.

"Tart."

"Floozy."

"Harlot."

"A shameless tramp."

"Oh jeezus," he says, "I hope so."

Then she removes his hands from her rear end. "Can we stop all this now? All this *what if I can't get it up anymore, what if I croak, however will you manage* business?"

He tries to nuzzle her neck.

"Sorry," she says, pushing him away. "I admit you've helped a bit with my orgasms, but right now I just don't have the time. Obviously everything still works and will for a while. Plus I'm getting married tomorrow. To a man who doesn't worry about such things. And I have to save myself for *him*."

He stands there with a look on his face that could almost be pain. And then she turns and walks away. "Do a little rearranging on your percentages, Chris. Believe it or not, I can stand your hands being right where they are. Which is exactly where they'll stay for as long as you're being an idiot. Or at least until tomorrow night," she looks back over her shoulder, "if you're lucky."

CHAPTER ELEVEN

The wedding takes eight minutes. Lily checks the clock on the wall when it starts, and again when it's finished. Eight minutes exactly.

Chris is wearing a new collarless white cotton shirt, jeans, a tan corduroy jacket. And loafers. She's wearing a deep blue jersey dress with long sleeves, a pleated skirt, a slash neckline, and a pair of black ballet flats. In her hand are one white lily, a surprise from Chris, and a bouquet of violets, a shock from Anna. The flowers give her something to hold on to.

Chris won't wear a ring, but she has told him she will and wants it to be a surprise, which it is, and perfect, too. A wide black ceramic band studded with turquoise, which explains Chris' disappearance on Wednesday, practically from morning till evening. And she suspects he did not pick it out alone, especially since it fits perfectly. Though Anna, in her new A-line gold and brown paisley jersey dress, is staying mum.

During the ceremony, Lily has an out-of-body experience, her first. She is somewhere above and to the left of the town clerk, an ample woman who seems to take no notice that Lily is standing before her and hovering above her at the same time.

The hovering Lily is enjoying herself enormously. She wants to spin in circles and shout "It's about bloody time!" The Lily facing Christopher can barely breathe. What if it's all a dream, the non-floating Lily wonders. Will she soon wake up?

Chris, on the other hand, has lost all yesterday's foreboding. He's gone back to his old unflappable self.

After they have been pronounced husband and wife, Anna snaps three photos with her phone, and the second witness—she may be the town clerk's assistant—offers to snap one of the happy couple with Anna in the middle. Lily hopes Anna will smile. Then they get in Lily's car and drive for twenty minutes to a restaurant up on a hill, with a view of mountains and a village settled in the dale below and have a strange hour of Anna explaining to Chris why she'll never get married, while he tells her in thirteen different ways to never say never to anything, and Lily simply tries to not act gooney.

It's obvious watching them that Chris and Anna have developed an ease beyond that first Thursday dinner. Which confirms Lily's suspicion about the ring, which she can't stop looking at, and forces her to acknowledge a hint of envy that he has managed it apparently without much effort. But it also makes her curious. What have they talked about? What has Chris told Anna? What has Anna told Chris? Anna will never say; though Chris might, if she pushed. But why disturb a boat that seems to have stopped taking on water?

Chris, she finds, has developed a nod to certain amenities, and the first thing to arrive at the table is a bottle of champagne. He pours three glasses and turns to Anna. "To you. For your indispensable help..."

"I knew it," Lily says, smiling at Anna, holding up her left hand. "Nothing this perfect could have been sheer luck."

"...and," he turns to Lily, "to you, my sheer luck."

By the time she and Chris have taken a sip, Anna has drained her glass.

The food is a blur, though Lily remembers the textures and the colors—the purple of the beet salad with tiny dollops of sour cream; the crusty brown rolls; the bright orange flecks of lobster in the creamy Newberg sauce; the blackened green of the asparagus; and the tiny cake with its creaseless white fondant topping, their names in dark chocolate beneath two piped wedding bells.

Lily laughs when she cuts the cake, passes the first piece to Anna, the second to Chris. "Remember the cake I made you for your birthday?" she asks him.

"Mmm-hmm," he says, his mouth full of cake.

"My first ever," she says to Anna. "And it was supposed to be very impressive-looking. Three tiers. A ton of icing. But I knew as soon as I took the layers out of the oven I'd screwed it up because they were about this high." She holds her fingers an inch apart, "and when they came out of the tins they thunked. But he was going to be there in twenty minutes, and there was always the chance they'd soften under the icing."

"It looked good," Chris says, "kind of fancy. But I've had an easier time sawing through wood."

Anna laughs.

"So," Lily says, "Chris decided it was something for the catapult."

Anna looks up from her cake and Lily nods at Chris. "You tell."

His cake is gone and he sets his fork down. "The school of mechanical engineering," he says, "had built a catapult. Giant thing called a mangonel. And they were keeping records, figures on the projectile, pre-firing projections and post-firing accounts."

"They catapulted a piano," Lily says. "You should have heard the sound it made as it flew."

"Not to mention when it landed," Chris says. "But not all of its use was purely scientific. They launched a ton of cow shit as I remember, a barrel of Jello, and at least one dead cat."

Anna grimaces.

"So Chris called up a colleague in that department," Lily says, "and asked if they could launch my cake."

"The idea of which," Chris says, "Jacob found interesting. So we took the cake to the catapult, and it seems word had got around that Lily Shea's cake was being launched. No one wanted to miss that. Must have been a hundred people there and more arriving." He winks at Anna. "Your mother was infamous on campus."

"Please," Lily says. "If I was infamous, it was only because of you."

Anna looks from Chris to Lily and back again. "Why," she says, eyebrows raised, were you *both* infamous?"

Chris looks at Lily and smiles. "Am I so old that the idea of me being infamous is impossible to imagine?"

A rhetorical question, she decides.

"Anyway," he says, giving Anna his attention. "I was what you might term an iconoclast in those days. Some people would have simply called it arrogance." He shrugs. "Bans on grad student/teacher liaisons had been abandoned long before, but the puritanical attitudes that established them in the first place were still very much in evidence. And I didn't like the way certain members of the faculty treated your mother."

"So he was hell-bent on rubbing their faces in it," Lily says, taking over. "He dragged me to every faculty event there was — parties, barbeques, lectures, readings, basketball games."

"I knew you played basketball," Anna says.

"You did?"

"Yeah. For one thing, you're pretty tall. But mainly, I saw the pictures."

"There are pictures?"

"The white album," Lily says to him. Then she says to Anna, "Most of the faculty just ignored me."

"A quarter ignored you," Chris says. "The rest hardly did." Then he says to Anna, "A quarter of the people at those events were women."

"Angela was always nice," Lily says. "The Dean's wife."

"Yes." Chris nods, "she had class."

"So what happened with the cake?" Anna asks.

"There we were," Chris says, "with two dozen boomboxes all tuned to the same rock station and too many people to fit, so they bypassed the math and just cranked the thing tight, placed the cake..."

"And then," Lily says, "there was this hundred-person countdown: five, four, three, two..."

"And they let her rip." Chris shakes his head. "It might have been heavy for a cake, but nothing for a catapult, and it flew over the field, over the pond, over some trees, and smashed into the Congregational Church steeple three football fields away."

"Wow," Anna says. "And what happened then?"

"A lot of cheering," Chris says.

"Did you get in trouble?"

Chris frowns. "Actually, about five months later, I got fired."

"You got fired because of the cake?"

He shakes his head. "No, there were lots of other reasons."

"Because of my mother?"

Chris looks at Lily. "It was more complicated than that."

"How?" Anna asks.

"Some day we'll fill you in."

Then Anna's phone vibrates atop the table. She picks it up. "I gotta go," she says. "There's something going on tonight."

"What kind of something," Chris asks, and Lily thinks how easily it comes out, that question, when she hesitates to ask it herself.

"Some of the girls," Anna says, "are hanging out with some of the ghost-busters."

"Polite, smart, and responsible ghost-busters, right?" he asks.

She smiles. "I guess."

"Okay then." He turns to Lily. "Ready to go?"

She isn't really. It's been everything she could have hoped for and more, and she doesn't want it to end. But she nods yes.

Chris drives, and after they drop Anna at her dorm with the boxed cake, it takes Lily a while to realize they're not heading home. "Chris, where are we going?"

"On our honeymoon," he says. "The thought never occurred to you that it's an accepted convention following a wedding?"

"Perhaps it would have if I'd married someone conventional." She feels a shiver of what can only be delight. "Is it someplace far? Are we staying overnight? I have to go home first and get some things."

"Not so far. Yes, two nights. And our bags are in the trunk." That's all he'll say no matter how hard she tries.

They drive for two hours, arrive after dark in the White Mountains at the Mountain View Hotel, a place she's always wanted to visit, but never has.

Their room is luxurious. A king-sized bed, elegant décor, a Jacuzzi, a well-stocked refrigerator, high-end art prints on the walls, a walk-in closet, and although it's too dark to see, "a view that'll knock your socks off," according to Chris.

"I can't believe you've done this," she says, making her third circuit of the room. "It's perfect." She walks up to him and kisses his chest.

"Let's go for a swim," he says. "I think it's been too long since we've done that."

"I don't have a suit."

"Yeah, you do. Look in the bag. Anna saw to it."

She searches, finally finds a two-piece stuffed into a side pocket. "This?" she says, holding up a piece in each hand.

"It's Anna's. She said you wear the same size."

"This is something a sixteen-year-old wears on the Italian Riviera. And I doubt we're the same size in a bathing suit!"

"So pretend," he says. "Besides, there won't be anybody in the pool at this hour. C'mon, Lily. It's our honeymoon!"

"And what are you wearing," she asks, "a thong?"

He pulls black and white trunks out of his bag and waves them in the air.

He's right about the pool. They are the only ones. And it's very dark, except for the underwater lights that give the place the feel of a hidden grotto. Chris immediately dives in, kicks his way to the other end and then back again. He pops up and rests his arms on the white vinyl pool deck. "Coming? Water's nice and warm."

"I can't swim, remember?"

"Yes. But I also remember that you know how to float."

"Okay," she says, "get ready to save me," and drops her robe across a nearby lounge chair. But then she discovers that she can't make herself jump. "I can't," she says, "I think I've forgotten how."

He starts to laugh.

"I'll come in the mature way, so this two-piece whatever-I'm-wearing won't end up flying north and south on its own." She gives him a stern look. "And you can stop laughing now."

"It's just because I'm having such a good time watching you right where you are," he says.

She enters the pool via the steps and takes her time in the shallow end before she finally goes horizontal. And, yes, the water's warm and, yes, she can still float, and, ohmygod, the ceiling is glass and there's an amazing view of the stars. "Look," she says, pointing up, and they float for a while side-by-side, his hand under her back so she can relax, as he tries to locate the points of the compass and the quadrant of the sky they're seeing. "This time of year we should see Andromeda, Aquarius, Pisces. Here's a question: what year was the Orion Nebula first studied in a detailed way?"

She considers an answer. "1888," she says, guessing.

"1659," he says, "by a Dutch scientist who thought he'd discovered it, but hadn't. Turned out two others, A Frenchman and a Swiss had already seen it thirty years earlier."

"I wasn't sure they even had telescopes in the seventeenth century."

"That's when they were first used. Imagine how the world opened up. By 1700 there were logarithms, electricity, microscopes, gravity...."

"Shakespeare died."

"The Inquisition."

"Harvard."

"The Plague."

"The Salem witch trials."

"And William and Mary was opened. I know because I taught there."

"When it was first established?"

"Cute," he says, and pulls his hand out from under her back, which makes her sink, which makes water go up her nose.

CHAPTER TWELVE

Chris does three more laps and she sits on the top step watching. His motion looks effortless and she keeps reminding herself that he belongs to her. That they belong to each other now.

Back in their room, they share the shower, almost as large as her entire bathroom at home, with double showerheads opposite each other, and she senses this intimacy is different somehow, and it makes her feel almost shy. He finishes first, dries himself, then takes a towel and dries her off, too, gathers her hair and twists the water out, and there's a tentativeness in him that tells her he's feeling it, too.

He drapes the towel around her shoulders. "It shouldn't be different, should it," he says, "but it is." She smiles. "It's been quite a twenty-one day ride, Mrs. Cheykin."

"Oh yes," she says.

His face goes serious. "But a good ride, right?"

"Best in the world."

"Remember our first night?" he asks. "Back then?" He pushes wet hair off her cheek. "I think maybe we have at least as much to catch up on, don't you?" And a kind of silent agreement passes between them.

Yes, she remembers that night, so unexpected but strangely right. Remembers how she'd developed the habit of lingering after his seminar for weeks before, working at her table until everyone else drifted away. He would linger, too, always available for a question or further discussion over what had come up earlier: *was Tolstoy's representation of Karenin as a sour and officious man a manipulation of the reader's ultimate feeling that a tragedy, and not justice, had occurred? Was Oblonsky's unfaithfulness a requisite to Anna's? A kind of permission that would otherwise have not been granted?*

It became their convention every Tuesday and Thursday. And somehow they would manage to 'bump' into each other around campus—at the quad, the book store, the coffee shop they both began to frequent every evening. Until finally one night, after the usual three cups of coffee that always left her completely unable to sleep, he casually asked her back to his place. And she said yes.

There was no question in her mind about what would happen. They'd both pursued; they'd both responded. And she fully expected he'd take her to bed, and she was more than willing to go. There'd been too many looks between them, too many accidental touches and sly smiles for things that night to be anything less than crystal clear.

Except what she knew would happen did not. Instead, they sat on the floor in his living room above the deli, a bowl of M&Ms between them, and talked until the sun came up the next morning.

Months later, she asked him, "Why didn't you make love to me that first night? Why did you wait?"

He laughed a little. "I don't know. I fully intended to. But then when you were there, where I'd wanted you practically from the first day I noticed you, my dick was saying one thing, and my head, which usually stayed out of those things, was saying something else entirely." He shrugged. "I don't know, Lily. You were so young, so perfect. Much too fine for just another conquest. Suddenly I wanted more than your body—though, god knows I wanted that— but at the same time I wanted more. More for you, and more *from* me. I wanted to know you in a way I'd never wanted to know anyone in a very long time."

Now, in bed, he puts one arm around her, the other crooked on the pillow beneath his head. "So, Mrs. Cheykin," he says, "tell me everything I don't know about you."

She tells him that she wrote him a dozen dozen letters, none of which she mailed. That she would call when she knew he wasn't home just to imagine the phone ringing in the empty apartment; tells him how she felt when she got the 'service disconnected' message ... so empty she was sick to her stomach.

She tells him that his friend Ryan Little visited her in San Francisco after she'd been there a month, asking to meet at an expensive restaurant ("sounds like Little," Chris says, sourly), where he told her Chris had already found someone new. ("that's absolutely not so," Chris says.) After which Little had come on to her, and then had the nerve to leave her with the check when she told him to go fuck himself. ("sounds like the bastard," Chris says.)

"About six months later, I met David," she says. "I'd never known anyone quite like him before." She sighs. "He seemed so ... solid."

She tells him about being pregnant with Anna, the endless vomiting, the joy. About the time Anna fell and needed six stitches under her chin, how she started reading at three, and was a most graceful ballerina at six. And she tells him that she almost did it a second time, almost married someone named Nicholas, but called it off the night before because she was tired of disappointment.

He tells her there was never anyone else like her. No one at all for a long time after she left, despite what that bastard Little said. How those he did meet were just ways of passing too long nights.

"I went to North Carolina one summer," he says, "the Outer Banks. We should do that together."

"Did you go alone?" she says.

"No, actually," he says. "I went with Cass." He hesitates a second. "Cass was an eighty-pound Labrador retriever."

"You had a dog?"

"Yeah. She turned up one day. Lost and scared. Had her for almost ten years."

"She had you longer than I have."

"She was a great dog. Maybe we should do that, get a dog."

She thinks about it. "Maybe."

He tells her about the succession of jobs —Virginia, Texas, Ohio— all of them steadily downhill thanks to crazy Denise and her paranoid obsessions. And how he felt when he heard she was dead. Immense relief followed instantly by guilt. About his book on

Tolstoy, and how the fact it was well-received led to job offers, solid offers, so that after fifteen years of drift, his career stabilized. And he tells her that sometimes he wonders if he sent her away for another reason.

"What?" she asks.

"Because Denise was out there having a hellish life. And maybe I didn't think I deserved one all that much better. It used to hit me sometimes, how unfair it was. That I should be happy when she was so constantly in misery."

"In her right mind," Lily says, "she would have told you to not be such a complete ignoramus." Which makes them both go quiet and then sends them into a laughing fit.

"Tell me her name," Lily says, "the adjunct."

"What difference does it make," he says.

"It doesn't. But you met Paul. You shook his hand, invited him to breakfast, embarrassed him. Don't you think I at least get to know her name?"

He sighs. "Connie."

"As in Constance?"

"Constance? I don't know. She calls herself Connie. Everybody calls her Connie."

"Does she love you?"

"No. And I thought we were limiting this to her name."

"Okay," she says, "then tell me a story."

"I haven't had to do that in a long time."

She snuggles against him. "Good," she says. "Just what I wanted to hear."

"Once upon a time," he says, "there was this kick-ass woman named Alexandra."

"My middle name," she says. "Good again."

"Stop interrupting," he says. "Every man in the kingdom desired her, but she would have not one of them. And then one day when she was jumping out of her window—that's the way she always left her house because a spell had been cast upon her when she was a newborn that she would always land softly—so she jumped out the window, as usual, and, of course, landed in the back of a passing hay wagon. Once she was in the wagon, she got very busy thinking about black holes, since they were her hobby, but after a while, she noticed a toad sitting on the hay beside her. Well, she really didn't like toads very well, so she picked it up to throw out of the wagon, but as soon as she touched it, she fell instantly in love."

"With the toad?"

"Yes, because this was a magic toad and anything that touched it would, of course, fall madly in love with it."

"And did it love her back?"

"It did. And she said to the toad, 'isn't this where you turn into a handsome prince?' *No, said the toad. I'm a toad, and a toad I will remain, because it's very important when you love someone to see them as they are. With clear eyes.* The End."

She presses her ear against his chest so she can hear his heart beating. "Do we see each other as we really are?" she asks. "With clear eyes?"

He hugs her tighter. "Yes," he says, "I think we do."

For a while they don't say anything, and then she whispers, "Are you asleep?"

"No," he says, "I'm strangely wide awake."

"Me, too." She listens to the slow, steady beat of his heart. "I did try to work on the book," she says. "*Mackerel Sky*. In Paris, believe it or not, when I visited Anna. We'd had two weeks together in an apartment David rented on the Rue de la Harpe."

"The Latin Quarter."

"You know it?"

"I did a lot of walking around the city those nine months I was there. We should do that. Go there for a long period. It's the only way to get to know a city. So okay, sorry I interrupted. Go ahead."

"The visit was mostly not okay. But I was happy to just have her in touching distance, although all she talked about was a skiing trip with her father and some of her friends at the end of the two weeks. Actually, David asked me to go, too, but it was pretty clear that was not going to make Anna happy. And the apartment he'd rented was available for another month, so I stayed on. Partly because I wanted to see Anna again when they got back, and partly because Paris was so beautiful." She laughs a little. "And partly because I think I still had a vision of myself as a writer. A *real* writer. Living the writing life. You know." He shifts in the bed slightly. "I'd sit at a table overlooking the street and write."

"Did you get far?"

"No. I couldn't write that book anymore. It was stuck in a different time and I couldn't find it. Everything I wrote was false."

"And you didn't try writing something new?"

She shakes her head. "There was nothing new."

"Maybe it's time to try again."

She stretches and yawns. "Maybe."

Gradually, the room lightens to deep gray, then becomes pearly, and when the sun comes up, the puzzle of twenty years apart feels almost complete and they fall asleep.

CHAPTER THIRTEEN

It's noon when they wake up, a brilliant blue-sky day. They eat yogurts out of the fridge, pull on jeans and heavy sweaters, buy the trail meals the hotel prepares, and take off for Mount Willard and its views. The air is crisp as they hike along an abandoned carriage road, and on the way up they stop to catch glimpses through the trees of far-off views. At the summit, Chris goes to the very edge and whoops, his voice echoing out over nothing, while she silently wills him to *step back, step back, step back, please step back.* A bird, bluish and about the size of a robin, cavorts around them, begging for food, landing twice on Chris's shoulder while they eat lunch. They throw the sandwich crusts on the ground, and the bird, when they start the hike down, follows them, flitting from tree to tree for a good half-hour before it finally gives up and flies away.

They drive into North Conway village and stroll the main streets, stop for hot chocolate and a home-made donut, browse a book store and an art gallery, where Chris buys a small, impressionistic oil on canvas of Tuckerman Ravine. "Your wedding gift," he says.

"Uh-oh. Now I'll have to think of something to get you."

"I already have everything I want," he says.

They pass a lingerie store and Lily tells him to wait for her. Then she goes in and comes out with a shopping bag. "Your wedding present," she says, but won't let him see what's inside.

They find a quiet restaurant for dinner, toast each other with some good red wine. Lily's legs ache dully, their faces are sunburned from the hike, but they linger at the table, reluctant to end this marvelous day.

"So when do I get to see my present?" Chris asks.

"When we get back to the hotel."

"I'm ready when you are."

They walk out of the restaurant into a cold night topped by a black sky studded with stars, and he instinctively puts his arm around her and pulls her against him as a shudder goes through her. "It's freezing!" she says.

"Winter comes earlier here."

"I'm glad I'll have you at night," she says. "The handy-dandy Cheykin bed warmer. No plugs, no wires, just good reliable heat all night long."

"I have no choice," he says, "now that I'll have this little ice cube applying herself to me October through May. Nothing more than an autonomic response to ice-age survival."

"You're nuts," she says, laughing.

After they're in the car, she asks, "Did I tell you there's a prerequisite to the presentation of your present?"

"Actually, no. Does this prerequisite apply to you or to me?"

"You."

"I have to do something to get my present? That's not fair, Lily. I just handed you the painting and said *here*."

"I know," she says, "but who ever said marriage is fair?"

"But *fair* should be the exact definition of marriage ... a union that grants mutual rights and responsibilities."

"Don't be silly. Right now we need to review a little history."

"I have to get ready to pass a *test*?"

"You have to remember the longest fight we ever had."

"We never had a long fight."

"Which involved a stag party and two strippers."

"Oh that," he says. "Why would I want to remember that?"

"Because of the discussion we had afterwards."

"We had a discussion?"

"We always had discussions after fights."

"I have to remember one particular discussion we had twenty years ago? Do you know how old my brain is?"

"Your brain won't get its present until it remembers."

"Shit," he says. And then he's silent the rest of the way back to the hotel, and every time she says something, he says, "Shhh. I'm thinking."

They'd had a huge fight, one that raged on for almost two days after he'd gone to the stag party.

"Strippers?" she'd said. "And you actually enjoyed it?"

"Well, I didn't *not* enjoy it. What was I supposed to do? It was a stag party!"

"Leave?" she'd said.

"You've got to be kidding. I think I'm old enough to handle myself with strange naked women in a room. It's not like I found it particularly arousing."

"Which means what? That you found it arousing, just not *particularly* arousing??"

It had gone on and on. She'd thrown words like demeaning and chauvinistic at him. He'd called her a false feminist and Victorian.

"Those women make more in one night than I do in a week," he said.

"So the exchange of money frees us all from moral concern?"

And when they'd both run out of steam, when their sense of indignation had been trumped by their need to not be mad at each other, the usual discussion had followed. This one about strippers and desire and what constitutes arousal.

"For you," she said, "anything constitutes arousal. All I have to do is put my hair up or take my hair down and you're aroused."

"That's not true," he said. "Well. Maybe. But that's because it's *you. You* arouse me. The lady at the post office is a perfectly fine-looking woman, but she could wait on me stark naked and it wouldn't arouse me. The young women in my class don't arouse me. Even those strippers didn't arouse me."

"Naked women didn't arouse you? Seriously? Seems to me you were pretty aroused when you got home."

"But that was *you. You* were the one I wanted to have sex with. Not them. They were in their all-together, and it was a fine thing to see, but when it came down to it, it wasn't such a big deal. Then I came home, and you were there in your flannel nightgown. That long thick thing you used to wear."

"Well, I was always cold."

"...and I mean, I couldn't wait to get under it. It was like the sexiest thing I'd seen all night."

"So, even though what's *actually* there, what's absolutely available and in-your-face is sexy," she said, "the *hint* of what's there is even sexier?"

"Dance of the seven veils," he said. If Delilah had walked out stark naked, would Herod have been so charmed? When Cleopatra rolled out of that rug, was she naked, as in some versions, or suggestively veiled, as in others. What's sexier?"

"Veiled," Lily said.

He'd closed his eyes. "Yes, definitely veiled."

She'd smiled. "We should conduct an experiment. To see what best leads to the point of maximum arousal. Skin or just a hint of it."

But they never had.

CHAPTER FOURTEEN

All the way from the parking lot, through the lobby, and into the elevator, Chris is quiet. Then, as they're passing the third floor, he says, "I remember. Imagination is the most powerful aphrodisiac. To a point."

"Correct," she says, though I think we never actually discovered the *point*.

"Which we will try and discover tonight?"

She nods.

"I think I'm beginning to like this marriage thing."

In the room, she sits him on a love seat, starts a Ray Charles' album on Pandora, and turns off all the lights except one. "Relax," she tells him, I'll be out in a sec." And then, just before she closes the bathroom door she says, "You're not going to fall asleep, are you?"

"You get funnier every day," he says.

She takes four very short nightgowns out of her mystery bag — each one sheer white nylon with thin satin shoulder straps — and puts them on, one over the other. She takes her hair down, sprays it with volumizer, works it with her fingers until it's as wild as she can make it. Then she looks at herself in the mirror. If she squints, what she sees doesn't look half-bad, despite the harsh lighting, so Chris, practically in the dark, should find her downright tantalizing. Plus all he has to see is what he needs to.

She puts her hands behind her head, elbows spread, and bumps to the right, then the left. She used to be able to do it pretty convincingly, but her range of motion feels a lot less fluid than it once was. Still, how energetic does a middle-aged striptease need to be?

She remembers her one moment of stardom. An end-of-exams beer bash just before she got her B.A. That was before Chris. Before, pretty much, everything. Everyone on their feet screaming while she gyrated her way through an imitation of Gwen Verdon. *And little man, little Lola wants you!* It was the last time she ever danced in front of an audience, which meant an undergrad drunk fest was the culmination of twelve years of dance lessons. And now, the only thing she's sure of is that she can keep time to the music.

She closes her eyes for five seconds and listens to Ray singing—*The Midnight Hour*. Perfect. She starts to sway, and, leaving a single light on behind her, opens the door.

"Am I sufficiently back-lit?" she asks Chris. "Sufficiently front-lit?"

He peers at her. "If you're asking if what you're wearing is see-through. It's not." Then he laughs. "But I think I get it."

"Get what?"

"What you are. A butterfly coming out of a cocoon. Right?"

"A cocoon?" She stands there for a second. "I am not a cocoon." She puts her hands on her hips. "How can I do this now when you think I'm a cocoon."

"Uh ... that's not what I meant. You don't look like a cocoon, Lily. I have no idea where that came from. Just go ahead and do what you were going to do. Great legs, by the way."

"Thanks. But the whole idea's gone a little flat for me. I mean, does this do anything for you?" She puts her hands behind her head, bumps in one direction, then the other.

He puts his head in his hands. Her hands go back to her hips.

"Okay. Done," she says. "This was supposed to be burlesque à la Gypsy Rose Lee, not the Marx Brothers. And you're not even trying to cooperate."

"I am," he says, looking up, trying hard to look serious. "I just don't know what, exactly, I'm cooperating in."

"Oh for heaven's sakes! I was going to strip for you! And you're supposed to tell me when you get to the *point*."

For a second they stare at each other. "Okay," he says, then don't just stand there. Strip!"

"I don't want to now. You laughed. You said I look like a cocoon. It's all ruined."

He leans forward just as Ray starts singing *Come Rain or Come Shine*. "Baby," he says. "Take off your clothes."

She pouts. "Now you're going to give me orders?"

I'm gonna love you like nobody's loved you...

"Try to think of it as a command."

"Oh really. And what will happen if I practice non-compliance? If I ignore you and your *command*?"

"You're going to make me say it in Russian?"

"That's not fair."

Razdevysya, Liliya. *Seychas*.

She closes her eyes. "What did you just say?"

"Take off your clothes, Lily. And do it *now*."

...high as a mountain, deep as a river, and won't it be fine...

She shivers a little and starts to sway with the music. Then she fingers the hem of the top nightgown and slowly inches it up until she pulls it off over her head and tosses it at him. It floats and he grabs it out of the air.

"Point?" she says, spinning slowly in one direction, then the other.

He shakes his head, and she goes over to him, bends close enough so her hair touches his face. For a second, he doesn't move, but as soon as he reaches for her, she pulls away and shakes a finger at him.

She starts to pull up the second nightgown just as Ray goes into *Night Time is the Right Time*.

...say now oh baby when I come home baby...

She tosses the second nightgown behind her and the air in the room seems to develop a buzz.

...right time to be with the one you love...

She stretches her arms up to the ceiling. "Point?" she asks.

He makes a noise she takes as a maybe. She goes up to him, puts her foot on his knee, then pushes her heel along the top of his thigh until he's sitting back and her foot is against his chest. This time he doesn't try to touch her, just sits there looking at her, and she gives one small push against him and moves away. She lifts the third nightgown, pulls it over her head, tosses it, and this time, when she looks at him, his eyes are fixed on the single transparent nightie.

"Point?" she says.

"Point."

She puts her arms over her head and turns slowly twice, then moves toward him, kneels on the love seat straddling his lap.

She puts her arms around his neck. "There really was no point, was there," she says.

He kisses her. "Not really. I was already aroused just waiting for you to come out of the bathroom. But you make a great stripper."

She rubs his nose with hers. "So our experiment was a failure."

He takes a deep breath, lets it out. A sigh of deep contentment, she decides.

"I think it's something that probably defies experimentation."

"Too complex," she says.

"Oh yeah." He kisses her three times in quick succession. "Some strange naked woman might stir my so-called reptilian brain. But who wants to go around being a reptile? On the other hand, when I see you, dressed, undressed, cocoon, no cocoon ... " He laughs a little. "My response is extremely complex. I feel affection..." he kisses her, "I enjoy expectation..." he kisses her, "and my imagination goes way off the meter." He kisses her again. "But no experiment fails. There's always a result, even if it's not the one you expected." He leans away from her a little and looks at her. "What did you do to your hair?"

She reaches up and fluffs at it. "I volumized it. To make it big and sexy. Like it?"

"It takes my breath away. *You* take my breath away." He nuzzles her neck. "You have this knack, Lily, this extraordinary knack."

"Which is?"

"For making life fun. For making me happy. For making every minute of my life feel important."

"Mmmm," she says. "I think we have a result! All it takes to make you say wonderful things is a little strip-tease!"

For a second he squeezes her very hard.

"I don't need an incentive. I just need you. Though I enjoyed the strip-tease immensely. And by the way, it isn't quite finished, is it?"

She pulls away from him, does a shimmy-shake. "Oh this little thing won't be in our way."

He leans forward and rubs his cheek against her breasts, whispers, "my darling Lily, *moya prekrasnaya zhena.*" And before she can ask, what? ...he says, *"My beautiful wife."*

The love seat is too small and the bed is at least eight feet away, so they just slide onto the rug.

"I guess I'll have to go out and buy a long flannel nightgown for winter," she whispers into his ear, "since you seem to appreciate just about anything I wear. Or don't wear."

"I think, Mrs. Cheykin, we should both shut up now and concentrate on what we're doing."

"Aye aye, sir."

... Still in peaceful dreams I see the road leads back to you ...

CHAPTER FIFTEEN

After the honeymoon, they spend half the week moving her out of her house. It takes every day, all day long to clean the place out, throw things away, pack up what she wants to bring. Chris comes every evening and they load up her car and his truck and drive together back to South Hadley.

On Wednesday, they stop at a restaurant on the way home and he hands her a hand-written envelope that reads Professor and Mrs. Cheykin. Inside is an invitation to a Saturday night cocktail party.

"Are we going?" she asks.

"Definitely. The hosts are Ken MacDonald, head of my department—great guy, great cook—and his wife Sandy. They're good friends. You'll like them both. Besides, it's a special event ... so people can meet my new wife."

"The wife whose last name you didn't know when you were getting the license?"

"Exactly. You're a surprise to them and a surprise to me."

"They're really surprised? People have said that?"

"Yes. Nobody's seen me with you. I suddenly show up married. That's a surprise. And when *you* walk in, that will be a surprise, too. I will once again bear the dubious label of cradle-robber."

She forks a piece of her Caesar salad. "Ohhh, I've been out of the cradle a looonnng time."

A half-minute of silence goes by although she can see he's thinking. And then he says, "Lily..." and she stops eating, looks at him.

"Speaking of ... well, whatever. I mean, it's a little late to bring this up, I guess. And you're probably taking care of it. At least you always used to." He frowns. "Though I haven't noticed that you're doing what you used to do."

"What on earth are you talking about?" She takes a sip of her water.

"Are we using birth control? Or not?"

"Oh," she says. "I get it. That little round case is no longer in the bathroom. *That's* what you're talking about, my omni-present pills."

He nods.

"I don't use them anymore," she says.

"Really." He pushes his water glass back, pulls it forward. "Does that mean you could …?"

"Get pregnant?"

He looks at her.

"And how would you feel about it if I did?"

"How would *you* feel about it?"

"I asked you first."

"Well, it's not something I've thought about a great deal, but it's probably not what a little kid would need. A grandfather for a father." He shrugs. "Heck. I could almost be his great grand-father, in a pinch."

"So you've decided it's going to be a boy already," she says. And then she smiles. "It's not an issue, Chris. I had complications after Lily. The doctor said I would never get pregnant again. And I haven't."

He nods. "Did you want more kids?"

"Part of me did. But not with David. Single parenting wasn't the kind of parenting I ever had in mind." She looks at him. "With you, though… " She goes quiet for a second. "With you I would have wanted three. Two girls and a boy." Another half-minute of silence, and she says, "I seem to have rendered you speechless."

"No, I ... no one's ever said that to me before. I don't quite know how to take it. On one hand I feel quite honored." He bows his head to her. "And on the other, there's a touch of regret."

She reaches across the table and puts her hand on his. "Because we never had the chance."

***

She follows him the rest of the way home. Her view, the boxes in the back of his truck. She keeps thinking about the thing at dinner. It's something that comes up between them every once in a while and always leaves this hollow spot in the middle of her chest. So much time without one another. So many opportunities lost. All those hours, months, years they can't get back.

But she's trying to take Chris's advice, trying to be positive instead of negative. With Anna. And with this. So she gives herself a mental shake. She will not waste this new time they've been given on regrets.

She focuses on the boxes, wondering where she's going to store them and how she's ever managed to collect so much stuff.

In bed that night, she can sense him fully awake after they say goodnight.

"Lily?" he says.

"Yes."

"I just wanted to say that if I were to have had children—two girls and one boy—I would only have wanted to have them with you."

She turns her face and meets his lips on their way to hers.

***

She wakes up late on Thursday morning, tired from all the clearing and packing. Chris is gone, but downstairs, there's coffee, and he's left the oatmeal container on the counter. The boxes they'd brought in the night before and left in the living room are gone. When she goes back upstairs and opens the door to the extra bedroom, she finds them there, in five neat stacks. But she finds much more than that.

Apparently Chris has been busy this week, too. While she's been in Stockbridge packing, he's been providing her with a brand new place to work. There's a big new desk, a new swivel chair that bounces a little when she sits in it. Her computer is set up on the desk, and there's a new lamp, even a new wastebasket. Against one wall stand not one, but two new book cases, so now she understands why he insisted she leave her old desk and shelving behind. "Too small, not enough drawers, just leave it all," he said.

So today, instead of shopping for furniture, she can start making the room her own. She unpacks several boxes, puts her books on the shelves, decides where to keep her computer stuff, her printer paper, all the other thousand things she pulls out of the boxes.

In one, she finds copies of her published stories. A half-dozen copies each of a half-dozen stories in thin, literary journals with sophisticated covers, selects the best copy of each of the six and carries them downstairs, puts them in the bookcase next to Chris's publications and then pulls out his book on Tolstoy.

His photo on the back cover shows him outdoors, looking out at a forty-degree angle from the camera into some interesting distance only he can see. It strikes just the right combination of charisma and seriousness. There's no credit beneath the photo and she wonders if the adjunct took it. Connie Constance Whatever. Because that's what he usually did when he needed his photo taken … hand a camera to whoever was nearby.

"Well, you're mine now," she says to his photo, "and don't you forget it."

She settles into a corner of the couch, just to read a few pages of his introduction, and is still sitting there three hours later—his writing, it turns out, as seductive as his Russian—when the door opens.

"Anna!"

"You both said it was okay to come whenever."

"Of course! I'm so glad to see you. Come and sit down. Can I get you something? Did you have lunch?"

"Yeah, I don't want anything." She drops her backpack onto the floor.

"There's still an unopened bottle of ginger ale."

Anna shakes her head no. "Maybe later," and she sits down next to Lily. "So New Hampshire was fun?"

"New Hampshire was great. Really perfect. You got the photos? The bird at the top of the mountain?"

"Yeah, that was weird."

"How about you? How was your weekend?"

Anna shrugs.

"Something wrong? Something happen?"

Anna leans back, looks at the ceiling. "Are all men idiots?" She turns her face toward Lily. "Are they?"

"Well, everybody's an idiot sometimes. And, yeah, I guess males catch it a little more often than females. Especially young males. Does this have something to do with your ghost-buster?"

Anna looks back at the ceiling and nods.

"Tell me," Lily says.

"I hung out with this guy Friday night. We really hit it off. Then I saw him again Saturday afternoon, sort of accidentally-on-purpose; and he came over Saturday night, and we went to the game. Then he had to go to work. He works the all-night shift at a convenience store on weekends, and he said he'd call me Monday around noon, and here it is *Thursday* and do you think I've even heard from him?"

Lily waits.

"He's like the first real person I've met since I came back, and then he turns out to be a complete asshole."

"And you haven't called him?"

"Mom, please. Why would I do that?"

"Because there could be an explanation. And you seem to like him. And if he really were an idiot, I think you would have spotted it a hundred yards away."

"Beside alien abduction, what could possibly be an explanation for a complete three-day disappearance."

"He could have had to work a double-shift; he could have lost his phone; he could be sick...." She makes a face. "I don't know. It *is* a long time, isn't it. Three days."

"Would you call someone if they did that to you?"

She thinks for a second. "Yes. If it felt important I would. I'd either want to find out the reason or at least make him face the fact he's an asshole. Let's turn things around. If you'd said you'd call him, but didn't, for good reason or bad, would you think more of him if he called you or if he didn't?"

Anna considers. "If he didn't call, I'd think he didn't care and that it was probably for the best, and then I'd just go out of my way to avoid him for the rest of my life. And if he did, then I'd think he had a tolerable amount of self-confidence. And I'd probably feel bad for being rude."

Lily looks at her and raises her eyebrows.

Anna gives an exaggerated shrug. "I guess I could think about it," and just as she's saying it, her phone rings.

Lily can tell by the way she says "oh it's you," that she should give the conversation some space, so she goes into the kitchen and makes noise opening a bottle of ginger ale and a package of cinnamon crackers, pours a glass for Anna, one for herself and puts some crackers into a bowl.

She hears Anna, a completely different Anna, say, "Okay, see you then," and even the living room, when she returns, seems bathed in a whole different light. Lily hands her a glass, sets the crackers on the table.

"Would you believe," Anna says, looking up at her, "that the convenience store—the one where he works—" got robbed early Monday morning!"

"Robbed? No! While he was there? Is he okay?"

"Yes. He's fine. But there were two guys and they had guns, though he's not sure they were real, but there was no way he was going to find out … and he had to give the police descriptions of the guys, and then he had to try and identify them looking at pictures, and then they caught them and he had do an identification through one-way glass. He said it was awesome!"

"And you're getting together again?"

"Tonight."

Lily has this momentary struggle between wanting to reach out and being afraid to. *Pretend she's still fourteen*, she hears Chris saying. *Be that mother.* She bends down, puts her hands on each side of Anna's face. "I knew my daughter could pick out an idiot at a hundred yards," and then she kisses Anna on the forehead.

Anna's eyes smile back at her. Oh to see that smile again in her eyes. But at the same time, she realizes there's a dark space the smile doesn't quite cover. And Lily knows she has to go there. But not now, not just now, when things feel almost glorious. She'll do that soon, but not now.

"Come with me," Lily says, "I want to show you something." Anna brings her glass and a cracker, follows her upstairs. "Would you believe Chris did all this and never said a word? My new office!"

Anna plops into the chair and spins it around twice. "Nice," she says. "He's not an idiot, is he. Chris."

Lily shakes her head. "No."

"Was he ever?"

"I guess we both were. He was paternalistic and stubborn. I was impatient and unforgiving. And I think I somehow felt entitled. As though I deserved everything that was good, nothing that was bad—which made it all the harder when things went wrong."

"Like with Dad?"

"I don't know. Things were completely different with your dad. I'm not sure I still had expectations then. We were just from two different worlds."

Anna nods. "Yeah, I know."

"You do?"

"Of course. I was your kid."

Lily opens one of the boxes, takes out a photo album, holds it up so Anna can read the cover. *Anna from birth to six months.*

"I was looking through it this morning," Lily says.

She flips the pages while they both point and laugh. "You were so cute," Lily says, "look how you were sitting up. And you were barely five months old. You did everything early."

"I guess I was impatient even then."

Lily looks at the new clock Chris has hung on the wall. "Stay for dinner," she says. "Chris will be home any minute. He's getting pizza and there'll be plenty. Yes?"

"Okay, but I have to leave by seven."

"To see...?"

"Max."

"Max. That's a great name. Maybe you could bring him here some time."

Downstairs, the door opens and closes. "I'm home," Chris calls, "where are you? I've got dinner."

"Up here. And I have company. We'll be right down."

***

"So it went well?" Chris asks, after they've gone to bed. "You were certainly in a good mood."

"Was I gooney?"

"What's gooney?"

"Something I'm trying not to be."

"So gooney is bad?"

"Actually, I'm not sure. It's just ... gooney."

"As in the bird?"

"Maybe. How does a gooney bird act? I forget."

"I think they have an odd courtship dance, make strange noises and duck their necks a lot."

"Oh," she says, "I hope I didn't do that."

"Not that I noticed."

"Good," she says.

CHAPTER SIXTEEN

On Saturday they leave for the cocktail party around seven. Chris wears what he always wears. The usual collarless shirt, no tie, jeans, the ubiquitous corduroy jacket; this one, dark brown. So she does what she always used to do, tries to blend with him and still manage to look somewhat dressed up. A white sleeveless top with a wide, square neckline and a long, vari-colored, blue skirt that reminds her of a stained glass window. Sandals. "You look great," he says, as they walk out the door into an unusually warm early November evening. "I like your hair that way."

She pats the bun at the nape of her neck. "Rather prim, wouldn't you say?"

"Not really." He transfers the bottle of wine he's carrying from one hand to the other, so he can open the car door for her, and as she slides in, he leans down and kisses her neck. "It's the kind of thing that whispers, *unpin me.*"

The party is at one of the big old colonial houses on Main Street, every window lit, the outer door propped open, the inner door ajar. It's the kind of elegant welcome she admires, and would never have the forethought to do herself.

They enter a large foyer decorated with floor vases filled with hydrangea blossoms, black-eyed Susans, purple ornamental grasses. A staircase at the far end curves up to the second floor.

"My goodness," Lily says, "I feel like I've stepped through the looking glass."

"Wait until you taste the food," Chris says. "Ken makes most of it himself and it's great."

"The guests of honor!" A slim, gray-haired woman comes toward them, hands raised, a welcoming smile, a confident face. She looks at Lily and the smile only grows. "Lily," she says, "I'm Sandra McDonald. Call me Sandy. It's wonderful to meet you."

"Our host," Chris says, leaning down and greeting her with a kiss on the cheek. "Yes, this is my wife Lily."

Lily puts out her hand and Sandra takes it, holds it for a second. "You're quite lovely," she says. "No wonder Chris spent no time swooping you up."

"We've actually known each other for many years," Lily says. "So you might say, it took some convincing on my part." And the three of them laugh.

It's an exchange Lily will take part in at least a dozen times before an hour goes by. Names fly at her and she tries to permanently attach each one to a face, but it's too overwhelming and she eventually gives up.

Chris disappears, and she finds herself surrounded by four very curious women, who take turns talking while she looks from one to the other. It seems each of them, at some time, made it her mission to find Chris a mate.

You're going to think we're terrible, but all of us tried very hard to find someone for him. Not that he wasn't entirely capable himself.

I introduced him to my best friend and my sister and my sister's best friend.

I mean, how can someone so fantastic stay single like that?

And, trust me, not one of them took, not one. I tried at least five times, and most of them were very good candidates, believe me.

Well—I wouldn't say it didn't take ... it just didn't take on his side.

And then you come along and BOOM!

Yes, but you knew each other in the '80s, right? Well, obviously he was just waiting to find you again. I mean, how much more romantic could anything be?

They want to know everything. Where they first met (Connecticut, they were both at Yale). How old Anna is (eighteen, nineteen in January). Where Lily's lived (San Francisco and New England, with New England her favorite). What she does (writer). Will they look for another place to live? (it hasn't come up, but she likes his house). Does she play golf? (no). Where did she buy that lovely skirt? (if she remembers, it was a little shop in Monterey).

Other people wander over, introduce themselves, stay to chat for a while. Then Ken McDonald, husband of Sandra, introduces himself and invites her to the buffet before "all the good stuff is gone."

She likes him. He asks only one question, does she like spicy guacamole? He tells her he makes it hot enough to make a big man cry, because that's the way *he* likes it, and when she tries it, yes, it does make her eyes water, and they both laugh. She tells him Chris has already introduced him as a great cook, and now she sees it's true.

"I'm happy for you and Chris," he says, "but frankly, happier for Chris. He and I have known each other for a while now, and I've never seen him like this before. I keep threatening to attach a tether because it's as if his feet don't quite touch the ground." He smiles, lifts his glass to her and she nods her thanks.

He refills her wine before he excuses himself, and she moves along the table taking a little of each of the four salads—egg, potato, pasta, green—feeling overwhelmed by all the attention and by what Ken has just said.

She retreats with her plate to the end of the table, a space momentarily empty of guests. Chris, hard to miss with that mop of white hair, is across the room talking to two men, and seeing him at a distance like this, is almost like seeing him for the first time.

A little taller than anyone else, a little larger than life, he's still the person you notice in a crowd. What does Hollywood call it? Screen presence. He had it before in spades, but even now he still does.

She watches a dark-haired woman slowly approach the group, watches as the men open their triangle to her. The woman acknowledges the others, but it's clear her attention is only aimed at Chris.

Lily bites on a piece of carrot, but the tip of her tongue gets in the way and she grimaces until the pain eases.

So that's the adjunct.

Hardly the 'older woman' Chris described. Yes, older than Lily, but still dramatically attractive. Good hair, good figure, a smart dresser. Sophisticated comes to mind.

Lily watches as the other men casually melt away, and a small electro-magnetic field seems to pop into place around the two of them, the way the party moves around them but lets them be. In her imagination, she sees them at other affairs, a couple, part of the set, and as two people who are now in some degree of pain because the intimacy they shared may never be again.

Her eyes, however, tell her something else entirely. There's Connie, standing fully facing him, open, unshielded, not even attempting to hide her vulnerability. And there's Chris, who stands obliquely to her, turning his head toward her only when he speaks, listening with his shoulder, the side of his face, every inch of him proclaiming *this is so over, if it ever was at all.*

Lily feels a rush of unexpected sympathy almost immediately trampled by a flame of indignation. Why do women do it? Why is Connie allowing herself to be pathetic, when it's so evident that what she wants to give is all out of proportion to what Chris is—or probably ever was—willing to give in return. And what about him? How can he *do* that? Not even *pretend* to care?

She feels the sting of her irritation, the warmth of an unexpected empathy. And then she feels something else—a sliver of understanding. It *is* usually women, but not always. The ache to couple, touch, be heard, be simply human, and, reluctantly, she sees herself in Chris's stance. Sees herself withholding from David, turning away from him. David, who was willing to wait such a long time for her to love him back, and never understood that his willingness to wait constantly sabotaged the thing he waited for. And what about Paul? Who was willing to fit himself into whatever small piece of her life she gave him.

It's she and Chris who are the odd ones. Two who would rather be alone or occasionally make do with what's available. At least until just the right miracle comes along.

She sets her plate on the table and walks toward them, knowing there's no easy way out of that lop-sided duet across the room, determined to finish what she unwittingly started and break that awful asymmetry once and for all.

When he notices her, Chris becomes animated, smiles, holds out his hand. "Lily," he says.

She touches his fingers briefly, then turns to the woman. "Hello. I'm Lily, Chris's wife."

"Oh yes," Connie says, "Lily." Her eyes widen for an instant, then become unreadable, and what, Lily wonders, was she expecting. Helen of Troy?

She holds out her hand. "I'm Connie. A colleague of Chris." Her mouth smiles. "Congratulations on your marriage," she looks toward Chris, then back at Lily, "to both of you. Everyone is happy and surprised. I mean … it all happened so quickly."

"I think we're still a little surprised, too," Chris says, looking at Lily.

"I hear you knew each other a long time ago?"

Lily nods. "And now this. All because of a chance encounter." She laughs a little. "Life is very unpredictable."

By now, Chris is effectively out of their tableau, his attention on something behind them, and she wonders if a kick would wake him to the dynamics here or if he'd merely rub his leg with a bewildered *hey, what did you do that for?*

"Oh, it's a cake, I think," Connie says, looking beyond and behind Lily. "In honor of the newlyweds." Her lips smile again. "So nice to meet you," and then she's gone.

Chris puts his arm around Lily's waist. "Looks like we're getting a second wedding cake."

Ken McDonald was right. He does seem to float. And he doesn't seem to notice Connie is gone. Apparently has forgotten she was ever there. Perhaps, that he ever knew her at all.

"How could you do that?" Lily whispers.

"What? I didn't ask for a cake."

She stares at him, astonished. But then she's not sure herself what she meant. *How could you sleep with that gorgeous woman? How could you cheat on me when I wasn't even in your life? How could you be so insensitive, so casual with someone who obviously cares for you? How could you? How COULD you?*

But the crazy thing is, it's all very familiar. They've had this same inane interaction many times before. Because for all his exquisite erudition, there are some things, some simple basic things, he just doesn't get. As if he completely lacks a receptor that's overly exaggerated in her own brain, sensitive to things impossible for him to even conceive.

The cake and guests move toward them—a sense of celebration and genuine good feeling in the air. And really, does it make a difference? Is sex for sex's sake wrong? Is there some rule that demands both participants feel identically? Is there a kind, painless, simple way to tell someone who cares about you that you feel essentially nothing in return?

And just like that, she decides to let it go. Because men are men and women are women. Because Connie is a grown-up and love is risky. And, for whatever reason, Chris belongs to Lily. He always has.

CHAPTER SEVENTEEN

"Here," he says, taking off his coat and putting it around her shoulders as they walk to the car. "Man, it got cold. And feel that wind."

He puts his arm around her and she leans into his warmth. "It was a wonderful party," she says. "I can truly say it was one of the best faculty parties we've ever been to."

"It's a good group." He looks at his watch under a streetlamp. "And it's not even late."

"The food was wonderful. Especially the cake. Do you think he made that, too?"

Chris shakes his head. "No. I don't think he bakes. But Sandra packed us some to take home." He holds up a small brown bakery box.

"Maybe I'll tell Anna to come by tomorrow and have some?"

"Definitely."

"We haven't talked yet. Not about the thing we need to talk about. But I have the sense that I can bring it up now without her shutting me out."

"Good." He pulls her closer.

The drive home takes just long enough for the car to begin to warm up and then it's back out into the wind. They run up the walk holding hands and he checks for messages while she goes upstairs.

He's in bed reading when she comes out of the bathroom, doesn't look up from the book, says, "that took you a while."

She stands there until he finally looks up at her. Then he takes off his glasses, closes the book and drops it on the floor.

"I bought it a while ago," she says. "I've been waiting for appropriate weather conditions." She does a complete twirl, and when she stops, she holds up a piece of paper. "But it comes with rules."

"Aw christ," he moans, "again?"

"Well, it's a game. And games have rules."

He crosses his arms and waits.

She steps up onto the bed and sits down facing him in a loose lotus. She points to the buttons that run from the neck of the white flannel nightgown down almost to the waist. "See these?"

"I do see them."

"Well, I have a list of questions. And every time you answer correctly, you get to undo one."

"Tell me these questions have nothing to do with economics or analytic geometry or nuclear physics."

She laughs. "None of those things. And you won't miss even one, because they all just happen to involve Russian literature."

He uncrosses his arms, rubs his hands together. "Do I start at the top or the bottom?"

"Top. Are you ready?"

"More than ready."

She reads the first question: "What is the name of Anna's brother's wife in..."

"*Anna Karenina*," he says, before she can finish, "and the answer is Princess Darya Alexandrovna Oblonskaya." He reaches over and unbuttons her top button.

"This," she says, "is very win-win. You get to undress me; I get to hear you growl Russian."

"*The Brothers Karamazov*," she says. "Name all three of the brothers. And the illegitimate son, too."

"Aw, c'mon," Chris says. "That's worth four buttons right there."

"Two," she says.

"Three. And I'll throw in the meaning of the fourth brother's name."

129

"Okay," she says, scooting closer to him. "Four."

He ticks them off on his fingers. "Dmitri Fyodorovich Karamazov, who's married to Adelaida Ivanova Miusov. Ivan Fyodorovich Karamazov, who falls in love with Daterina Ivanovna. Alexei Fyodorovich Karamazov, the youngest. And the ublyudok is Pavel Fyodorovich Smerdyakov. Smerdyakov, by the way, means 'son of the reeking one.'"

"That was so much more than I asked for," she says, leaning toward him, "that you have to re-button the button you just unbuttoned."

"Yeah right. There is no going backward in this game, young woman. And my intention is to speed things up, not slow them down. How about five buttons?"

"How about three?"

"I'll take it."

She smiles at him. "Now say the first paragraph of *A Tale of Two Cities*."

"That's not Russian literature. That's an English guy."

"You didn't let me finish. You have to say it in Russian."

He shakes his head. He starts. And before two minutes have gone by, Lily has unbuttoned three more buttons herself. By the time he stops, the nightgown is on the floor and Chris has passed third base. "You cheat," she says. "I love it when you cheat."

"You drive me insane," he says.

And afterwards, when she's lying there against him, wondering how much better things could possibly be, she asks, "What is it between us? What is it that makes us love each other so damn much?"

He doesn't say anything at first, then, "I don't know ... we just *click*."

"You've never clicked with anyone else?"

"I used to think so. Until I met you. And then after you, I never heard another click until October 9 at 3:20 PM."

She smiles. "You remember it to the minute?"

"To the precise minute."

"I've never clicked with anyone else." She comes up on one elbow and looks down at him. There are certain things about you that get me right here." She pats her stomach. "Like a slow uncoiling of warmth. The way your wrists look when your shirtsleeves are slightly turned back. The way you always smile a little slower than everybody else."

"Slower?"

"Always. Which makes your smile more noticeable." She shrugs. "Maybe it's something primal. Maybe I just like the way you smell. And vice versa." She looks at him. "What do I smell like to you?"

"You really want to know?"

She nods.

She starts to laugh as soon as he starts to sniff her. Her cheeks, he says are cinnamon, her neck lemon, the space between her breasts licorice, the inside of her elbow clover, her stomach vanilla. He stops between her stomach and her thighs and lays the side of his face against her. "Can I just stay right here for the rest of my life?"

She runs her fingers through his hair. "You could, but wouldn't it get awkward?"

"Possibly," he says.

He tells her the top of her thigh smells like jasmine; her knee, like a band aid; her ankle like popcorn; her toes like bacon. "Other side?" he says.

"No. I think that's enough. So I really smell like all those things?"

"Plus the overall faint aroma of trouble."

"Okay," she says, "my turn," and he settles into horizontal.

"Sawdust," she says, smelling his chest. His arm is tobacco, his stomach, skunk. "Down boy," she says, moving to his leg.

"I can't help it," he says, "do you have any idea what it feels like to have someone sweep their hair across your body?"

"Baseball glove," she says, her nose to his thigh.

"How come everything you smell of is good," he asks, "and everything I smell of isn't."

"Because you're a boy and I'm a girl." She gives him one long aerial whiff from his toes up to his chin.

"Promise me one thing," he says, "that you'll never cut your hair."

"Promise," she says.

"Well, what's the verdict?"

"Chris," she says. "You smell like Chris. And I have to say it was a strangely satisfying experiment. So maybe there's something to it after all."

"Satisfying," he says, "yes." He pushes her hair back from her face. "But in scientific terms, our experiment was archaic. Science has already done the research. It's already been tabulated and processed—the reason a person is attracted to another certain person and only that person. You don't know about it?"

"No." She settles into the crook of his arm. "But you're going to tell me, right?"

"I am. It seems people make connections—or fail to—on many many different levels. For instance, two people might connect on, say, three levels, eight levels, fifteen levels, even a hundred and thirteen levels, but not on the rest, and those levels they connect on? ... not enough to even rate a notice."

"Why? How many levels are there?

"Four million and three."

She laughs. "Four million and *three*?"

"It's a very complicated thing, Lily. I mean, think of all the facets of an individual's personality and then double that by bringing in a completely separate and unique individual. All those traits, genetic and learned, all those conscious desires, sub-conscious desires, experiences, brain patterns. It's huge!"

"It does sound huge."

"But the interesting part of the research is that every once in a great while—a millennia, never less, sometimes more—two people come along and mesh, quite extraordinarily, on almost every single level. They have a name for it. *Shchelchok*."

"It's Russian research?" she laughs. She repeats the word, "*Shchelchok*."

"Very good."

"What does it mean?"

"It means they *click*."

"As in you and I *click*?"

"Right. And you and I really *shchelchok* because we connect on three million nine hundred and ninety-nine levels. Our brain patterns hum along in perfect symmetry. Our genetic traits are synchronistically geared. Our conscious and sub-conscious desires are essentially indistinguishable."

"Wow," she says. "Even though I'm not vaguely Russian and you're not vaguely Irish?"

"Shhh," he says, "my story. You can go next, if you want, but right now you're a listener."

"I am listening.'

"Now I want you to be very quiet and see what you hear." So she goes very still, they both go very still. "Hear that?" he whispers.

"What?" she whispers back.

"That tick tick ticking. Very hard to hear but it's there. It's the perfect beating of our life forces, yours and mine. Extraordinarily simpatico."

"But what about the three levels we don't connect on?"

"Oh, those are so esoteric they hardly matter. I think, in fact, they only exist in some far-off universe that we can't even imagine."

"So they've researched compatibility in other parts of the universe, too?"

"Of course. Everyone knows Russian scientists aren't alien-averse."

She yawns. "I'm so glad," she says.

"About Russian scientists?"

Her eyes close. "That we *schlektok*."

"*Shchelchok*."

"Mmmm," she says. "Click."

CHAPTER EIGHTEEN

Chris sets his side of the recliner down onto the floor. Lily notes that he looks exasperated, has for most of the last hour. "Didn't we just try it here five minutes ago?" he says. The tone of his voice is sheer frustration.

"Yes," Lily says, "but we couldn't get it close enough to the wall because of the bookcase, and now that's moved." She steps back, picks a couch cushion up off the floor and wraps her arms around it, looks at the recliner, the way it blocks one side of the couch and juts into the room. "It still doesn't work, does it."

He doesn't even look, just stands there giving off bad vibes. "Nothing seems to work *any*where. Let's just leave it here, Lily, okay? It's fine."

"No, it's not fine. It sticks out too far into the room and it blocks one side of the couch."

"What *difference* does it make?"

"Oh, okay. No problem, Chris. People can step up onto the sofa and walk over each other to get to the other end. Or maybe vault over the back onto the seat."

Why, she wonders, is he acting like such a royal pain in the ass? "It makes a difference, Chris. Especially if we have to detour around the recliner every time we walk across the damn room."

"People?" he says. "What people? It's you and I, Lily. *We're* the only people who live here. And in the past two hours, the people who live here have moved everything in the damn room thirty times. And thirty times you haven't been satisfied. Can you just settle on *some*thing and we'll learn to live with it?"

"Thirty times? *Thirty*? And whose idea was it to move this goddamn recliner here in the first place?"

"Well I didn't think you were going to be so fucking fussy about how the room had to work!"

That's it. She takes the cushion and flings it at him. Unfortunately he's far enough away and quick enough to catch it.

"What the hell," he says.

Then the door opens and Anna is there. "Whoa," she says, stopping inside the doorway. "What are you two *doing?*"

"We two," Chris says, flopping into the recliner, "are *restructuring* the living room, while your mother tries to kill me with a pillow." He throws it onto the couch. "We've been *restructuring* for two hours, and if you can figure out where this thing I'm sitting in should go, even if it means tossing three other pieces of furniture out into the yard, I'll send you to Bimini on your winter vacation." He closes his eyes. "With your new friend ... the guy who got robbed."

"Max," she says. "Really?"

He opens his eyes, frowns. "Did I say Bimini? No. I meant Brattleboro. I'll send you both to Brattleboro."

"Hi, honey," Lily says. "You'd think moving a few pieces of furniture was equal to being *shot at dawn.*" She directs the last three words at Chris with what she hopes is precise meaning. "And guess whose idea it was to move the recliner from Stockbridge in the first place?"

"Only because I thought it looked comfortable. I didn't realize it was eighteen-feet-long when you stretched it out."

"Oh for heaven's sake, stop being such a baby. And stop exaggerating everything out of all proportion."

"*If,*" Anna says loudly, you move that bookcase over there," she points to the one wall they haven't tried yet, "and put the couch and the two brown chairs opposite each other in the *middle* of the room, then the recliner will fit in that corner next to the window."

For a few seconds, no one says a word. "And," Anna looks directly at Chris, "you said Bimini first."

Lily lets out a hoot and in about seven minutes, they're done.

"That was masterful," Chris says.

Lily smiles at Anna. "She has a very good eye and very good spatial sense."

"Which she definitely doesn't get from you," Chris says. He looks around the room. "Thank you, Anna."

"You're welcome." She looks at Lily. "You said something about cake?"

"In a plastic container on the counter. And there's part of an omelet left over from breakfast in the pan on the stove, if you want to heat it up."

Anna leaves the room, comes back with a fork and a plate of cake, and sits down on the couch. "But now you need a table here so you have someplace to put stuff."

Lily picks up two rattan cubes and plunks them down between the couch and the two chairs. "Nice," Anna says, and Lily sits down in one of the chairs.

"It's not a small room," Lily says, "but the shape is odd. Long and not very ...." But before she can finish the sentence, a picture lodges itself in her head and she starts to laugh.

Anna stops eating, Chris glances up. Lily laughs and can't stop.

"It was the look on your face," she finally gets out, pointing at Chris, "... when I threw the cushion."

Chris frowns and Anna just looks confused, which starts Lily laughing all over again. "The cream," she manages to say, "the whipped cream. Same look."

Chris sits there watching her, but his face softens a little, and he says. "I still say that was no accident."

Which makes her howl, and now Anna's laughing, too, even though she has no idea why.

Chris waits until the two of them have regained some control. Then he says, "Years ago your mother and I had company for dinner. It was a big deal because we'd never invited anyone for dinner before, never cooked for anyone before." He looks at Lily. "That's what's so funny?"

All she can do is nod.

"So just before dessert, she called me into the kitchen and said I had to run out and get whipped cream for the dessert."

"Bread pudding," Lily says."

"So out I went. The store was only twenty yards away, and back I came."

"Except it wasn't whipped cream," Lily says. She shakes her hand in the air. "You know, it was the stuff in a can..." and she makes a noise like an aerosol. *Wissshh*

"I was in the kitchen," Chris says, "ready to top the pudding when she comes in and starts on me — *how could you buy this junk. We need cream, real whipping cream.* And I said *what difference does it make? It'll be fine...*"

Lily takes a deep breath. "Which is exactly what you said about the living room." Her stomach hurts from laughing.

"And then she grabs the can out of my hand and next thing I know, I have whipped cream all over me. All over my shirt, all over my face, in my hair..."

Lily starts laughing again, and so does Anna.

"I know you did it on purpose," he says.

"I didn't. It was an accident, Chris, I swear it was an accident. I would never have done that to you." She takes a deep breath. "At least not with two guests in the next room."

"I'm not so sure about that," he says. "But all this is starting to remind me that I pretty much owe you one."

They look at each other. "Yeah," Lily says, "maybe you do." Then she frowns, sniffs, jumps up. "I think the omelet's burning."

When she comes back, she sets the plated omelet on the cube in front of Anna, along with a glass of milk, and sits down again. "It didn't really burn," she tells Anna, "just a little around the edges."

Chris clears his throat. "My mother," he says, "stayed home and took care of us when I was very young. Like most mothers in those days. Except she wasn't like most mothers. I mean, she cooked, kept the house clean, belittled my father, but she hated her life and was mostly miserable." He looks at Lily. "As you probably remember."

Lily shrugs, looks at Anna. "She was not a charming woman."

"Anyway," Chris says, "another thing she did was rearrange the furniture. Constantly. Unendingly. Almost without interruption. Every few days, you came home from school and nothing was where it had been when you left. Not your bed, not your stuff. The rugs changed rooms, the curtains changed windows. The living room became the dining room, the dining room became a sewing room. One day I came home and found all my brother's things in my closet and all mine in his. And it's a classic, right? If you can't rearrange your life, you rearrange the furniture. But I was seven, and I didn't know that then, so it was just plain … unsettling." He takes a breath. "One day, after my father had worked a double shift and came home at four o'clock in the morning, he went into the bedroom and threw himself down on the bed. Except the bed wasn't there anymore. Because my mother had moved it to the other side of the room."

After a second of silence, Anna snorts and Lily has to bite down on her lip.

"It's okay," Chris says, "in retrospect, it's funny. Although my father didn't think so because he broke his elbow, which meant he couldn't work for two months, and so he was home all the time with my mother, except about half-way through, he walked out of the house one day and never came back."

"Whoa," Anna says. Did you ever see him again?"

"I used to run into him sometimes. He didn't go far."

"How come I never knew any of this?" Lily says.

"Moving the furniture seems to have unearthed the memories from some crypt where they were buried. I didn't realize until today I had such a distinct aversion to moving furniture. And, more importantly that I couldn't control that aversion." He looks at Lily. "I apologize."

"It's okay. We'll never move a piece of furniture again."

"Yes, we will. Whenever it's necessary. And I'll try to act like a grownup about it."

"What did your mother do after your father left?" Anna asks. "I mean, did she just keep moving furniture?"

"No. She got a job. She went to work as a lunch lady. You know, one of the women in the cloth caps who dole out the spaghettios at school?"

Anna nods.

"She complained about that, too, but I think she was actually a little happier. Or maybe I should say a little less unhappy. She hardly ever moved the furniture after that."

No one says anything, as if they're giving everything he's said a second of silence.

Then he stands up. "I'm off to the Library." He looks at Anna. "You'll still be here if I'm back around four?"

"I think so."

"We could do Chinese for dinner then. Or Thai. Or Indian."

"Indian," Lily and Anna say together.

"Good." He looks at Lily. "I'll text you when I'm on my way, and maybe you and Anna can meet me there?" Then he walks over to her and kisses the top of her head. She takes his hand, squeezes it.

After he's gone, Anna says, "that was pretty cool." She's finished the omelet and the milk, is scraping what's left of the cake off the plate.

"There's more," Lily says. "There should be at least one more piece in the container."

"I ate it all," Anna says.

"Oh."

"It's okay. I have a quick metabolism. Like you."

"I know. You're fine. What was pretty cool?"

"What he did. You know, getting mad and then figuring out why and apologizing. Usually people just let whatever the fight was about kind of shrivel up and crawl under something."

"That's true," Lily says. "I suppose I should have apologized, too. For throwing the cushion at him."

"I don't think it bothered him much. I mean, you can't hurt anybody with a cushion."

"He just made me so mad." She looks out the window. "I wonder why he had to go to the library?" Then she looks at Anna, and Anna looks back at her, and what Anna said about letting things shrivel up and hide is the third image of the afternoon she can't ignore.

"Anna, can we talk?"

Anna makes a face. "Isn't that what we're doing?"

"I mean really talk. Because there's something we've never addressed. Or something *I've* never addressed with you. And I don't want it sticking between us anymore. Is that okay?"

Anna shrugs. "I guess."

Lily leans forward a little. "The thing is, Anna … ever since you came back from France, no, before that … ever since you went to live with your father, we've been *different* with each other. And I haven't known what to do about it. How to try and fix it. And I want to. Can we try to fix it?"

"I thought that's what we've been doing."

"Yes. Me, too. And that's been huge. But like you just said…"

"We shouldn't just let it crawl off somewhere?"

"No. We shouldn't do that." She hesitates. "I'll go first?"

Anna nods.

"I hated it when you went off to be with your dad. I didn't want you to go."

Anna pokes at the edge of the wicker cube. "Then why did you make me?"

"I didn't make you, honey. I thought that not letting you go was unreasonable. And selfish. You'd gotten to know him, right? Those six months he lived nearby? He wanted you to spend more time with him. Just him. And he wanted it very badly."

"But you never *said* you hated it. You acted like you wanted it."

"Well of course I did. If I'd acted like I didn't want you to go, you wouldn't have gone. Or you would have felt guilty about going. And it wouldn't have been fair to your dad. And maybe not to you, either. Was I supposed to keep you from him? Just because I didn't want to let you go? It was the only logical way for you to really get to know each other."

She stops for a second, gets her bearing. "You don't remember, Anna, you were too little, but in the beginning, when we were first divorced, the only way he could see you was if I were there, too. You wouldn't go off with him alone. You threw tantrums and screamed for me. One time, he strapped you into your car seat and drove off and was back in three minutes. He was in tears, I was in tears, you were hysterical. It took half an hour just to calm you down. It was horrible for all of us. So after that, he'd come to the house and play with you in one room while I tried to stay out of the way. But you hardly ever gave him more than ten minutes before you went looking for me. You were so young, and he'd always been gone too much." She stops. "It wasn't fair, was it. For any of us."

"He said you could have come to Paris, too. He said that was an option, but you said no."

"That's true. I did. And maybe that was a mistake. But I would have been completely dependent on him, and I didn't want to be. And he always had the option of staying in the states. Being near you."

She lifts her shoulders, lets them fall. "We did the best we could with a very hard situation. And maybe we made some wrong choices. But you grew to love being with him, didn't you?"

Anna shrugs. "Sometimes I thought you just figured it was easier without me. You could do what you wanted."

"Anna, what I wanted was to be your mother. That's who I was. Who I am. And when you left ... I was nobody for a really long time." She leans forward, rests her hands on top of a cube. "I missed you so much. And I am so very very sorry for making you unhappy. It's the last thing in the world I ever wanted —or ever want— to do."

Anna sits there, looking at her lap. "I was just mad," she says. "I really wanted to come home at the end of that first school year. I mean, the school was good and I had friends, but everything was so different there, and Dad ... the only way he knew how to be with me was to take me places and bring my friends, and buy us all stuff. It was like he was always afraid I wasn't going to be happy enough."

"Why did you say you didn't want to come home then?"

"Like I said, I was mad. At you. And it was a way of getting back. It was the only way I had."

Lily gets up and sits down next to Anna, puts her arms around her. "I'm sorry I hurt you. And I'm sorry you hurt me. But can it be over now? You know I love you more than anything, and so does your dad. And now you have both of us."

Anna buries her face against Lily's shoulder, and they stay like that for a long time. Just sitting, just holding on to each other.

CHAPTER NINETEEN

On the day of their one-month anniversary, Lily is sitting at her desk working, finally in a routine that accommodates Anna, Chris, her work, herself, when she hears Chris coming up the stairs. But it's Tuesday, it's three o'clock, and he doesn't get home until five on Tuesdays. "You're early," she says.

"I am," and he slides a newspaper clipping onto her keyboard. "But we have an appointment in a half-hour."

She looks at the photo in the clipping. "It's my house!"

He points at the picture. "Not a triple window above the porch, just a double, but everything else more or less fits."

She looks up at him. "We're going to look at it?"

"Of course. It's the only authentic Craftsman-style bungalow that's been on the market around here in ten years. Let's go."

"Right now?"

"This minute."

***

The house is set far back off the road, so it doesn't come into view right away, and when it does, a hundred yards up the driveway, Lily lets out a little 'oh.'

The outside paint is faded, but the colors are typical—cocoa brown walls, mahogany trim, and deep green accents.

They get out of the car at the top of the driveway.

"It's a lot overdue for a lot of things," Chris says, "but don't let that discourage you. It's mostly superficial."

"Have you already been here?"

He nods. "This morning. I've had a call in with the realtor for a while. The house isn't officially on the market yet."

She looks at him in wonder. "Chris? Is this really you?"

"No. This is some guy who's willing to do just about anything for the woman he loves."

She grabs him around the waist and hugs him hard. "You're leaving me breathless."

"That's exactly what I'm after."

They walk around the outside, and he's right, the house is in a state of genteel decay.

"Very old couple," he says, "lived here all their lives. Family just moved then into a nursing home after the husband fell and broke his hip. They're together in the same room."

"I guess that helps a little."

When they get back to the front of the house, they climb six broad wooden steps to a large open porch, and Lily goes over to one end and looks across the yard. It's full of mature trees, out-of-control shrubs, overgrown gardens. But in her head, she sees it as it should be.

"Ready?" Chris says, taking a key out of his pocket, and she crosses the porch and they go in together.

"It's musty," he says, "but I don't think it's mold. It's been closed up since May."

The wood floors are darkened, without even a sheen, but she's pretty sure they're walnut, and all the woodwork is still natural.

The two bathrooms are dingy and antique, but the walls are white-tiled and authentic; the floors, white and black mosaic; the towel bars, original; the sinks, set onto white porcelain pedestals. The dining room has one wall of big windows, and a gumwood built-in storage unit at one end that consists of twelve drawers with brass pulls below and glass-fronted cabinets above. From the nine-foot ceiling hangs a marvelous glass and lead light fixture in the middle of the room.

Lily touches the smooth-grained wood around the doorways, realizes neither one of them has said a word since they entered.

The kitchen is a seventy-year-old disaster, with cheap upgrades that were probably new in 1950, but there's a pantry between the kitchen and dining room with all original glass-front cupboards and its own soapstone sink surrounded by what looks like a real ceramic counter.

The living room has a stone-faced fireplace and a vaulted beamed ceiling. "Which means you lose a bedroom upstairs," Chris says, breaking the silence, "but we don't need four bedrooms anyway, right?"

She shakes her head and follows him to the stairs, catches sight of another first floor room with high windows, a fireplace, and floor-to-ceiling bookcases on three walls.

"Library?" Chris says.

The stairway is extra-wide, with a landing half-way up and a stained glass window that looks out over the side yard but is mostly obstructed by a yew, and then the stairs turn back on themselves and continue up to a large landing at the top, where four short hallways take you to a bathroom in one direction; a small bedroom in another; and each of the others to a large, multi-windowed bedroom. "One faces east," Chris says, "the other west."

"East is nice to wake up to in the morning," Lily says, and her voice sounds loud in the emptiness.

Back in the landing hallway, she opens one of the four doors. "Linen closet," she says. "And look … it's as finished as a piece of fine furniture."

"That's the thing about this style. It didn't get it's name for nothing." He opens a door on the opposite wall. "You'll never guess what this one is."

"A dumbwaiter?" Lily says.

"Some kind of lift. Laundry?"

The third door is a closet filled with old-fashioned wire hangers tilted at odd angles to one another.

"And this," Chris says, opening the fourth, "has the stairs to the attic."

She looks at the narrow steep wooden steps that disappear into dark, sees the two sets of footsteps in the dust. One set going up, one coming down. "You've been up there."

"Yes, but it's completely unfinished and you need a flashlight. The roof seems tight. No obvious leaks."

They do another complete walk-through and end up sitting at the bottom of the stairs. Even though the windows are streaked and dirty, light floods in everywhere.

"Well," Chris says after a while, "what do you think?"

"I'm overwhelmed."

"Because it's daunting?'

"Because I'm sitting in the house I've always dreamed of."

"Then you want it?"

"Want it? That makes it sound like we're buying a waffle iron or an ice cream cone." She looks at him. "Chris ... it could be such a wonderful house. But it would cost a fortune to fix up, and the price is certainly no bargain."

"But actually it is," he says, "considering its innate quality and the fact it comes with twelve acres. Did I mention it abuts a wildlife sanctuary?"

She covers her face with her hands, shakes her head, looks up at him. "It's too much, Chris. It's lovely, but it's too much."

He leans his elbows on his knees. "Okay, look. You're selling your house. I'm selling mine, or maybe we won't sell mine, maybe we'll rent it. We're not going to find something like this ever again." He takes one of her hands in both of his. "We've done without each other for twenty years, Lily, let's live large for a while." Then he shrugs and looks almost bashful. "Besides, I've discovered something about myself that you don't know."

She smiles. "You're a wizard?"

"Almost as good. I have a knack for investment. I own a couple of other houses in town. We can do this, Lily. All you have to do is say yes, and it's a done deal."

She looks around. "Shouldn't we think about it first?"

"We don't have time. I put down a twenty-four hour deposit this morning. And there are four other deposits waiting. I just happen to know the realtor and she called me first."

Lily looks at him. "She did, huh?"

"Look, she's seventy and she has eight grandchildren."

"Ah, just like the adjunct."

He gives her a look. "C'mon, Lily. Do I ever bring up what's-his-name. Do I ever?"

"No. But you're *much* more mature than I am."

And then, in an effort to put the conversation squarely back where it belongs, Chris gives her his best, no-nonsense, professorial look. "If these stairs we're sitting on are going to become *our* stairs," he says, "we need to make a decision now."

She puts her hand on the banister, feels the smoothness of the wood. "Then I say yes. I say definitely yes."

CHAPTER TWENTY

In the next few weeks, Lily discovers something else about Chris. He really is a wizard. He knows how to put a complicated project together in a matter of days and arrange for an absolute deadline. The electricians, the plumbers, a window crew, an insulation crew, a roof crew, a foundation crew, a chimney crew.

"Run another hundred hours of juice through those old wires and the whole house would have burned down," the head electrician tells them. "Lead pipes," the plumber says, "you don't see them much anymore." And as soon as he says it, the pipe he's touching collapses in on itself. "Roof underlayment is sound, like you thought," the head roofer says, "but those shingles are fifteen years past their end date."

They watch their poor house get quickly deconstructed and then slowly put back together. Stronger, newer, cleaner, brighter, quieter, warmer.

They all go to Bimini for Christmas break—Lily, Chris, Anna, and Max. And just before the beginning of spring break in March, the house is done.

With a moving van coming in three days, Lily starts packing closets and bookcases and cabinets and cupboards, and is grateful most of her boxes never got unpacked at all. She goes down into the basement, and, as Chris said, there are about a dozen boxes he has to go through before they move. Most of it, he said, can be thrown away. But he hasn't done it yet, and so she pulls one box off the pile and then sets it on the floor because the box beneath it has her name on the top in Chris' handwriting.

She carries it to a table and opens it. Clothes. Her clothes. Everything she left in Connecticut twenty years ago. Everything neatly folded. He's moved half-a-dozen times during those years, and he's taken this box with him every time.

She recognizes a skirt, a pair of sandals she used to love to wear, a crazy-colored floral head scarf, a sheer, black nightgown, underwear, a parka, a baggie full of hair elastics. He packed every single thing she left behind and then kept it all.

Two more boxes are marked with her name, another one full of clothes, and one smaller, lighter than the others. Inside that box, she finds a framed photo she'd forgotten. It's the picture Steve McNally took at the first faculty party she and Chris ever went to. And for the first time she understands what the others must have seen. The picture shows an incredibly young girl and an incredibly handsome man. The girl is looking at the camera, the man is looking at the girl, and Lily stares at it for a long time, alternating between feelings of warmth at the way Chris is looking at her, and regret that what they had was lost for so long.

Then she sets the photo down and lifts out a folder. Inside, she recognizes her manuscript. *Mackerel Sky* across the first page, above *A Novel in Progress by Lily Shea*. In another folder are dozens of cards and notes, some on proper paper, others on napkins, post-its, the backs of envelopes. *Dear Chris – can you pick up my cleaning? - XXXXXX. - Where are you? I miss you? - Be back soon, warm up the bed for me. - Lily, don't you ever slam a door on me again!!! - Running late, don't wait. - Prof. Hicks is an ASSHOLE! - I think I love you more than anyone has ever loved another person.* He'd saved them all.

She carries the box up to her office, puts the photo and her manuscript on her desk, sits down and starts to read. Thirty pages in, she hears the door open downstairs and Chris calls, "Hey, I'm home."

She calls back, "Up here."

"You found your manuscript," he says, perching on the corner of the desk.

"I thought for sure I'd give up in disgust after a page-and-a-half," she says, "but it has something."

"It needs you to get back to it, or back to something new. You're a different writer now, better in many ways, I'm sure."

She looks up at him. "Chris, you kept all my stuff. All of it."

"It stayed where you kept it for a long time. But then I moved. So I decided to take what I still had of you with me. I mean, there was always the outside chance you'd come back. Right?"

She lifts her hands off the desk. "And I did. But I think the clothes have to go now."

"If you say so." And then he notices the photo, turns it so he can see it. "That actually stayed out of a box for a much longer time. In one of my desk drawers."

"You kept it in a drawer?"

"A nearby drawer."

"Why?"

He shakes his head. "I don't know. It was complicated. For one thing, you'd taken the album, so I had no pictures of us, except for this. For another, I didn't want it out all the time, because I didn't want to get so used to it that I stopped seeing it. But at the same time, seeing it..." He shakes his head. "Seeing it, hurt. But I still needed to look at it relatively often."

"We really screwed up, didn't we."

"No," he says, "we just did what people do. But we have to forget all that. Because we got lucky again, right?"

She nods.

"And the reason I'm home," he says, "is because we need to see a lawyer. Any chance you can do it later today?"

"About what?"

"She's going to need your signature on a bunch of stuff. I'm adding you to everything. Life insurance, deeds, bank accounts, the whole schlemiel."

She smiles. "Which means what ... that I'm loaded now, too?"

***

At the lawyer's, she signs her new name so many times it starts to feel entirely normal that she's Lily Cheykin. The lawyer goes over everything very thoroughly, but the only thing that sticks in Lily's brain is when the lawyer says, "And the trust that was in your name, Mr. Cheykin, and the name of your first wife, Denise M. Cheykin and then revoked following her death, is now in a trust for you and your present wife, Lily Cheykin."

On the drive home, Lily says, "You put money aside for Denise?"

"I did that a long time ago," Chris says. "If she outlived me, the money would at least have kept her off the street."

"Meaning you were always supporting her. Even when we were together."

He nods. "She was helpless, Lily. It was a terrible life, but at least she didn't go hungry or roofless. And no matter how bad she got, she always managed to get those checks and cash them."

So it all suddenly made sense. All the cheap vacations, the trips not taken, the tightfistedness.

She leans toward him and kisses him on the cheek. "I love you," she says.

He takes his eyes off the road to glance at her. "*Ya tozhe*," he says. "*Me too*."

***

The van follows them to the new house, and Lily carries their photo inside and places it on the mantel. By the end of the day, every room is filled with boxes to be unpacked; the furniture is more or less in place; and it's snowing.

Chris starts the fireplace in the living room, turns on the front porch light so they can see the snow, turns off the lights inside, and they settle down in front of the fire on the couch. The flames throw light and shadow against the walls and ceiling, and Lily says, "Pinch me. This has to be a dream."

"No dream," he says, "I have the backache to prove it."

"I made up our bed," she says.

"Not yet. It's too good right here."

They stare at the fire, and after a while, she says, "Chris?"

He looks at her.

"Is it too good?"

He says, "You just put a completely different slant on what I said." And then he looks at her more closely. "Jesus, Lily … are you *crying?*"

She doesn't answer. She can't. Yes, she's crying.

"Lily." He sits forward, turns and puts his hands on her arms. "What's the matter? What's wrong?"

She shakes her head. "Nothing." She takes a deep breath, wipes at her nose. "Nothing's wrong. That's the problem. Look at us. We have each other. We have this wonderful house. Anna's coming tomorrow, and doing it happily." She sniffs. "I'm not used to things working out, Chris. Not like this."

She sees him almost laugh, but then he stops himself. "So everything that should be making you happy is actually making you unhappy."

"It doesn't make me unhappy. It *scares* me. I don't want to lose a single piece of it."

"But why should you even think about losing any of it? You just got it, for christs sakes."

"Because you're right. I've become this pessimistic, expect-the-worst person. Was I always like this? I don't think so, but was I?"

He sighs, kisses her on the forehead, sits back and puts his arm around her. "Not pessimistic. Not expect-the-worst. Not then, and not now. You were in a situation that would try anyone's soul. And I said those things in a dumb attempt to help."

"It was not dumb."

"Yeah. It was dumb. You're as good as anyone at taking things as they come. And the way I look at it, we had a pretty lengthy negative column going for a while. Which means we still have a ways to go before we get close to breaking even. And this is one pretty goddamn perfect moment." He looks at her. "Let's not worry about losing it. Let's just enjoy the hell out of it. Okay?"

She nods. "Okay."

"You'll try?"

"No, I'll do it."

"No you won't."

"I will."

"No you won't. Because one thing I've always been able to rely on is you being contrary. Ergo ... tonight." He says it matter-of-factly, evenly, no trace of accusation or annoyance. "Put a hundred people on this couch, Lily, and fifty would be content and the rest, ecstatic." He looks at her. "Unless one of them is you."

"Which is going to drive you crazy eventually."

"No. It makes me love you. The only thing predictable about you is your unpredictability. You're the antithesis of dull and I'll never figure you out if we live to be two hundred." He gets up and pokes the fire, adds another log. "What do you think made me notice you in the first place?"

"Leaping naked into a snow drift."

"Memorable, but not it."

"My hair."

"Also memorable, but not enough in itself."

"Criticizing your hand-writing."

He shakes his head.

"What?"

"You don't remember the first time we shared a table at the co-op?"

She frowns. "Maybe."

"Well, I remember it very well."

"Tell me."

"I walked in; place was a zoo; I almost turned around with my coffee to head back to my office; but I spied a table for two in a corner with one empty chair and you, somebody I recognized from my seminar. I walked up to the table, stood there for a second, but you didn't look up because your nose was in your book. So I cleared my throat. *All right if I sit here?* I said. And what I expected to hear was *Hi Dr. Cheykin. Of course. Sit down.* But instead, the contrary Lily Shea looked up at me as if it were a question that required some degree of thought."

She laughs. "You surprised me. I had my nose in a book. I was concentrating."

"Leaving me to stand there thinking you might actually say *no.*"

She pats his hand. "Poor you."

"But then you rallied: *Oh, hello Professor Cheykin.* And I repeated ... *may I sit here?*"

"And *then* I said *of course.* And that makes me contrary?"

"No. What came next proves you contrary. You obviously knew me, right?"

"Right."

"And I knew you as a member of my seminar who had been consistently challenging me for a good six weeks."

"I never challenged you. I asked questions. I was curious."

"Questions that often forced me to prove my statements."

"Which you misinterpreted as confrontation?"

"That's *your* word. I said *challenging.* Just like you're being now. But we're getting off the theme."

"Go ahead," she says, "make your point."

"So I sat down. Expecting what usually happened when I sat across from one of my students. Talk. Conversation. Chat. Dialogue. Banter. Ex*change.* Because I'm the friendly one in this duo."

"Mmpff," she says.

"But all I got was your nose back in your book."

"You were reading, too. And as I recall, we happened to look up at the same time once or twice and smile quite nicely at each other."

"After which you immediately put your nose back in your book. And then when your coffee…"

"It was tea."

"…*tea* was gone, you stood up, and to your credit, you did say *good bye Dr. Cheykin*. And that's when I said, *Good bye. We should do this again sometime*."

Lily laughs.

"And that's what you did. You laughed. Just like you laughed now."

"We'd done nothing."

"But I wasn't expecting you to laugh. I was expecting a quizzical look at best, based on our shared ten minutes of nothingness. But because of that nothingness and because you laughed, I watched you walk away until you disappeared, wondering why you hadn't talked to me and bewitched by the fact that you'd laughed. *Does she not like me?* I wondered. *Does she think I'm unworthy of interaction outside the seminar?* And after all my wondering, when I finally got back to the paper I was reading, I found I'd written the word *puzzle* at the top of it and then had to cross it out."

Lily laughs again.

"I don't like crossing things out on papers. It's disconcerting to the student."

"So what you're telling me is because I didn't swoon or gush; because I got your deadpan joke, those things made you *notice* me."

"I've always been intrigued by puzzles."

They watch the fire in silence for a while, but she can almost hear him thinking.

After a while he says, "It's not possible you did that on purpose, is it?"

She yawns. "Did what on purpose."

"Ignore me."

"Chr-is. First of all, I did not ignore you. I said hello, we exchanged at least one smile, I said good-bye. That's not ignoring someone. Do you think I *planned* it? Arranged to keep an empty seat just on the chance you might wander in and choose to sit in it so I could then ignore you?"

"It's always bothered me."

"Because it's inconceivable that someone might prefer reading a book to your scintillating companionship?"

"It had never happened before."

She lets out a hoot. "Vanity, thy name is Christopher."

"It has nothing to do with vanity. I was your professor. You were supposed to find me at least interesting enough to engage in a friendly chat."

"We did nothing but chat for two years after that."

He takes her hand. "True."

She smiles. "We should go to bed. It's late. It's been a long exciting, *puzzling* day. And you may notice I never rebuffed you during it. Not once."

"A rebuff is an intentional rejection."

"Not if it's only a *perceived* rebuff."

"My plan was to make love to my wife on our first night in our new home."

"You could adjust your plan to our second night and we could go upstairs and go straight to sleep."

"Deal."

He follows her up the stairs, and on the landing, she sees snow beginning to collect on the windowsill. Downstairs, the fire snaps. "You first," Chris says, motioning toward the bathroom.

She turns and looks at him. "I really am happy, Chris," she says. "So very very happy."

CHAPTER TWENTY-ONE

When she opens her eyes the next morning, Chris is gone and the snow has stopped. Downstairs in the kitchen he's left a note on the table – *shoveling, walking, be back by 10*. She looks out the windows to find the driveway clear, the trees frosted, and a cardinal sitting on a holly branch. "Bird feeders," she says aloud and finds a pen in her purse, tears off a paper towel and writes it down before she forgets.

She could probably find Chris, follow his footprints, but she feels lazy, and realizes that if there weren't a hundred things to do today, if Anna and Max weren't coming, she might actually talk herself into going back to bed.

It's already late, eight-thirty, but she can't help wandering through the first floor, seeing the house for the first time at this particular hour, with a brightening sky casting faint slants of sun across the floors. She knows some day it will be as dependable as a pair of old slippers—the house and the way it accepts the sun, the wind, gray days, summer nights, but right now every corner and plane and surface is strange and new and intriguing.

The library, they've decided, will also house the stereo and television. The small second-floor bedroom will become her office, and she goes upstairs and wanders into it now, looks out the windows. There's a view of distant hills through leafless trees, and she shivers a little. Is she coming down with a cold? The flu? She takes a hot shower, dresses, and then remembers that she never ate breakfast.

Downstairs in the kitchen, she thinks about making oatmeal, but the pots are in a box, as is the oatmeal, and she's not all that hungry anyway, so she moves boxes around until she finds the one marked *appliances*, pulls out the toaster, finds the bread and then the box marked *spices*, sprinkles sugar and cinnamon on the toast, and then after she's finished, makes another, which she finds she doesn't want, after all.

The refrigerator hums softly, the snow begins to drip off the roof, and the lingering taste of the sugar in her mouth suddenly begins to cloy. She goes upstairs and brushes her teeth again, looks at herself in the mirror and notices that the usual color is gone from her cheeks. She looks, in fact, almost ashen. Which means she *is* coming down with something. Or maybe it's nothing more than the wrong kind of bulbs in the long fixture above the mirror. Not a good time to get sick, she thinks, with so much to do.

But then she hears a door open downstairs and Chris calls out *hello.*

"I'm coming down," she answers.

"I found a great trail," he tells her, his cheeks red from the cold. He hangs up his coat in the back entry, pushes off his boots, "out back and through the preservation land. About four miles, nice big loop, varied topography. It's great, Lily ... and right in our backyard!" He looks as if he's found a pot of gold. "We'll do it later," he says. "With Anna and Max."

"Okay," she says. "I guess you had something to eat?"

He points to a bag of apples on the counter.

"I'll start unpacking the boxes in here," she says, "so we can at least feed ourselves. I had some cinnamon toast, but now I'm beginning to wish I hadn't."

He puts the back of his hand against her cheek. "You look pale, sweetheart. You okay?"

"Yeah. I think so. Overtired. But I'm fine."

He goes off to the library and she starts opening boxes and spreading the contents onto the counters, and by the time Anna and Max are at the door, she's feeling fine, whatever it was, gone. And suddenly she's famished.

"We stopped at the bakery," Anna says, bringing into the kitchen the smell of fresh cold air and just-baked bread. "Croissants, donuts, muffins, take your pick."

"Hi honey," Lily says, giving her a hug. "Are the roads clear?" She grabs a blueberry muffin.

"Perfect," Anna says. "It was only four or five inches."

Then Max is there, too, depositing a pack of water bottles on the counter. "Wow, some house," he says.

Chris comes in. "Welcome you two." He gives Anna a hug and slaps Max on the back. "Your knee okay?" he asks.

Max nods. "All back to normal." And then to prove it he does three deep knee bends, and they all laugh.

"I'll remember that flip you took for a long time," Chris says.

Anna makes a face. "Yeah, water skiing isn't exactly Max's forte."

"Well," Max says, grinning, "it could be if I hadn't grown up in Vermont. I just need some ocean practice, that's all."

Lily looks at the way they are together, Anna and Max. Easy, comfortable. Not like they've known each other for a few months, but all their lives. She likes his confidence, his sense of humor, the way his face goes still and serious when he's listening. He seems to have the right combination of boy and young man, still capable of play, but aware that the balance of his life is slowly changing. And Anna is happy. Not depending on him to fill up her life, but choosing to give him a significant place of importance. Plus, as Anna has pointed out a dozen dozen times ... he has the most amazing blue eyes.

Lily starts unpacking the boxes in the pantry—dishes, bowls, baking utensils, tablecloths, dish towels, napkins. She has to decide how the pantry will be used. Storage only? Food prep? And while she's trying to figure it out, Chris comes in, puts his hand on the back of her head and leans around to kiss her on the lips. Then he crosses his arms and leans against the counter near the sink. "Feeling okay?"

"Fine," she says. "Some funny thing that didn't last very long."

"Um..." he leans toward her and says in a lowered voice, "France still a no-talk issue?"

"Yes. Definitely."

He raises his eyebrows, looks at her, turns to leave. "Max and I are doing the … what did you call it?"

"Entertainment center."

"Right. Entertainment center. That's what we're doing."

"Try to hide the wires, if you can," she says.

He salutes before he disappears.

"Anna," she calls out, "I think we'll keep the less-used appliances in here."

Anna carries them in one at a time. A blender, a waffle iron, a popcorn maker. "We should make popcorn later," she says.

Lily nods.

"You're kind of quiet, Mom," Anna says, after a while.

"Yeah, I guess I am. I'm a little tired, sweetie. It's been a whirlwind." And on cue, she yawns, which makes them both laugh. "I just need to get to bed early for a couple of nights in a row."

"Did you know where you were when you woke up this morning?"

"You know, I did. And I slept like a log. Except I think I heard a coyote sometime during the night. It's so quiet here. No car doors slamming. No customers buying bread and donuts at five a.m. And the house seems to have a peaceful presence. Like an old soul that's seen it all and isn't surprised by anything anymore."

"As long as it's not haunted," Anna says, and laughs. Then she takes off the hat she's been wearing, wool, purple and blue and red, with a long yellow pompom hanging down the back.

"You're letting your hair grow!" Lily reaches out and touches it. "Wow, it's already below your ears. So thick and beautiful. Though I liked it short, too."

Anna shrugs. "I got sick of having to cut it all the time. Sick of it short." Then she glances at Lily. "Mom? Are you crying?"

"No." Then she sniffs, laughs. "I don't know. Maybe." She wipes at her eyes. "I've been ridiculous lately. Chris must think I'm losing my mind. It's everything that's happening. All the changes. *Good* changes. Or maybe I'm just going sentimental in my old age." She laughs again.

"You're not old," Anna says.

They work side-by-side for a while without talking, and then Lily says, "Anna, I'm so glad you're here today. You and Max. It makes everything just about perfect."

Anna stands motionless for a second. "Love you, too, Mom." Then, "So where do you want to put stuff like peanut butter and jelly?"

***

Pretty soon there's music coming from the library, then the sound of the TV, and then the theme song from an old Clint Eastwood movie.

"Which movie?" Anna asks Lily.

Lily listens. "*A Fistful of Dollars*, I think."

"Who can name this movie?" Max calls out.

"*A Fistful of Dollars*." Anna calls back.

Silence.

"Who's the director?"

"Sergio Leone," Lily tells her.

"Sergio Leone!"

Max comes into the kitchen. "How did you know that?" Then he says, "You didn't. Your mother told you."

Max is a film buff. And although he knows more than Lily, she can almost keep up with him. On the other hand, the last American film Anna saw was in 2003. And it was probably by Disney.

"Just because I haven't seen *some* of them doesn't mean I haven't seen *all* of them," Anna says.

Lily concentrates on the jar of tomato sauce she's putting on a shelf. This is Anna's business and she'll handle it her own way.

Lily had known nothing about it until they were at the airport, Chris and Max off buying snacks, all of them waiting for their Bimini vacation to begin. Lily had sensed Anna was on edge from the moment they picked her up, all through the car ride to the airport, the bus ride from the parking lot, the security check.

Had Anna and Max broken up? Were they going through with this trip because they felt compelled to—the tickets bought, everything arranged? Though Max had hopped into the car like a nine-year-old, excited, happy, almost giddy. He'd never been anywhere before this trip.

Then perhaps it was Anna having already decided it was over, and now she was facing seven days with a boy she only *used* to like.

But when it finally came out, it had nothing to do with any of that. What Anna asked, although it felt more like begging, was something Lily wouldn't have guessed in a thousand years.

"You don't want him to know about France? But why?"

"Because," Anna said, "I don't want *anybody* to know about it."

"Anna..."

"Mom, do you have any idea how people look at you when you've done something so different? For four years I was different. And I'm sick of it. Every time I opened my mouth someone said...*oooh, you're American!*...and I'd have to say the same things and answer the same questions over and over and over...*have you ever lived in California? Hollywood? Have you been to Ground Zero? Are there still cowboys in Texas? Do you know Lady Ga-Ga?* It was all so *stupid*. I was always the *American* girl. And if people here know where I've been it'll be the same thing all over again, except reversed. I'll be the *French* girl. And it'll be ... *Anna, how do you say this in French? How do you say that? Why are the French so rude? Oh Paris, is it really as romantic as everyone says?* I don't *want* to be different, Mom. I want to be just like everybody else. And you'll tell Chris, too, right?"

Which she did. Behind a column near the boarding gate. And of course she had to deal with his straight-arrow logic.

"It makes no sense, Lily. She should be proud of that experience. It's part of who she is. Every kid should be so lucky."

"Chris. It's not an argument and it's not something up for discussion. Anna has asked us not to mention it. So we won't. When she's ready to share it with her friends, I'm sure she'll let us know."

"But..."

"*Chris. Just do it, okay?*"

He'd put his hands up. "Okay, okay," muttered something in Russian that she probably didn't want to know the meaning of. And then later, in the plane, they'd had a quiet conversation and she'd explained. "It's not just the being different," she'd told him. "It's more complicated than that. She's dealing with everything that's happened. She wants to keep them separate—her life with me, her life with her father—maybe it's been her way of handling it, of keeping herself from flying apart. And now those two lives have switched again. She's only eighteen, Chris. We have to help her, not challenge her. Let her feel her own way. She'll begin to knit things together when she's ready."

***

When they're finished with the kitchen, Lily and Anna move into the library, where everything that can be listened to and watched is sitting on three shelves in one bookcase half-way between the floor and the ceiling. She smiles. No wires visible. They can hear Chris and Max in the basement banging storage shelves together.

"Now this is very important," Lily says. "All the books are arranged by literary period, and within each literary period by nation and author, and within that, multiple books by one author are arranged by publication date."

"Seriously?"

"Oh," Lily says, "you have no idea how seriously. Chris processes the arrangement in a completely different way than we would. NEVER NEVER alphabetically by author. I remember the first time I removed a book from a shelf and, when I was finished, stuck it back in the wrong place. You'd have thought I'd torn out pages and stuffed them back in upside down."

"So he actually got *mad*? I've never seen him mad."

"He doesn't really get mad. Not the way you and I get mad. He gets ... steely and silent. And terrifically offended. Plus he breaths funny." She sets her lips hard together and forces air out through her nose.

Anna laughs. "Like a bull?"

"As a matter of fact, yes. And you know what I did? I bought a bright red handkerchief and left it on the bookcase. Whenever I removed a book, I put the handkerchief in the empty spot and let it hang off the edge. He didn't say anything, but I think the handkerchief bothered him almost as much as ruining his sacrosanct order."

Anna looks at the box of books in front of her, as if touching one might provoke mayhem. "So what if we screw this up?"

"We won't. The boxes are numbered and the books went into the boxes in perfect order. Chris did it himself. We'll work together, and not switch a thing."

They open one box at a time, taking turns removing books and putting them on the shelves. They listen to jazz. They talk. About Anna's father, who's coming to visit in the spring and seems to miss her more than she misses him; about Mandarin Chinese, which is a hundred times harder than Anna thought it would ever be; about a sketching class she's surprisingly good at; about her roommate, who's dating a twenty-three year old grad student and learning to do things in bed she and Anna didn't even know existed. Which makes Lily want to ask what, although she doesn't.

In two hours, the three walls of bookcases are filled, with space left over for additions.

***

When Chris comes upstairs, he stands in the doorway. "Wow. It looks completely lived-in." He inspects one wall of books, and Anna and Lily exchange glances.

"Great job," he says. "Very nice. Thank you both." He looks at his watch. "Two-thirty, ladies. If we want to hike that trail, we should do it now before it gets too dark. It'll take a good hour."

"I'm ready," Anna says.

Lily throws herself down on the couch. "I think I'll pass. I feel fine, really, but I don't want to push it —all this *and* a hike. The three of you go, and I'll drive into town in a half-hour or so and pick up a couple of pizzas for when you get back. Yes?"

Chris looks unhappy or concerned, or maybe both.

"How about you stretch out on the couch," he says, "and I'll go get the pizzas."

"No," she says. "*You're* going with *them*. I'm fine. We'll all be back here by four."

After the back door closes behind them and the house goes quiet, she falls asleep for what feels like just a little while, but when she wakes up, the late afternoon sun is casting a reddish glow along one bookcase, and she closes her eyes and almost goes back to sleep before she remembers. Pizza!

She calls the order in on her way there, picks the order up at three-fifty, and is half-way back to the house, the pizzas sitting in the back seat, when the smell of them starts to make her stomach churn. She waits for it to get worse, to the point where she has to pull over and throw up on the side of the road, but the nausea hovers just below that, and then a flush of heat rolls through her and she breaks into an instant sweat. She rolls down her window, which helps, but only a little.

What she really wants to do is throw the damn pizzas out of the car, and as soon as she pulls into the driveway and stops in front of the garage, she gets out and gulps at the fresh, cold air. Then the back door is banging shut and Chris is coming down the back steps. She points inside the car. "Could you get them? I can't."

"Max is hoping you got sausage," he says, and Lily presses her hand against her mouth. In a single moment, the world reels and she remembers the last time she was this way. Remembers walking past the open kitchen window, David grilling sausages on the deck

166

outside, and the smell that usually made her mouth water hitting her in a sickening mash of grease and sourness. Remembers how her stomach heaved, how she was cold and sweaty at the same time. And then sick part of every day for two awful months. But that can't be it. It can't be. It can't.

By the time Chris reaches her, she's ready to slide down against the car onto the ground. Not from the nausea, but because the shock has made her knees buckle.

"Jesus, Lily … what's wrong."

"I'm okay, I'm okay," she says. 'But oh god, Chris. I can't believe this. I think I might be pregnant. Oh god, I think I might be pregnant!"

CHAPTER TWENTY-TWO

She didn't know that Anna was right behind Chris. And she'll always remember the look on Anna's face as Lily looked up and saw her there. Disbelief. Shock. The two of them standing there looking down at her as she sat on the driveway.

Chris was open-mouthed until he snapped into action, pulled her up and more or less carried her up the stairs and inside.

Sitting at the kitchen table, Lily looks at them all looking back at her. Could she have handled it any worse, she wonders? "I'm sorry if I worried you," she says. "I fell asleep and was late getting the pizzas, and then I got a little sick driving home." She looks at Max, who seems somewhat concerned but not as shocked as Anna and Chris. "Could you bring in the pizzas?" she asks him. "They're in the back seat."

He seems relieved to have something to do and goes outside.

"Let's get through dinner?" Lily asks.

"You're going to have a baby?" Anna says.

"I don't know. No. I don't think so. It was a bad moment and I should never have said what I did. It just all of a sudden struck me so hard … remembering how I felt when I was pregnant with you and I made a crazy leap that it was the same thing. But it *is* crazy. I can't be pregnant. I can't."

Anna bends down and puts her arms around Lily. "It's okay, Mom. It's okay either way," and Lily's eyes fill with tears for the third time in less than a day. She looks up at Chris, who seems to have turned to wood, and Max comes in with the pizzas, which makes Lily's stomach turn over, so she buries her nose against Anna's shoulder.

"C'mon, Mom," Anna says, "lets go in the other room." Then she says to Max over her shoulder " Put the pizzas in the oven, okay, Max? Like four hundred for five minutes?"

Lily stretches out on the living room couch. "I'll get you a blanket, Mom," and Anna runs upstairs. Lily closes her eyes. She hears Chris come in. He sits down on the table beside her and puts both his hands around hers.

"Sorry about this," she says, opening her eyes.

"You have nothing to be sorry about. Still feeling lousy?"

"I'm okay right now. It comes and goes. Odors bring it on."

"And that's the way it was with Anna?"

She nods. "But that doesn't mean anything." Her eyes fill again.

"Lily," he says. "Everything's going to be okay."

"Is it?"

"Yes, it is."

"I should never have blurted it out like that. What on earth is wrong with me? Such a stupid thing to do."

"Meaning you should have kept it to yourself? Walked around with it and spared us all? For god's sake, Lily, how do you think I'd feel knowing you'd done that. Remember what happened the last time one of us kept something to himself? When I kept you in the dark because it seemed wiser than sharing the truth?" They look at each other. "We don't do that to each other anymore."

Then Anna is there with the blanket and Lily is sure she's been standing in the doorway listening, giving them their moment.

She gets covered to her chin, which is a good thing because she can pull it up over her nose to lessen the smell floating in from the kitchen.

"Go eat your dinner," she says, "And can you please eat it fast so I don't have to smell it anymore?"

***

The pizza odor gradually disappears and the air gets cooler and she knows Chris has opened a window in the kitchen. After a few minutes, he comes in with a cup of tea, sits down. "A sip?"

"Yes. I'll try it. Thank you." It's just right, not too hot or too sweet. It goes down. Her stomach handles it.

Then Anna comes in, and behind her is Max. "Um…" Anna says, "I'd like to tell Max something, but I want to do it with you two here, if it's okay."

The room gets very quiet and Lily feels her face flush hot. What on earth is Anna about to say?

"Max," Anna says, "I didn't live in Massachusetts with my mother for the last four years. I lived in Paris with my father."

Lily takes a breath. Chris looks down at the floor. Max says, "Really? That's pretty cool. So you mean, if we went backpacking in Europe like we've talked about, you could get us through France? You speak French?"

Anna nods.

"That's great. I mean, the language-thing has always really bothered me."

'I speak Spanish, too."

"You're kidding."

"Not kidding."

"O-kay. Hey, wanna watch that movie?"

Anna hesitates. "All right."

"Professor Cheykin? Mrs. Cheykin?"

Lily shakes her head. "Thanks, Max, I think I'll stay here."

"Me, too," Chris says.

Anna hangs back until Max is out of the room. "That was a lot easier than I thought it was going to be," she says. She makes a face, starts to leave, turns back. "You know, Mom, you can find out tonight."

"Find out?"

"Whether it's true or not. A pregnancy test? At the drug store?"

"Oh," Lily says, "I never thought…"

"It takes three minutes," Anna says. "And I'll be here a couple more hours. I mean, if you want to know for sure."

Lily and Chris look at each other after she's gone.

"She did that," Lily says, "because of what you said, you know."

"Did what? Said what? I don't even know what a pregnancy test is."

"Not about the test," she says, "telling Max about France. She heard your little *tell everything to each other* speech."

"I'm getting really confused here, Lily. Can we really do a pregnancy test?"

"I guess we can. I've never used one, but yes."

Chris swallows. "Should we?"

"Do you want to?"

"Do *you* want to?"

"I'm not sure."

"I think we should," he says.

"Okay. As long as the car doesn't smell anymore." She shivers. "It's getting cold in here."

"Oh shit," he says. He goes into the kitchen and slams the window shut.

They don't speak on the way there, except after he parks. "I guess I'll get it," he says, when she makes no move to open her door. "Where do you think they keep them?"

"I don't know. You'll have to ask."

He doesn't say a word, but the look on his face tells her he'd rather have vultures eat his entrails than ask where they keep their pregnancy tests. He sits there for a second girding himself, gets out, and then comes back in less than five minutes carrying a white plastic bag that's all out of proportion to the item inside. "That was quick," she says.

"I played a hunch. They were right next to the condoms."

She opens the bag, takes out a small rectangular box. "Wouldn't you know it would be pink," she says. And then takes out a pack of gum. "When did you start chewing gum?"

"I don't. I didn't," he says. "I have no idea why I bought it. Out of habit, I guess. Like when you buy a pack of condoms and the gum mutes the message somewhat. Somehow, it felt similar."

"A habit with you, huh? Buying condoms?"

She hears him sigh. "Lily..."

She pushes her elbow into his arm. "I'm kidding. Just because I may be pregnant doesn't mean I've lost my sense of humor. And it doesn't mean you should, either."

He sighs again.

At home, he reads the directions out loud twice, and Lily sits in the kitchen with the test in her hand for fifteen minutes, before she finally goes into the bathroom. Then she comes back and grabs his hand. "You have to come, too."

When it's done, she sits on the closed toilet with her head in her hands. "Tell me," she says.

The two minutes feel like two lifetimes.

"Two lines," he says. He swallows. "That means yes."

"Oh my god," Lily says.

"Mom?" Anna knocks softly on the door, and Chris opens it. "Might as well ask Max to come in, too," he says. He holds up the wand.

Anna lets out a gasp. "I can't believe it."

"No honey," Lily says, her head still in her hands, "I don't think we can, either."

"I kind of stopped wanting a little brother or sister a long time ago. But maybe it's just because I stopped thinking about it."

Lily raises her head and looks at Chris. "Is it all right if I tell Max?"

Lily shrugs. "If you must." She's not sure Chris has even heard what Anna said.

Anna and Max finish watching the movie. Chris gets the fireplace going and he and Lily sit on the couch and stare at it.

Lily shakes her head. "Remember last night … when you said things would get complicated soon enough?"

"I figured we'd have more than twenty-four hours." He rubs his hands through his hair. "I knew we were having too much sex."

She looks at him. "What?"

"Well you weren't supposed to get pregnant, you said it yourself. You haven't got pregnant in eighteen years. And now you're pregnant."

"I've had sex, Chris. I've had plenty of sex in eighteen years."

"As much as we've had in the last three months?"

She closes her eyes. "No. Maybe not *that* much. But I don't think that's the reason. I mean, of course it's the reason, but it's not the *reason*."

Then they don't talk again for a while.

"Look," she says. "I'll call my doctor in the morning. There's going to be a lot of things to think about. I'm old for this."

"*You're* old!"

"Can we please not think about it anymore tonight. This thing is going to take over our lives. And we're going to have to deal with it. But tonight, can it please just be our second night in our new house? Can we put off worrying until tomorrow?"

"Frankly, my dear," he says, "I've never seen you as the Scarlett O'Hara type. I mean, how can we do normal, when nothing's probably ever going to be normal again."

"Because whatever happens will become the *new* normal. We'll adjust. But for tonight, can we just pretend that the only thing we have to worry about is deciding where to put our new lamp? Because I can't take any more today."

He scoots over and puts his arms around her, hugs her so hard she can barely breathe. "I love you, Lily," he says. "I'll do anything.

Anything you want. You want me to pretend, I'll pretend." Then he lets her go. "More tea?"

"Yes." She smiles. "That would be nice."

***

When Anna and Max leave, Anna gives Lily what the two of them used to call a bear hug, one almost as hard as the one Chris gave her ... big and tight and long. Max stands there looking nonplussed, so she guesses Anna did tell him. Anna and her newfound policy of full disclosure.

"Did you see the way that kid looked at me?" Chris says after they're gone.

"Max?"

"Yeah. It was like he'd heard something he couldn't believe. A kind of *old guys can still do that?* look."

Lily smiles. "He should only know what old guys can do."

"So," he says. "Another cup of tea?"

"Thanks. I'm fine."

"Sure?"

"Sure."

He takes a few steps in one direction, then a few in the other. She's never seen him quite like this. Unable to settle, all his nerves on high alert. She looks at the clock on the mantle. "It's just a little after nine. We could let our new entertainment center entertain us. Maybe watch a movie? Though the way I've been going, I'll probably fall asleep half-way through. Still, you can always fill me in tomorrow on what I miss."

He goes to the window and looks out. Then he shakes his head. "No. I don't think I could sit still that long, Lily. I'm all..." He turns around and looks at her. "...jumpy."

"Well..." She walks over to him. "Sometimes, when one is jumpy about something, it's a good idea to concentrate on something else. "Wasn't your original plan to make love to your new wife in your new home tonight?"

He looks at her as though it has to be the worst suggestion he's ever heard.

"Well?"

"Jesus, Lily. I..."

"Chris. I'm already pregnant. What more can happen? Right now I'm feeling perfectly fine, but in need of a very big dose of normal attention. The next few days, the next few weeks may be filled with questions and decisions and, probably, me throwing up. Right this minute, I need normal. I need to be as close to you as I can get, as close as the two of us can be together. So could you talk yourself into it, please?"

"You're sure it's okay?"

"Of course it's okay."

By the time they've turned off the lights, turned down the thermostat, locked the doors, brushed their teeth, and gotten into bed, he seems to have not come to terms with any of it.

Facing each other in bed, he says, "Never in my wildest dreams."

"I know," she says, "me neither." And then she does something she's hardly ever had to do before, she touches him first.

"It's just me and you," she says, when he finally takes her in his arms. "Tonight, it's just me and you and nothing else."

CHAPTER TWENTY-THREE

Lily swims through the next four days until their doctor's appointment on Thursday. She vomits twice every morning; once around nine and again around eleven. Then she's fine until late afternoon, when she either vomits again, or just feels like she has to.

She falls asleep at her desk, gets essentially no work done. And she wishes Chris would disappear at least half a dozen times a day, annoyed with the way he looks at her (as though he's not quite sure who she is), and by the look on his face when his guard is down (as though life as they knew it will never be the same.)

But then he goes back to work on Tuesday, and she's so lonely she calls him before he even gets onto campus. Which, she can tell, scares the shit out of him.

"I'm fine," she says, "I just wanted to see what time you'd be home."

"The usual," he tells her. "But if you need me sooner, I can do that, too."

"No," she says. "Today's a good day. I'm doing great. See you this evening." Then she goes into the bathroom and vomits, after which she lays down on the bed and cries.

That night she attaches a typed note to the refrigerator under a Bimini magnet in the shape of the island. *I'm going to try very hard to not be unreasonable*, it reads, *but until my hormones settle down, I may be difficult to live with. Please understand. It won't be you, it'll be me. Most of the time. Love, Lily*

She has to laugh at the way he looks at her after he reads it. As though he's waiting for snakes to grow out of her skull, for her teeth to turn to fangs. "Maybe it won't be so bad this time," she tells him. "Maybe my hormones don't roil quite the way they used to."

On Thursday, they have a completely silent ride to the doctor's office. A completely silent twenty minutes in the waiting room. And when the receptionist says, "Mr. and Mrs. Cheykin?" Chris jumps.

The doctor talks about tests to determine Lily's overall health, to check out Chris' sperm. "My *sperm*?" Chris repeats. So Dr. Wright explains about age-related breakdown; about DNA fragmentation that may result in fetal defects. "According to what you've told me about your lifestyles, you have no obvious confounding factors— neither of you smokes; you're not overweight; you're healthy; you both exercise. But a sperm test is quick and non-invasive, and based on your age alone, Mr. Cheykin. I recommend it. It will be another bit of information to base your decisions on." Then he talks about chromosomal testing and amniocentesis for the baby, although those, if desired, will have to wait several more weeks.

He explains that Lily's age, her complications with Anna's birth, and her doctor's prognosis that she'd never get pregnant again are signals she needs to be closely watched. "I'll want you in here every two weeks. And if anything feels wrong—anything at all, you're not to call me, you're to go directly to the hospital. Understand?"

They leave the office after two hours with their heads spinning. Lily's exam says everything's in good order. She's about six weeks pregnant; her due date September 1. She leaves the office with a small brown bag that holds three bottles of vitamins she knows she won't be able keep down.

"I need a drink," Chris says, as soon as they're in the car.

"I can't drink," Lily says, "so you can't either."

"That's not fair."

"Get used to it." Then she falls asleep on the way home.

***

Anna texts her early every morning. *Hi Mom how are u doing?* Then she calls in the afternoon and tells Lily everything she's done since they talked the day before. It becomes the high spot of Lily's day.

Lily writes to her sister and tells her everything, but tells her not to tell their mother. She'll do that herself. Then she writes and tells her mother that she and Chris Cheykin (from Yale, Mother, remember?) have reconnected and are now married. She stops there. It seems sufficient for now.

On Wednesday night, Chris makes what's become his standard dinner—two peanut butter and jelly sandwiches, a glass of milk, and a banana for dessert. "You can go ahead and cook yourself something," she says.

"No way."

"I can go in the other room."

"That doesn't quite seem to work, does it."

"I'm sorry."

"Jesus, Lily, don't cry. I *like* peanut butter and jelly sandwiches."

She sits with him while he eats, wondering what he sees when he looks across the table. The only thing she's done today is brush her teeth. Her hair is loose, uncombed; she's wearing a pair of flannel pajamas she found still cellophane-wrapped in a box. He'll never wear them, and they're very expensive, very warm, and she doesn't even care who gave them to him. Over the pajamas, she's wearing her raggy old bathrobe.

For no reason at all, she remembers a thirteen-year-old Anna with chicken pox, walking around the house with a veil over her poor, bumpy red face, moaning *I look like roadkill!! I look like roadkill!!* over and over. Roadkill, she thinks, and puts her hand over her mouth.

He finishes one sandwich, and as soon as he starts the other, she goes into the bathroom and throws up. "See?" she says, when she comes back to the table, "you might as well have cooked yourself a smelly, delicious steak."

She sits down. And then she says what they've both been avoiding. "We don't have to do this."

He puts his sandwich down. "I know."

"Should we?"

"I don't know. I think that has to be *your* decision."

"It can't just be *my* decision, Chris. It's half your situation and it has to be half your decision."

"How can it work that way, Lily? What if I say yes and you say no or vice versa? The way it has to work is you make the decision and I say *yes* to whatever you want. I'm not the one throwing up every half hour, crying if the tea's too hot, falling asleep sitting up. But I am the one watching and that's not easy, either."

"So I have to do all that and make the decisions, too?"

For a long moment, he says nothing, then, "No. Of course not." He takes a deep breath. "Okay. Here's where I am. I'm not thrilled it's happened. It wasn't supposed to. Still, it *has* happened and, believe me, I'm not taking it lightly." He hesitates. "I can't remember the last time I was afraid of anything, Lily, but this scares the hell out of me. I've listened to the doctor, I've looked online, I've become way too familiar with things I've never thought about in my entire life— miscarriage, eclampsia, birth defects, risks to the mother." He leans toward her a little. "I just got you back, Lily. I can't bear the thought of anything happening to you."

He gets up, goes into the bathroom, comes back with a box of Kleenex and waits until she's blown her nose and wiped her eyes.

"As far as I'm concerned, nothing is worth that. Nothing. So I follow this thinking to its logical conclusion —that we can make all the frightening scenarios go away just like that."

He lifts his hands off the table. "And then ... I get very hung up on one thing." He lowers his hands to the table, leans toward her. "This baby we've started is part *you*, and making something that's part Lily go away would be something I could probably come to terms with, but it wouldn't be easy." He doesn't say anything for a second. "I could do it, though, Lily, if it's what you need, if it's what you want." He falls silent for a minute. "I don't think this is something that can be a fifty-fifty decision. It needs to be sixty," he points at her," and forty," he points at his own chest.

She hasn't taken her eyes off him once. She nods. "I'm almost sure that making it go away is not what I want. You said it wasn't supposed to happen, but it has ... well, I take that a step farther and say it's happened for a *reason*." She shakes her head. "I know, I know that's not the way you think, and I agree it's no reason I can successfully argue, but I *feel* it. I *feel* there is one."

She expects a challenge because she knows there's no clear logic to what she's just said. But all he does is nod. "Okay then," he says, "it's settled."

They sit there for a while holding hands across the table, and then she gets up and starts opening and closing cabinet doors. "I could swear we had pineapple," she says. "I could swear I put a can away just a couple of days ago."

"I don't eat pineapple," he says, "and I haven't seen any."

"I'm going to the store to get some. All of a sudden I'm hungry as hell and I have pineapple on the brain."

"I'll go," he says, "or we can go together."

"Together," she says. "I'll get my boots."

"There's a theory," he calls into the front hall, "that so-called morning sickness is the way your body protects the baby at its most vulnerable time from things that could hurt its development."

She comes back into the kitchen with her long down coat on, and boots. She twists her hair into a pony tail. "How do you know that?"

"I've been on-line. I've been on-line a lot."

She puts her hood up, anticipating the temperature in the car before the heat kicks in. "Do you think pineapple's okay?"

"It's probably fine. It's fruit." He stands up, goes into the entry and grabs his coat. "And look, if we're going to approach this in a kind of Zen cloud..." He zips the coat, takes his gloves out of the pockets, "which I'm fine with ... then whatever you don't want to eat, you shouldn't, and whatever you do want to eat, you should."

In the car, their breaths making clouds in the ten-degree air, she says, "I feel like we're Lewis and Clarke encountering the

Rockies. We've just climbed the first mountain, which we had no idea was even going to be there. No preparation for it. Hard as hell to climb. But at least it's a relief to be at the top."

"And, Mr. Clarke, what do you see when you look out?"

"Oh," Mr. Lewis, I'm afraid I only see a lot more mountaintops." She smiles at him. "But at least we have this one under our belt."

At the store, she buys a few things that appeal to her, Chris puts four cans of pineapple into their cart, and as soon as they're back home, she eats half a can. Until the thought of even one more piece drives her into the bathroom, and she imagines Chris sitting by himself in the living room, staring into the fire, thinking Zen Zen Zen Zen...

***

Two weeks later, they're back to the doctor, who pulls out Chris' test results first. "You're how old?" he asks Chris, then, before Chris can answer says "oh yes, I see it here, fifty-nine." He scans the page again. "Excellent," he says, looking at Chris, "no problems here. If your birth date said you were thirty, I wouldn't be surprised. Though I'm not sure I'd suggest you look at this as the start of a large family."

He and Chris smile at each other, and Lily feels like raising her hand and waving it around. *What about me, guys?*

Dr. Wright doesn't call her tests excellent, but there are no problems, and her exam shows everything progressing normally. "Let's have you come back in two weeks and we'll do an ultrasound then," he says. "It's a little early, but we might be able to see if it's a boy or a girl. That is, if you want to know."

In the car, Lily says it's okay with her either way. "Anna was a surprise," she says, "and I remember how I loved hearing the nurse say, *It's a girl!* But for once, Chris is definite. He wants to know. "Why?" she asks.

"Because," he says, "there's already too many unknowns. It would be a comfort to be absolutely sure of one thing."

"Okay," she says. "Then we'll do it."

"That's a whole new realm, isn't it," he says. "A girl. A boy."

"Plus," she says, "knowing will make picking out a name only half as hard."

"A name," he says. "It's going to have a name." He doesn't say another word all the way home.

CHRISTOPHER

CHAPTER TWENTY-FOUR

He wishes he could remember every second of the six months before Sophie was born. He lies in bed at night and tries to recreate them. At least as long as he can stay awake. At the same time, though, it's beginning to scare him. Because sometimes it feels too much like magical thinking. A way of escaping the empty space beside him.

But at least that's preferable to the couple of nights he's spent wallowing. Thinking ... unfair, monstrous. Wondering why it couldn't have been him. Railing against another future snatched. Wasn't one tragedy enough for one lifetime?

Thinking about Denise. That beautiful, high-energy, quirky, dark-haired girl. Watching her gradually devolve into madness, and god knows he'd tried to hold on to her, assure her, protect her, help her. Which only made her leave him, blame him, hate him, and then spend most of the rest of her life trying to destroy him. Wasn't that enough for one person to carry around for one life? Apparently not. Because now there was Lily. Who was everything he could want and more. Lost to him once. How could he bear to lose her again?

It takes every ounce of strength he has to get out of that quicksand of thinking. But he has no choice. He has to do it for Sophie. For Lily.

So instead, he goes back to the day of the first ultra-sound, Lily waking him before dawn, whispering, "I can't sleep," in his ear.

He'd struggled out of a dream, opened his eyes. "So I see," he'd said, assuming it meant he shouldn't sleep either. "Feeling okay?"

"Yes. I'm just nervous, I guess."

He put his leg over hers under the covers. "I think it'll be fine," and she put her hand against his chest and kissed him on the chin.

"You were in my dream just now," he told her.

She smiled. "It was a good dream then."

"Well, that depends. I think you were a kangaroo."

She laughed her one-note laugh. "How did you know it was me if I was a kangaroo."

"I was driving some gigantic off-road vehicle. There was dust everywhere. Australia, right? A kangaroo?"

She nodded. "Did you *hit* the kangaroo? Because of the dust."

"No. It was just suddenly beside me on the passenger seat. And it had a baby kangaroo. I could see its head sticking out of the pouch."

"A mother kangaroo. So definitely me."

"Right. And then this mother kangaroo leaned very close and said, *I can't sleep*."

"Seriously."

"Yeah, you know how dreams get mixed up with what's happening in the moment."

Her knee rubs against him provocatively, but he ignores it, because she's obviously a Fido right now. Which means intimacy, but no sex.

It was a thing she'd confronted him with early on in their relationship, their initial relationship, and it had put him through a good six months of something close to agony.

"You're always jumping on me," she said, one night in bed, bringing him to a collapsing halt. "And there are times when I do want sex. Lots of times. But there are also times when I don't. When all I want is to be close."

"You mean like just now? Foreplay with no climax?"

"No. I mean intimacy, you idiot. Cuddling, skin on skin, talking, sharing, just being close. Do you think you could try to understand that?"

"I think I do understand it, Lily. It's just that it would be nice to have a little advanced guidance. Like those PSAs on the radio? *Sex alert, no sex alert*?" He rolled over onto his back. So, okay, he was aggravated, maybe even a little pissed-off, and it was in his voice. He could hear it himself.

"Chris," she said. "This isn't about you. It's about *me*. I want you to pay *attention* to me. *Me*. Instead of that constant buzz in your gonads."

"Christ, Lily, all I *do* is pay attention to you."

"Not when it comes to *this*."

He felt a distinct sinking feeling in his stomach, almost a kind of fear. Because he really did have no idea what she was talking about.

"Do I climb on top of you when you're studying?" she said. "When you're prepping for a lecture? Did I do a fan dance the night before you introduced me to your mother? No. Because I *read* you. I intuit things and act accordingly."

"But that's not what you're talking about," he said. "I know enough to leave you alone when you're working or distraught. I'm not idiotic enough to make love to someone with a fever or two broken legs." Which at least made her laugh. "But you're talking about something invisible. Just *tell* me, Lily. One word. That's all it takes. *Sex* or *nix*. One three-letter word. Is that too much to ask?"

"Yes. Because I want you to *know* me. I want you to *get* me without having to explain myself to you."

So they embarked on his journey to true understanding. Which was nether easy, nor fun. He pictured them on a road, the same road, but with divergent paths only Lily seemed able to see. Yet she expected him to not just follow, but know which path to take, even though they were invisible.

He was wrong more than he was right. Constantly getting caught up in the moment and pissing her off. And when he pissed her off, it not only ruined the intimacy she wanted, it ruined the sex he'd *thought* she wanted. Sometimes for days.

But then, slowly, he began to see something in Lily he'd never noticed before. She wasn't simply human. She was also feline, mostly feline. But sometimes she was canine. And seeing that, understanding that, saved him.

When she was a cat, she wanted sex. She licked her paw, stretched, arched her back, purred, rubbed against him with purpose and a kind of cunning. But when all she wanted was intimacy, she was a dog. She bounced, ran in circles, panted, barked, wagged her tail. She might touch him, even rub against him while she was doing all this, but it meant something completely different. And once he had a handle on all that, the problem essentially disappeared.

Anyway, all of that was easier the second time around. His libido wasn't on high octane any more. There was room for other things he knows he missed back then. Subtlety was less puzzling. But Lily was different, too. More forgiving, less demanding. The feistiness and the fire were still there, but the heat was cooler, the fuse longer.

So on that morning, with Lily wide awake at five a.m., wanting to talk and touch and nothing more, completely unconscious that her breasts were teasing him, that her knee kept invading his crotch, on that morning he knew exactly what was expected of him.

"I never saw Anna before she was born," she said. "Tell me, really *tell* me ... do you want a son, Chris, or a daughter? And don't say it doesn't matter."

He thought for a second. "Maybe a son needs a young father. Someone to run around with. Coach his soccer games, teach him how to surf, hang from a tree."

"You used to surf. I bet you still can. Anyway, I think a boy would grow up to be a better man with a father who's learned patience and understanding."

"Siddhartha Buddha at your service. But if you're insisting I choose one or the other ... I think a daughter would be good. Besides you've already done that once; you're an expert. But if it *is* a boy, I'll do my best to keep in shape. So he won't be able to out-wrestle me until he's at least four."

"Okay," she said, pulling closer, taking his hand and holding it against her stomach, "now tell me something you've never told me before."

It was an old game, and if he came up with something good, then she had to come up with something better. And if what he said wasn't just good, but excellent, she sometimes transmogrified from a canine into a feline.

He considered for a minute. "Between the ages of ten and eleven I began my career as a thief."

"You stole things?"

"Yeah. Lots of things. I think I started off with a comic book. Just stuck it under my jacket one day and walked out of the drug store. It was terrifically exciting. A real adrenaline rush. And it was so easy."

"What else did you steal?"

"Candy, toys. Once I stole a pair of binoculars that probably cost a fair amount. I was good at it. And once I stole a box of tampons because I had no idea what they were and I wanted to find out. And a box of condoms, too. Same reason."

"Did you use them?"

"The tampons?"

She kicked his leg.

"I was ten, Lily. Why would I need condoms?"

"And then you got caught."

"No. I never did. I just stopped doing it."

"Why?"

He thought about it. "I think I had a premonition. Or maybe it was a moment of perception. In any case, I saw that it was starting to control me instead of the other way around, and I didn't want to go there. Somehow I knew it wasn't what I wanted to be." He stops, looks at her. "So ... was that good?"

"Yes. That was very good."

"Your turn. And remember, it has to be something better."

She was silent for a while. Then she smiled and he knew whatever she was going to say was going to knock what he'd said out of the park.

She stuck her chin out, looked him straight in the eye. "I admit it. I ignored you on purpose that day in the co-op."

He looked back at her. Then practically yelled, "I knew it! I knew you did that on purpose!"

She let him enjoy his moment.

"Just to get me onto you, right? Just to make it a hunt and a chase."

"Oh," she said, "don't flatter yourself, big boy. I did it because I thought you *deserved* it. All those students of the female persuasion ... and some of the faculty members, for god's sake ... hanging on your every word. *Professor Cheykin this and Professor Cheykin that*. It was disgusting. I thought you deserved to be taken down a peg or two. Or three or four. And it worked, too, didn't it? Made a lasting impression. Poor you sitting there like a little boy whose mother wasn't paying any attention to him."

"You were after me, after all."

"I was most definitely *not*. At least not at first. Not when you sat down. Not while we sat there opposite each other. I mean, I wasn't completely immune, but at the same time I thought you were so stuck on yourself. Cocky. Conceited. Smug."

"I was like that?"

"Well, no. That's the thing. You weren't. But I didn't know that until you said what you said when I got up to leave."

"We should do this again sometime."

She put her hand on his cheek. "Hmm. Yes, it was you being funny and real. Not trying to impress me. And the fact that you were sad."

"I was not sad."

"Yes you were. A little. Because you'd been snubbed. For no reason. But the sadness came out as a joke. On yourself. As in *why would anyone want to do this again with me.*"

"Well, like I told you once, it had never happened before."

"You'd never been snubbed?"

He shook his head. "But then love was born?"

She nodded. "I guess it was."

They'd talked until sunshine filled the room and Lily had to get up and pee. And it's those moments, those aching moments, he's not sure he can live without.

He turns over and sees the four sonograms still lying on top of Lily's bedside table. But it's that first one that sticks with him. Maybe because they looked at it at least a thousand times. Sophie. The rounded head, with a profile of nose and forehead and mouth, tiny arms, legs, hands, fingers. A miniature person afloat inside Lily.

And then that slight wave of a hand that made them all laugh.

A girl, the technician was pretty sure. And if Chris had to bet, he'd have guessed that, too. Something about that tiny image on the screen already feminine.

He closes his eyes and the memories continue to unfold.

By sixteen weeks Lily was over the nausea, the sleepiness, the easy tears. They both began to lose their tentativeness. They were having a baby, of all things. Lily's stomach was bulging, it was real.

It took him longer than Lily, a lot longer, to get used to it, and even once he was, there were moments when it would suddenly be there, unannounced, at the center of his consciousness, and he'd feel momentarily stunned. More than once, the thought of what they were doing just plain scared the shit out of him. Though he never told her that.

It didn't seem to scare Lily at all. If anything, she was the one becoming the Buddha. Emanating waves of contentment he could almost feel. She seemed to be nesting. Decorating the house, hanging pictures, buying plants, painting the second bedroom, the nursery, a pale yellow. And she was writing. Every day. Had finished the memoir she was working on, told any new inquirers she was on sabbatical.

"You were right about *Mackerel Sky*," she told him. "It was much better than I remembered. But I'm not that person anymore, so I'm going to use these months before the baby comes to work on something new."

She said he could read it when she had a completed draft. And he watched it gradually take her over. From the two hours a day she set as her first goal, to sometimes four or more. The passion was back, and with it, her sense of humor.

The warning note, however, stayed on the refrigerator door. Is there still. With a couple of his own red-penciled stars for two exhibitions of unparalleled obnoxiousness. One, for the first meal she cooked after she could smell food without having to run into the bathroom —the end of his peanut butter and jelly sandwich dinners.

It was a jambalaya, half a million ingredients including chicken, shrimp, sausage. It was supposed to be spicy, but Lily had left out the hot sauce and the cayenne on purpose. He'd had jambalaya in Louisiana. He knew what it was supposed to taste like. It was supposed to be hot. Hell, it was supposed to broil the inside of your mouth. And Lily's jambalaya was delicious. But it wasn't spicy. Not even a little. So he'd taken a bite, then gone searching for the pepper. "Just needs a little heat," he'd said, flipping the lid.

"Let me." And she'd grabbed it away, dumped half the bottle on his plate. "Maybe it'll be hot enough for you now?"

The second star, he drew the morning after an impromptu stag party at a local bar, the first time he'd gone out with his colleagues since he and Lily had been together. Not that he went out all that much even before. But people were glad for him, you might almost say impressed. He hadn't been high-fived so many times since he'd stopped playing basketball.

He called from his office. "They want me to go," he told her, "I'll be home early."

She'd sounded fine. Even said something about *have a good time*. And yes, he did stay longer than he intended, but he'd been on his own clock for decades and wasn't in the habit of signing in or out. So when the pillow clocked him in the bedroom at half-past one, he had a hard time being tolerant. Besides, it caught him full in the face.

"What the hell was that for?"

"For not making it clear that you meant early Saturday *morning* instead of early Friday *night*." she said. "For making me lie here and worry about you for three hours. For not calling to say you'd be late. In short … for being an insensitive ass-hole!"

He'd stood there with a fire zipping through him, hadn't felt that kind of anger in a long time. "I'm not a child, Lily, you're not my mother, I don't have a curfew, and it's not like I do this on a regular basis. If I want to go out and have a couple of drinks with friends, I'll god-damned do it! And I'll stay out as long as I want!"

Then she'd made a noise. So now she was going to fucking *cry*? Which made him even madder, so mad he grabbed the covers and pulled them right off the bed.

"Chris!" She wasn't crying, she was laughing. "I can't believe I hit you! I couldn't even see where you were!"

But it wasn't *that* dark. He could see *her* very well. Against the white sheet. Her hair spread out across the pillow. And suddenly all his anger went straight to desire.

Never in his life had he found anything remotely sexy about a pregnant woman. Until Lily. He loved the fullness of her breasts, the way her nipples swelled against his tongue, the convex tautness of her stomach.

"I'm sorry," he said, her lying on top of him after the hot, quick sex. "You're right, I should have called."

"And here I thought the caveman was all out of you," she said, against his ear. "It was a good throw, huh?"

"Yeah, very precise."

She laughed then, and he remembers how the motion of her body made him hard again.

***

"It seems that I'm going to be a father," he told Ken McDonald, before someone saw Lily and put the news out on the campus gossip line. Ken went speechless for a good half-minute, then shouted, "My god, man, congratulations!" Lily told Ken's wife the same day. "Sandy almost choked," she told him that night. "She just kept saying, *no*. I'd say *yes*, and she'd say *no* again."

***

Weeks before the due date, she and Anna came home with a bunch of bags filled with baby stuff. "You wouldn't believe what they have for babies today," Lily said, pulling things out to show him —blankets, 'onesies, sleepers, bibs, diapers. "No frilly dresses or matching booties," she said. "And you'll notice not everything is pink?" Because she was determined this daughter of theirs was never going to be a *princess*.

The first time the baby kicked, Lily called to tell him during a lecture. But they had an arrangement that she could call him any time and he'd answer. Then that night, they'd sat on the couch for three hours, his hand on her stomach. Nothing. Until they went to bed, and then he'd felt it. He hadn't expected the emotion that rolled through him.

"Isn't it wonderful?" Lily said.

Yes, he thinks, opening his eyes, it was all pretty wonderful.

Across the room, he can see the outline of the poster Lily made still taped to her closet door. OUR BABY at the top, and a list she constantly added to: can blink; move; has fingerprints; yawns, sucks her thumb; kicks; gets the hiccups; can hear.

That last one was when Lily put him to work. "I want you to start talking to her," she told him. "In Russian, too."

So a few nights a week he laid his head on Lily's breasts and talked to her stomach.

"Hey," he said, the first time, "I'm your old man."

Lily tugged his hair hard.

"Cut that out," he said, reaching up to grab her hand. "It's a totally valid appellation. As in *hey, how's your old man*? Plus, don't you think she deserves a warning of sorts?"

"If she does, it has nothing to do with the year you were born." She patted his head. Gently. "Go on. Talk to your daughter."

He was never sure where any of it came from; he just riffed. "Even though you don't know it," he told her once, "you already have a history. You're part of a brooding tradition that invites suffering and torment."

"Oh god," Lily moaned. "She's as much Irish as Russian, you know."

"Fine," he said. "Teach her a jig when it's your turn. Right now, though, it's *my* time, Unless, of course, you'd rather write me a script."

She laughed a little, pinched his ear. "No, go ahead, say whatever."

"A great Russian philosopher," he continued, "once said that love makes you happy, but also makes you suffer; yet, at the same time, to *not* love makes you *un*happy, which in itself is a form of suffering. So to be unhappy is to suffer, but to be happy is to suffer, as well. So either way, kid, if you're Russian, you suffer."

Lily hooted. "And who is this idiotic Russian philosopher??"

"*Love and Death*," he said, "Woody Allen."

"You," she said, "are going to be *such* an impossible father. Have you never heard of *this little piggy went to market*?"

"*Etot malen'kiy prosenok*," he began, which made Lily go very still and then dig her fingers into his scalp.

"Uhh…" he said, "you realize I can't cater to you both at the same time?"

"I know, I know," she said, "I'll try and get used to it."

But the thing was, he didn't want her to get used to it.

Sometimes he counted to ten, recited the days of the week, the months, the seasons, the planets, tried to explain E=MC2 and Peter the Great's influence on Russian literature. Important things, he told Lily, for any baby to know.

But Lily had a favorite story she made him tell at least once a week. About a queen and a king who lost each other when a great rift opened across their land and the royal couple found themselves on either side of a giant fissure that couldn't be crossed. "There must be a way around," the queen said. "I'll search in this direction," and she pointed north. "You go south," she told the king. They searched for years for a way across and when they finally found it, they were overjoyed. They loved each other more than ever. So much, they were unable to contain it all within themselves. "And some of that extra love dripped into the queen's pocket," he said, "and created … you. And then the king and the queen and the little *mysh* lived happily ever after."

Mysh, mouse. Myshka, little mouse. But in actuality she was going to be Alexis or Fiona or Olivia or Chloe. Those were the names on the refrigerator.

He refused to weigh in. "It doesn't matter," he told Lily. "I like them all. You decide."

"How?" she said.

"Well, short of letting her choose her own name when she's old enough, you could simply put them all in a hat and pick one out."

She gave him a look. "You're absolutely no help at all, are you."

"No," he said, "I guess not."

Anna moved in with them for the summer and by the beginning of July, she and Lily had inexplicably settled on Sophie Alexis Cheykin. He was glad the endless discussions were over. He liked the name. Sophie.

Then Anna went to Paris for three weeks to visit her father, and when she came back, David came with her. He was going to be in town three days before flying out to San Francisco on business, and Lily invited him for dinner. Preparations were delegated. Chris: two good bottles of wine and a fancy dessert from the bakery. Anna: a salad and a hummus dip. Max was just supposed to show up. Which left Lily with the main course, a Greek lasagna of artichokes, eggplant, and lemons. It smelled great, but Lily had never made it before, and kept worrying that she should have stuck with something more familiar. A sure sign she was nervous.

He didn't share the nerves, and there was nothing about David that was unexpected. He was Brooks Brothers sharp, talked fast, smarter than average, had a benign intensity about him.

Max was nervous and unusually quiet, and David seemed to take a fairly obvious and immediate dislike to him.

"I hope it's okay," Lily said, as Chris carried the lasagna from the oven to the table.

"Just as long as no one goes for any extra *seasoning*," Chris said.

And despite her nerves, Lily laughed and put her hand on his back. "I still owe you another jambalaya, don't I?" she said.

After dinner, David asked Chris if he'd show him the land out back, and the first thing he said when they were a decent distance from the house was, "So what do you think of this Max?"

"Max? Max is fine. He's, uh, a little more serious than he might look. Does well in school. Works. Treats Anna with respect."

David cleared his throat. "His background, though. Vermont? Isn't his father a farmer?"

Chris nodded. "Beef cattle. Yes."

"Have you met them? His family?"

"Briefly. At the end of the last school semester. Seemed like good people."

"What I'd like to know, David said, "is where he's going. Anna says he's a history major. What's that going to do for him?"

"It'll get him a Bachelor of Arts," Chris said, "to start with. Then it could take him in several different directions depending on where his interest lies."

"A Bachelor of Arts?" David said it as though it were something very low on the evolutionary path.

"It's where I started."

"I thought you started out to be a physician."

Chris nodded. "That's true, I did. But I changed my mind."

David looked at him. "Whatever for?"

"I discovered I preferred interacting with ideas instead of people."

"You couldn't do both?"

Chris stopped walking, looked at him. "I thought we were talking about Max."

"Yes. Of course. It's just ... I guess there's no point in skirting it now, since it's a long-dead issue. But during those years I was married to Lily there was always somebody else there. I'm guessing it was you," and then quickly, "I don't mean you were there physically. She had told me a bit about you, that's all ... that it was over. But frankly, I can't help but be curious as to how that person ... you ... managed to stay so central in her mind, if not in her life, for so long. Because god knows I could never occupy that place."

"The heart is a curious thing," Chris said. "It can't necessarily be made sense of. But my relationship with Lily is my relationship with Lily. Your relationship with your daughter ... I guess it may include her relationship with Max. At least to a point."

"You have no idea," David said. "Wait until *your* daughter is nineteen. Maybe then you'll understand."

"I may not be a father yet," Chris said, "but I do know Anna. And she's a lot like Lily. She knows what she wants and more often than not knows what's best. You don't have to trust Max. You just have to trust Anna."

David looked at him, shrugged. "I guess I don't really have any other option, do I."

"The way I see it, you don't need any."

They shook hands when David left, and after his car was out of the driveway, Chris felt a surprising sense of relief.

***

At thirty-four weeks, Lily began to have short spells of false labor. She was tired all the time, began to have headaches, and the doctor seemed moderately concerned. The baby, he assured them, was over five pounds. "I think we shouldn't wait." So he set a date for a caesarian delivery on a Thursday morning, four days away. But on Tuesday, Lily woke him in the middle of the night. "Contractions," she said, holding her stomach. "not stopping, very fast, very hard."

Chris doesn't remember much about the drive to the hospital, except when Lily's water broke. That he remembers very well. Along with the sickening fear that she was going to have the baby right there in the front seat of the car.

But Sophie didn't arrive in the car, or on the gurney, or in the elevator. She waited for the nurses, the doctor, for everyone to don a blue gown, for Chris to be standing at Lily's side holding her hand, for someone to say, *here she comes!*, for someone else to say *she's just beautiful!* And then he was trying to organize it all in his mind. A baby. Their baby. An astonishingly tiny wet, dark-haired, screaming life, who ceased her crying almost as soon as the nurse deposited her into Lily's arms. "Oh," Lily kept saying over and over, "oh oh, oh."

CHAPTER TWENTY-FIVE

He remembers Lily looking at the baby, looking up at him, a look of sheer joy on her face, and then he remembers all hell breaking loose. The baby sliding toward him as Lily's body stiffened and convulsed. Sophie suddenly in his arms as he caught her. He knows he yelled when Lily's eyes rolled back in her head, remembers how everyone, except for himself, seemed to go into some kind of precise, mechanistic dance.

"Please wait out here," a nurse said, ushering him out, handing him a blanket for the wet, squirming baby in his arms. A small, windowless room. A chair.

"It wasn't supposed to go this way. He wasn't supposed to be in a separate area, his two-minute-old daughter wrapped messily in a blanket. He and Lily were supposed to be enjoying their first minutes with her together. Lily was supposed to be tired but okay. Except Lily wasn't okay.

He figured later that it was forty minutes before someone came out to explain. He held his daughter. He'd never held any baby for more than a moment, ever. And they were trusting him to not drop her, to not hurt her, to not hold her too tight or too loose.

After a while, she started to cry, and he watched it rise in her like a kind of desperation for something he had absolutely no ability to provide, and he was immediately reduced to feeling like a five-year-old. What was wrong with Lily? What was wrong with this baby? Nobody had even looked at her. She'd been born and they'd handed her off to him. Maybe she was in pain. He looked around. He needed help. He couldn't handle this by himself.

"I'll get someone for you," he said to his daughter, and as soon as he spoke, she stopped crying, opened her eyes, looked up at him. And that's when he saw it. Curiosity. A desire for something to hold onto. Her eyes searched his face, slid away, then back, the way you tried to see something in the dark by looking not at it, but at the space to its right or left. She was searching, trying to get this strange new reality into focus. "It's okay," he said, "I'm here. I'm right here, *myshka*," and suddenly, as though the moments of birthing and crying and searching had taken every tendril of strength in her body, she closed her eyes and was instantly asleep. Just like that, all the tension in her body gone. Her eyes moving under their lids. Her little chest puffing up and down.

He was afraid to move, almost afraid to breathe, until a shiver shook her, and without even thinking he maneuvered her against his chest, wrapped his arms around her to keep her warm.

Finally, a nurse came in with the doctor. "Oh," the nurse said, "I see you've done this before. We're going to go and get cleaned up now, and then, if you want, you can have her back." His arms ached from being in one position for so long.

"Your wife," Dr. Wright said, "has had a seizure. We think it's a result of an aneurism." He tapped his head. "She has a bleed in her brain."

Chris opened his mouth, but no words came out.

"She's being prepped for surgery and the surgeon, Dr. Bavier, is already on site. We must stop the bleeding as quickly as possible. The surgeon will keep me informed and I'll keep you informed throughout. It could take several hours. She'll remain under constant monitoring on the surgical floor for at least twelve hours, and then, if there are no complications, she'll be moved to ICU. You can see her after the operation is done. I'll send someone for you."

Chris finally found his tongue. "Why? How?"

The doctor shook his head. "A weakness in a blood vessel. Could have been with her since birth. We can't tell. But if it had happened anywhere outside these walls, there's an overwhelming chance she would have died." He stood up, put his hand on Chris' shoulder. "I know it's hard to take in, but believe me, we're lucky on this."

***

Chris got two updates within the next three hours. The first: *the bleed has been located and the operation's going well so far.* And the second: *The bleeding's been stopped, your wife is doing well.*

It was dawn when a doctor in green scrubs walked in, a heavy stubble on his face, his eyes bloodshot. "I'm Jack Bavier," he says. "I performed your wife's surgery. She's holding her own. We had to get to it fast, so it was necessary to do a craniotomy – you know what that is?" Chris nodded. "And the leaking artery was clipped. We'll control swelling as much as possible to avoid pressure on the brain. You may see her if you wish, but she is non-responsive and probably will be for a while."

"Prognosis?" It came out a croak.

"We won't know for a while. Every hour without a crisis, the odds go up for recovery." He sat there for a second more, seemingly out of exhaustion, then pushed himself up. "Come with me."

It was hard to believe it was Lily lying there. Still as death. Tubes and wires running to monitors, bags. Her face swollen, white as the pillow she lay on, her head swathed in a cap of bandages. People walked in and out. He talked to her, told her Sophie was beautiful, that he would take care of her until Lily was better again, that she didn't need to worry. "She has your eyes," he said, "and your temper. But I can handle her, I think. I handle you, after all."

At eight A.M. they asked him to leave for a half-hour. "Where's my daughter?" he asked, and someone brought him to the nursery. CHEYKIN, Baby Girl, 5 lb., 8 oz, 17 in. She was asleep, wrapped in a pink blanket, a pink hat covering her hair, and while he stared at her, she startled, made a face, opened her mouth as if to cry, then settled and slept again. Seventeen inches. For some reason that number astounded him. Anna. He had to tell Anna.

He called her cell and told her he was downstairs in her dorm.

"What's happened?" she said.

"The baby came during the night. She's fine. But your mother had some difficulty."

"What? What's wrong? What's wrong!" She yelled it, and he heard her in the phone and coming toward him down the stairs at the same time. He pushed her toward two chairs in a corner.

"But she's going to be all right, isn't she?" Tears spilled out of her eyes, dripped off her lashes.

"She's doing fine right now, Anna. They're watching her constantly."

Anna stood up. "We need to go."

***

They sat with her all day Wednesday and through the night. It makes Chris uncomfortable to remember that for twelve of those hours he essentially forgot about Sophie. Every few hours, the nurse would ask them to leave the room for a while, and sometime during that night—he had lost all sense of time by then—he and Anna took the elevator to the nursery.

Sophie was asleep, and a nurse opened a door, stepped out into the hall. "You're Dr. Cheykin," she said.

She looked vaguely familiar.

"I used to work on campus," she said. "I'm sorry about your wife. I hope everything will be fine very soon. Would you like to see your daughter? You can come in if you'd like."

"I don't want to wake her," he said. "Her sister hasn't seen her yet. Just through the window?"

She went back inside and pushed the bassinet close to the glass. Sophie lay on her side, her fist in front of her face. And looking at her, he felt almost dizzy. He closed his eyes, leaned his forehead on the glass. The cool against his skin helped. He needed order, always had. And now his whole world was in pieces on the floor.

He opened his eyes and looked at her. God, she was so small. Had he really held her within minutes of her birth? How in hell, he wondered, had he managed that, when right now all he could do was ask himself how he was ever going to manage anything ever again.

He glanced at Anna, standing with her arms folded, her back to the window. There was anger in the set of her jaw, in the rigid line of her shoulders. He knew exactly what she was thinking.

"Anna," he said, "some things just happen. Human beings are lousy in these situations. Because we need a *reason*. We need something ... or some*one* ... to blame. But there's sure as hell no blame here. Turn around and look at Sophie. Do you really believe it's her fault?"

Anna stood there, staring at the floor.

"Is that what your mother would want you to believe?"

Slowly, she turned around, looked at her sister. Then she shook her head. "No." She sighed. "Can we go back now?"

"Sure."

***

Early Thursday morning, they moved Lily to ICU. He couldn't remember the last time Anna had spoken.

"Let's go get some breakfast," he said.

She shook her head. "I don't want to leave her."

"You need to eat something, Anna. It's not going to do your mother any good if you end up sick, too."

She shook her head again.

"Okay. I'm going to the cafeteria. I'll bring something back. And you have to eat it."

She nodded.

But before he went for the food, he went back to the nursery. Again, Sophie was asleep, but this time when a different nurse came to the door, he said, "Can I hold her?"

Inside, he put on a blue coat, the nurse lifted Sophie out of the bassinet, put her in his arms. Then she walked off a ways and so did he. Sophie stirred, but her eyes remained closed.

There were no other babies in the nursery, Sophie was all alone, and he remembered Lily telling him that things had changed since Anna was born. That your baby wasn't taken away after a feeding and brought back to the nursery, but stayed with you in your room. Unless you requested otherwise.

He looked down at his sleeping daughter, tried to think what Lily would want him to do.

"Hi, mysh," he said, "remember me? You're not here because your mother doesn't want you with her. Things just got a little complicated. So she can't take care of you right now." Sophie sighed, her lips pursed, moved. "But you seem to be doing fine. And I'll be back to visit. And you'll be with your mom soon. Because everything's going to be okay." He leaned down and touched her forehead with his lips. "It has to be."

The nurse was off in a different area, and he held Sophie for a while longer, then walked back to the bassinet and somehow maneuvered her into it without waking her up. Although he did manage to push her cap to one side so it dipped down over her forehead and partly covered one eye. "Sorry," he whispered, and fixed it the best he could.

"She's an easy baby," the nurse said, coming up behind him. "Eats well, sleeps well. She's very sweet."

"I'm glad she's not giving you any problems," he said. "I, uh messed up her cap. I'm not very good at this stuff, I'm afraid."

"Oh, you'll get there," she said. "It's all just common sense."

He nodded, pulled open the door, looked back over his shoulder at Sophie in the almost empty room.

***

He brought four egg sandwiches, three orders of hashed browns, two bottles of orange juice, two bottles of water, and half a dozen donut holes back to Lily's room. The smell of it in the elevator made him weak. How could he have been so hungry and not even been aware of it?

Anna ate one of the sandwiches, one of the hashed browns, drank one of the waters. He left an orange juice for her, and then ate everything that was left.

The food seemed to rid Anna of her torpor, and all of a sudden she was crying.

"Anna," he said, getting up and moving his chair next to hers. But he couldn't think of anything to say that would help. She wasn't a one-day-old baby completely unaware of reality. She knew Lily was in trouble. So he just sat there with her, handing her a new tissue every once in a while.

"I was so mean to her," Anna said finally. "I was just awful."

"Things like that happen," he said. "Remember? No reason? No blame? Your mother never blamed you. Besides, it got straightened out, and that was the best gift you could have given her. Everything that happened before doesn't matter now."

She breathed a ragged sigh, and they both sat there watching Lily as the clock on the wall ticked off another hour, then two.

Lily looked so perfectly calm. But then something gripped him that made it impossible to sit still. He got up, walked over to the window. Outside there was a blue sky, sunshine, people walking along the sidewalks down below as though nothing was wrong. It all felt like an insult.

What if Lily was only calm on the outside? What if she was roiling inside? The thought tore at his gut. What if she was suffering? What if she was frightened, confused, utterly lost.

He went over to the bed, leaned his hands on the railing and bent over her. "Hi, beautiful," he said. "We're here, you know. Me. Anna. And our baby is perfect. Sleeping in the nursery like a log. She's doing just fine, Lily." He stopped for a second. "Remember that time on the Vineyard ... Phil McKenna's place? And you and I took his canoe out into that little bay? Menemsha, I think it was, or maybe Aquinnah. There were no life jackets, and you said *what if we tip over, I can't swim.* And I said *we're not going to tip over and besides, you can float now.*"

He leaned down a little closer. "Remember that, Lily. You can float. You don't have to swim, you don't have to struggle, and you don't have to be afraid. All you have to do is relax and let the water hold you up. Just float, Lily, float."

Then he stepped back and put his face on his hands. He hadn't cried since he was kid, and he'd never cried in front of anyone ever. But tears came now. Silent and burning. He didn't stop until he felt Anna's hand on his shoulder.

"Sorry," he said, wiping his face on his sleeve. "I don't usually do things like that."

"It's okay," she said. "You're the one who taught Mom how to float?"

He nodded.

"She taught me. When I was really little. And then when I was older I took lessons at the Y. She wanted me to be a very good swimmer because she said it was important. And when I asked her why *she* didn't learn, too, she said, she really didn't need to because someone had taught her how to float once and that was all she needed."

The rest of the day and night went by in a continuing jumble of cafeteria visits, fitful hours in the sleeping lounge, hallway walks, nursery visits, sitting by Lily's bed watching watching watching.

And then on Friday morning, a nurse came in to tell him his daughter was ready to go home.

"Home?" he said. "But my wife..."

"It's a terribly hard situation," she said. "I understand. You can arrange for home infant care. Or are there family members who can help out?"

His mind raced. "Yes," he said, "I'll arrange things."

In the nursery, the second nurse he'd seen there apologized for having to go through the list she held in her hand, "but of course it's hospital policy," she said. She smiled at him and he smiled back even though he had no idea why. She talked to him about the formula; told him it should be warm, but not too warm; that one or two ounces was the maximum the baby would want at any one feeding, at least in the beginning. "How many feedings?" he asked.

"When she seems hungry ... every three hours, maybe less."

"Even at night?"

She laughed, as though he'd made a joke.

She fished a pen out of her pocket and wrote something down. "This is a good agency," she said, "if you need someone to help with the baby. Of course you have a car seat, Dr. Cheykin."

He nodded. It had taken him two hours to install.

She looked at the paper. "And the umbilical cord," she read, perfunctorily, "...keep it as dry as possible until it falls off." She looked at him. "There. Finished."

Umbilical cord, he thought.

There was a birth certificate application to fill out, and then a third nurse brought Sophie in and settled her in Chris' arms. "Good luck, Dr. Cheykin," she said, and put her hand on the baby's head, like a blessing.

They waved him out the door and into the elevator, and it hit him, when the elevator stopped at the third floor and two people stepped in, that they'd assumed he was a doctor. An M.D., not a Ph.D. Someone who didn't need to hear the boiler plate of *taking your baby home from the hospital* because he was *Dr.* Cheykin. He looked down at Sophie, who made a face and a noise that sounded like "mmmpphh."

Outside the door to the ICU, he stopped and took a deep breath. He hadn't been home in three days, hadn't showered, hadn't had any proper food. "Okay," he said, looking down at his daughter, I guess we have to go home now." This time she opened her eyes, looked back at him, blinked, but with only one eye, so it was really more of a wink, and despite everything he smiled.

He found Anna asleep, her head on the edge of the bed, her hand on Lily's arm, and it hit him, looking at Anna, that all their worlds were spinning dangerously out of control.

"Anna," he said.

She lifted her head. Looked at him, at the baby, then at her mother.

"We can't do this anymore," he said. "I need to go home and make arrangements, and you need to get back to your classes. You can't get behind this early into a semester. Neither of us can do anything here. Lily's where she needs to be, and they'll let us know when things change. I'll come during the day for a few hours, and you can, too, if you have time, but you can't miss any more classes. Lily wouldn't want that. So c'mon. I'll drive you back to your dorm."

She didn't protest. She seemed to need being told what to do. It was the only sense of order left.

"Your mother's going to be okay," he told her in the elevator. "But it may take a while. When she wakes up, we're going to be able to tell her school's great, the baby's great, everything's great. That we took care of things while she couldn't. Okay?"

She nodded, and for the first time, looked at Sophie. "She's awful tiny," she said. "Do you know what to do with her?"

"I don't think it's that hard. I'll manage until I can find someone."

Anna shook her head. "My friend's mother had a baby when we were both twelve. You'd never guess how loud something that small can scream."

The elevator door slid open and the three of them left the cool, fluorescent-lit hospital for the hot, blinding sunshine of a late August day, and even though Sophie's eyes were closed, she flinched. Chris covered her face with his open hand. *Dobro pozhalovat' mir, myshka,* Chris murmured. *Welcome to the world, little mouse.*

He dropped Anna off at the door to her dorm. She started to get out of the car, then turned back and hugged him. "Call me if you hear anything. No matter what time it is."

"I will," he said.

Sophie slept all the way home. He carried her upstairs to the pale-yellow nursery, and put her in the crib, thinking this might possibly be doable, after all, until his elbow collided with the mobile Lily had hung there and it collapsed into the crib, right onto his sleeping daughter.

She made a face, then opened her mouth, and like Anna said, it was one damn big noise. He gathered up the mobile and dropped it on the floor, gathered Sophie and tried to jiggle her back to sleep. But she'd have none of it.

As he remembers, it was the longest day of his life.

He got her to drink from the bottle, although the nipple seemed three times too big for her little mouth and much of the formula leaked down her chin and ended up soaking his arm. Every ten seconds, she'd stop sucking, turn her face away, cry. Then, suddenly, gasping and choking, she threw up —it had to be far more than she'd taken in— all over herself, all over him.

Now what, he wondered, her stomach as empty as when they'd begun. But every time he tried to give her more, she cried. Cried if he tried to put her down. Cried if he walked around. Cried if he stood still. And just when he had steeled himself to the possibility she might never stop, she fell asleep against his chest.

He was afraid to put her down, but at least it was a chance to breathe, to sit down, to open his laptop and get on-line.

He watched videos of babies being fed, browsed BABIES, TAKING CARE OF. Discovered that it might be the sound of his heartbeat that had calmed her down. She'd been hearing Lily's all those months. Okay, that made sense. He looked up FEEDING YOUR BABY and discovered something else ... babies couldn't burp. Had a moment of anger at the nurse who had neglected to mention that one little thing, though why would one tell that to a doctor? Then watched ten U-Tube videos, and, christ, everybody had a different technique.

Sophie stayed asleep, and after a while, he started to nod off, too. Dangerous—at least no one had to tell him that—so he slid down onto the rug, holding her in place against his heart, put pillows on either side of them, so she couldn't slip off. He dreamed Lily woke him, on her knees beside them, looking wonderful, laughing at how ridiculous he was. "Lily," he kept saying. "You're okay. I knew it was all a mistake." And then Sophie made a noise, and Lily said, "oh, my beautiful baby..." and Chris opened his eyes and she was gone.

He fed Sophie again, a little at a time, like the videos showed, lifting her to his shoulder and patting her back. When she burped, it was the only good thing that had happened in three days.

He fed, burped, fed, burped. She didn't throw up. He put her on the couch and she didn't cry, and then he remembered that she hadn't had her diaper changed since she'd left the hospital. He watched three videos. Not that hard. Take off the old diaper. Soaked. Wash her bottom and then dry. Put on a new diaper. Except the diapers Lily had bought went all the way up to her arm pits. He tried folding them down, but that didn't work, so he searched through the hospital bag and found six tiny diapers. They looked like something for a doll. But that was about the size of her, wasn't it, a doll.

When it was on, he looked at her and she looked back. "Jesus," he said, "I haven't said a word to you since we got home." Lily would kill him. Babies needed talking to. Stimulation, sound, music. He was going to stunt her development single-handedly.

She fell asleep on the couch and he called the hospital. *No change. No change*, he texted Anna.

It would become the mantra of their existence.

CHAPTER TWENTY-SIX

He slept for a while, then called the number the nurse had given him. Mrs. Gallagher. But Mrs. Gallagher had no care givers licensed to tend newborns at this time. "Call back in a month," she said. "A month?" he said.

No one had asked him if *he* had a license. No one had asked if he even had a clue.

He left Sophie on the couch, since she'd shown no signs of being able to turn over, and fell asleep on the floor again. She woke him up in two hours, the sun setting, the sky orange, and they went through the procedure again—bottle, intermittent burping, new diaper.

He decided he needed a shower, but didn't want to leave her alone, so he put her into a plastic carrier, and brought her along into the bathroom. It didn't seem that people he'd known had done things like that with their babies, but he had this compulsion to look at her every five minutes, at least when he was awake, and it was the only way he could figure out to do that and take a shower at the same time. Besides, she seemed to like the bathroom. Maybe it was the warmth, the sound of the shower. She didn't cry, she stayed awake until he was almost finished, then fell asleep and missed watching him shave.

The night went pretty much like the day, except from 8:10 to 10:04, she never stopped crying. She cried when he tried to feed her, cried when he tried to burp her, cried while he changed her diaper.

Some babies have a fussy time. They just need to cry. Listen to your baby. There are different cries for different situations. There's a mountingly insistent 'I'm hungry' cry. A moaning 'I'm tired' cry. A cry that could also be described as a screech that says 'my tummy hurts' often accompanied by your baby drawing up his or her legs. Then there's the 'fussy cry' which isn't particularly alarming, but seems to have the purpose of venting your baby's tension. If your baby has been fed and changed and there's nothing obviously wrong, simply hold your baby in your arms and try to offer comfort. It usually doesn't last more than an hour or two.

He'd found a web site called *Ask the Nanny*. Nanny talked like a grandmother, looked like a grandmother, *was* a grandmother. She knew everything about babies. All you had to do was choose a subject—feeding, burping, bathing, crying, diaper rash, teething, rolling over, umbilical cord care—and Nanny talked about it *ad infinitum*. Plus, she did it in a British accent, which he found strangely comforting.

He took stock. Sophie wasn't doing anything special with her legs. She wasn't moaning or screeching. She'd eaten. There didn't seem to be any leftover burps. Fussy, he decided, wondering if he was the one providing the nervous tension.

He held her. He tried talking, but that didn't work. He tried Russian, but that didn't work either. He even tried singing. Wasn't surprised when that seemed to make it worse.

And then at 10:05, just when he was getting desperate enough to call somebody, anybody, Sophie stopped crying and fell instantly asleep. It confounded him the way she could go from one extreme to another in the time it took to blink. He set her on the bed. She didn't look like she'd been crying for two solid hours—her skin pink and clear, her body relaxed. *He* was the one worse for wear, had caught sight of himself in the dresser mirror as he comforted her from one end of the room to the other, and his reflection had scared him.

He stood there watching her for another few minutes, and when he was convinced she wasn't going to suddenly wake up and require more comforting, he went into the yellow room, took the crib apart and carried all the pieces into their bedroom and put it back together. It took him an hour, and when he was done he carefully moved her into it and threw himself on the bed. She slept for another five minutes before she woke up.

And so it went.

Saturday morning, Ken McDonald called, and it hit Chris like a ton of bricks that he was supposed to have been at meetings the day before, setting up TAs, okaying his dissertation list, filing lesson plans. The campus, his job, had simply ceased to exist.

"Ken," he said, "I don't know where to start..." It felt like the explanation should have taken a day, rather than the five minutes it actually took. Ken said he'd get grad students to fill in. Not to worry. And then Sandy was on the phone. "Can I help? What can I do?"

It was the lifeline he would have thrown himself onto with great relief just half-a-day earlier, but it suddenly hit him that he was fairly certain he wasn't going to outright harm Sophie. And there was something else, a new feeling he couldn't identify that had taken hold in him. Sophie was his daughter, and it was his job to protect her, to care for her. Not anybody else's. "If I need to have someone stay with her. Not for a long time, two or three hours," he said, "can I call you?"

When Sophie woke up, he found himself studying her face while he waited for her bottle to warm. Babies had tended to all look alike to him. The younger they were, the more alike they seemed. But Sophie, he recognized. She looked like ... Sophie. The way her hair curled down onto her forehead. The shape of her nose. The cupid bow of her top lip. The way her face settled into an intelligent frown when she was calm and he was speaking to her.

When she woke him up just as he'd seemed to close his eyes, it surprised him that he wasn't annoyed, that he was actually anxious to pick her up and hold her, say hello, glad that, despite Lily, despite her mess of an inept father, she was moving forward with life. Hungry, burpy, full of pee and poop. He looked at her little face and, every time, fell in love a little more.

And he talked, because as long as nothing else pressed too hard on her attention, she seemed to listen. He told her what he was thinking. *I think I'll call the hospital and check on your mom in a few minutes.* He told her everything he was doing. *I'm calling the hospital to check on your mom now. No change.* He told her everything they were going to do together. *I'll text Anna and tell her that nothing's changed, and then we'll go see for ourselves, okay?"*

At noon, he put her in the car and took her into ICU, waiting for someone to say *you can't bring a baby into ICU,* but no one did. On-line Nanny had said new-born babies had a well-developed sense of smell, so he held her next to Lily for a few minutes. "That's your Mom," he said, putting her back into the carrier.

The surgeon came in at two, as he'd said he would. "She's in a relatively deep coma, which has little bearing on her recovery. Her vital signs are good. All we can do is wait and hope that she begins to rise to consciousness soon."

"And if she doesn't?" Chris said.

"The longer the coma, the less the chance there will be for a full recovery."

"Are we talking hours or days or weeks?"

"I would like to see her beginning to emerge within the next fourteen days."

When they were alone, he told Lily everything that had happened since the day before, watching her eyelids, her mouth, her hands for any sign of response. And when there was none, he felt a well of emotion rise inside him, lodge itself in his throat, so that for several minutes, he couldn't speak.

She looked so small, lying there. So slight. She'd grown Sophie inside her, delivered her. And now this massive trauma to her body. How could she have the strength to fight back?

"Lily," he said finally, "you have to come back to us. We need you. You and I have all that time to make up for. Sophie needs you. Anna needs you. I need you. Lily ...."

Sophie whimpered in her carrier and he lifted her out. He took Lily's hand and touched it to Sophie's head. "Lots of hair," he told her. "Like you said, remember? *One thing for sure,* you said, *with us for parents she'll have great hair.* And she does, Lily, she does."

But it was almost too much to bear, that limp hand on their daughter's head, no response, no caress, nothing at all.

He fed Sophie, hoping her sounds, his murmurs, the physical manifestations of feeding, burping, diapering, would reach Lily wherever she was. But when he left, she was as still as when he'd arrived.

Driving home, he felt a depth of loss that almost made him physically ill.

Out loud, he said, "Snap out of it." He couldn't give in, couldn't give up. It wasn't allowed. He looked over at his daughter, reached out and touched her cheek with a finger, and drove the rest of the way with one hand resting on her chest.

***

That evening, Anna and Max came to the house. Anna had just finished sitting with her mother for two hours. "I just told her all the stuff I would have told her anyway," Anna said. Her lips trembled. "She doesn't look any different. Any better."

"She's not worse," Chris said. "Her body took a double hit. The birth, the aneurism. She's going to heal slowly, but she'll heal." He made himself sound absolutely certain. And then Max jumped in.

"She just needs a lot of rest, Anna. And this way, she's getting it. I mean, with the baby and everything, if she was awake, she'd be all stressed out. That would be hard for her. Thinking about Sophie and you and everything. But this way, she'll just wake up when she's ready." He looked at Chris. "Right?"

Chris nodded. "Right." But what he really wanted to do was go over and give Max a great big hug.

Instead, he put Anna in a chair and Sophie in her arms. "You two get to know one another," he said, and went into the kitchen, made a big batch of scrambled eggs and bacon, and when it was ready, he put Sophie in her carrier and sat her on the table so she would hear them talking and smell the food. Be with them.

"I think she kind of looks like me when I was a baby," Anna said.

Chris smiled. "That would make sense." And then he thought, *pictures*. She was almost five days old and he hadn't taken one picture. He got up and took a few with his phone. "How do I get prints," he said, "so Lily can see them when she wakes up?"

"Send them to me," Max said. "As many as you want. I'll make prints. And I'll take videos, too."

"How can you be so calm about everything," Anna said to Chris. "Aren't you scared?"

"Yeah," Chris said. "I'm scared. But Lily and I decided at the very beginning of all this that whatever happened was meant to be." He shrugged. "I don't usually follow that attitude, Anna, but, you know, I'm beginning to think she was right."

"My mom lying in that bed was meant to be?"

"Your mom had that abnormality in her blood vessel probably all her life. It may have never ruptured. But then again it may have at any time. If it had ruptured any other place except inside the hospital, she could very well have died. And the only reason she was in that hospital was because of Sophie. See where I'm going?"

Anna nodded.

"Yeah," Max said, looking at Chris, then at Anna. "We all need to trust that, right? Because your mom would."

Sophie started crying while Max was clearing the table. "Why don't you try to keep her happy for a few minutes," Chris said to Anna, "while I get her bottle ready." But in the kitchen, he heard the steady rise of her cries, from mere want, to downright unhappiness, to outright frenzy.

"Uh ... can you *do* something?" Anna called out, and then appeared in the kitchen, Max in tow, holding Sophie as though she were made of glass. "Whatever I'm doing isn't working."

"Hey hey hey," he said, testing the formula on the inside of his wrist, the way Online Nanny did it, "what are you so unhappy about, little mouse, huh?"

And instantly, the crying stopped.

They all looked at one another.

"I think she knows your voice," Max said.

And there it was again, that new feeling rolling through him. He took her, touched the bottle against her mouth, and she moved her head toward it, then frantically side to side, searching and making herself miss it, until she finally clamped on and began taking giant, noisy swallows. Not just hungry, famished. They all laughed, and Max took a video of the feeding and the burping, and then another one when Chris changed her diaper, and another of Anna holding her. "Say hi Mommy," Anna said, looking from Sophie to the phone, then "Hi, Mom," and luckily Max stopped the video before she burst into tears.

So now there'd be more to do. Pictures, videos. Maybe he should keep a journal, so Lily could see he'd taken care of their daughter. Done what he was supposed to.

On Sunday he called Sandy and asked if she could babysit on Monday morning. "I need to talk to my post-grads," he said. "It's not fair to them, if I don't. Just for two hours, Sandy. Then I'll come pick her up and take her to see Lily."

It was time, he decided, to start putting things back together. He was a good organizer, and he could organize this, too, if he could just get his head clear. Something a little more sleep would help fix.

That night, he fed Sophie at midnight. She was taking more formula every time. Her eyes focused on him now, no more searching, and he leaned close to her face. "Hey, *mysch*," he said. "You're Sophie. I'm..." He started to say Chris, stopped himself. "I'm Dad, I'm your daddy." Her arm flew up and caught him on the chin. "And you're just like your mother, huh?" He smiled; she grimaced. "You know," he started to change her diaper, "things would be a little easier around here if you could sleep a little longer than two hours at a time, at least at night. You see, there's this thing called REM sleep. Very important. And your old man's not getting any. Which is making him older by the minute."

She stared at him with an intensity that almost looked like understanding.

"You're mommy's going to hate that she missed any of this," he told her. He picked her up, one hand under her head, the other cradling her butt, light as a feather. He studied her, felt the way her body tensed and relaxed, watched her head move from side to side in random shifts, the way her long fingers clenched and opened.

"Your mommy," he said, "is the most fantastic person in the world. And you are a very close second." He thought about Lily, willed her to wake up, be well again, come home. "We need her, don't we," he said, feeling Sophie relax as her eyes closed.

That night they both slept for four hours. It was the longest stretch in five days, and when he heard her stirring, making the little noises that told him he had five minutes before the screaming started, he was downstairs and back with her bottle before she'd begun to really whimper. He kept the light off, hardly said a word. From now on, stimulation was something for when the sun was out. She ate, she burped, she got a dry diaper, and then she was back to sleep for another three hours, and when he woke up in the morning, he felt close to human.

CHAPTER TWENTY-SEVEN

Sandy arrived twenty minutes early with a back seat full of frozen dinners for Chris to retrieve and stick in the freezer. Ken had cooked all day Sunday. "And there'll be more when this runs out," she said. "Everyone will take turns keeping you fed, until things are back to normal."

"I put Sophie down about an hour ago," he told Sandy, "so she'll probably be out for another hour or so. There are bottles ready to go in the fridge..." He hesitated. "You don't mind warming them in a pot of hot water? I don't use the microwave. I know some people do."

"Not me," she said. "I do it the old fashioned way, too. Don't worry, Chris. We'll be fine."

He had to force himself to the door, the driveway, the car. He felt naked without her. Kept glancing at the empty car seat all the way to campus.

Once he was there, everything took way too much time, and instead of the three hours he'd planned on, it was over four, and he had to keep making himself slow down all the way home.

Half-way up the back steps, he heard the crying. Sobbing, really. An edge of hysteria on every high note, and when he found the door locked, he had an almost irresistible urge to kick it in. But then he heard the lock turn and Sandy was there, Sophie, red-faced and hysterical, in her arms.

"She was fine until about a half hour ago," Sandy said, "and then she just kind of lost it. I'd fed her, changed her. We even had a bath. And she was fine through it all."

Chris took off his jacket and tossed it onto a chair, took Sophie and folded her in his arms. "It's okay," he said, "it's okay, it's okay." She ratcheted down a few degrees, rubbing her face against his shirt, taking big swallows of air. He'd never seen her like this.

Within minutes, she was half-asleep, but every thirty seconds or so a ragged half-sob tore through her.

"Nothing I did seemed to work," Sandy said. "In fact, I think I was just making her mad." She shook her head. "But she certainly seems to know who her Daddy is. Sit down. I'll make us some coffee and a sandwich."

Chris held Sophie until the redness was gone from her face, until her breathing was calm and even, then he put her on the couch. But as soon as he did, she stiffened, her arms flew up, her face scrunched, her mouth opened. "It's okay," he whispered, "it's okay, Sophie." He rubbed her stomach until she was relaxed again, then watched a moment before he went into the kitchen.

"So," Sandy said, "looks as though you have another more-than-full-time job. Which you seem to be very good at, by the way."

"I guess she's got used to me," he said. "You gave her a bath?"

"Yes. She pointed to a light blue plastic tub on the counter. "Was it her first?"

Chris nodded. "Afraid so." Bathing Your Baby wasn't one of the Online Nanny links he'd clicked.

"She seemed to like it."

"How often should she have one?"

"Two or three times a week?"

"Could I take her into the shower with me?"

Sandy shrugged. "Maybe when she's a little older. Though you could try it and see how she does. As long as you don't mind taking a cooler than usual shower. Do you have a pediatrician?"

He took a bite of the grilled cheese sandwich she'd made him. "I think there's a name on the refrigerator. Should I make an appointment? She's only a week old." He held up the sandwich. "Great. Did you put pickles in it?"

"That's Ken's homemade piccalilli. There's a jar for you in the fridge."

"It's nice," he said. "Crunchy."

She nodded. "I think you should make an appointment. She's fine and she's healthy." She smiled. "Rather robust, in fact, with that little temper of hers. But the doctor will weigh and measure her. Look at her birth weight to make sure she's growing properly, eating enough. Plus a doctor will tell you when she needs inoculations, when she can start solid food … those kinds of things."

He sighed. "I know she's growing, because the diapers have stopped falling off. But what I'm hoping is that Lily will be able to handle most of that."

Sandy's face lost much of its vitality. "How is she, Chris?"

"They need to see signs that she's coming out of it soon. Otherwise…" He shook his head. "…but I can't think about that."

"Believe that she'll be okay. Keep that thought. And in the meantime, I'm available whenever you need me. Though it's definitely evident your daughter prefers you." She took several sips of her coffee. "Likes the masculine touch, I guess. But really, it's pretty amazing how you've taken to it. Ken never did. At least not like that."

He finished the last of his sandwich. "That was delicious. Thanks Sandy. For the food, for lunch, for being here this morning."

"You'll ask for help when you need it?"

He nodded.

"It will be good for her to get used to other people a little at a time." She stood up. "I'm going home. And I suggest you go and take a rest. You need to do that whenever you can."

That's exactly what he did.

***

He let the grad students handle the next few days, while he handled Sophie, who seemed to be rapidly developing a very small, but very definite will of her own, and a verbal range, as well. Added to the crying, the gurgling, and the tongue-smacking, she'd started grunting. And there was something else he could only describe as a glissando, a kind of upward vocal slide that consisted of at least five notes.

Plus, she didn't always wake up crying now. Sometimes she'd lay in her crib for as much as three minutes looking around before she remembered she was hungry. The outside world was beginning to tug.

When she was ten days old, he woke up before Sophie for the first time, his head filled with the realization that ten days ago, Lily had been beside him. That they had fourteen hours of normality left and not a clue that it was about to end. Then Sophie stirred and he turned to watch her in the crib, her feet in the air, her arms pumping. It was the first time he didn't have to spring out of bed completely asleep.

Lily's mobile was back up, and the movement of the black and white elephants and giraffes, as anatomically incorrect as they were, fascinated her for moments at a time.

His plan had been to head for the hospital once she was awake, fed, and ready to travel, but he found himself having a hard time managing it. It wasn't until early afternoon that they were finally on their way, and it occurred to him half-way to the hospital why. He was scared. As if all the hope that had kept him at Lily's beside was evaporating. How many times could he go and find her just as lost to them as the day before? How could he continue to bear that?

When he entered Lily's room, Anna was there, sitting by the bed, and Max was there, too, sitting in a corner. He could see by Anna's face that she was losing her hold on the situation.

He looked at Max. Max shook his head. *No Change.* There was something vaguely familiar on the TV, but it took him a second to make sense of it. It was Sophie. Anna. Himself. Max had made a loop of the three of them and it was playing constantly to Lily. Beneath the TV, taped to the wall, was a blowup of Anna holding Sophie, and the same smaller print was propped on Lily's bedside table.

"That's great," Chris said to Max.

Anna put her face against Lily's blanket. Her shoulders began to shake. "I can't stand this anymore," she said, "I can't."

For once, Chris couldn't think of anything to say. Because a very big part of him didn't think he could stand it anymore, either.

Then Max stood up. He walked over to Anna and put his hands on her shoulders. "There's a good chance she can hear you," he said. "I've been reading. She might hear you even though she can't respond. Think how hard it would be for her to know you're so upset and not be able to do anything about it." He looked at Chris. "We have to let her know that we know everything's going to be all right."

Chris set Sophie's carrier on a chair. He went to the opposite side of the bed and leaned down, gave Lily a kiss on the forehead. "Lily," he said. "We're all here. Sandy stayed with Sophie for a while a few mornings ago, and I'm afraid your daughter gave her a hard time. Poor Sandy. I don't think she was expecting so much trouble from someone who's not much bigger than a loaf of bread."

Anna looked up. "What did she do?"

"Your sister got mad. She seems to know the difference between kith and kin."

"As in...?" Anna said.

"As in friends versus family."

Anna smiled. "She prefers us."

"Calves know their own mothers right from birth," Max said. "They won't suckle from another cow."

Chris looked at him. "Even within the same breed?"

"Yup. People think cows are dumb, but that's not true. They recognize members of their own herd; they interact with each other; and they have personality traits. Some are confident, some are shy, some are smarter than others. And it's usually not the biggest, strongest cow that runs the herd, it's the one the rest of the cows like best."

"The most popular cow?" Anna said, and laughed.

"It's true. Cattle are smart. Ours know how to press a button with their heads to fill their grain troughs. Same with water."

He went on for half an hour, talking about cattle, and it seemed to completely relieve the gloom that had permeated the room.

"You'll all have to come up to Vermont and check out my dad's farm after your mom's better," he said. "He'd like that. And babies really seem to like watching them, too. The cows. They always seem to get this astonished look on their face. The kids." Then he made a face to show them and they laughed.

Sophie began to stir, and Chris fished a bottle out of her bag. "Want to feed her?" he asked Anna.

He stood there, watching over her shoulder, and when she handed him the bottle after three ounces, and lifted Sophie up, they all laughed again at the enormity of the burp.

"That sounded like one of our cattle," Max said.

Chris glanced at Lily. Felt the upbeat of the past hour drain away. Ten days and counting. No change.

***

The next morning, Chris was up at six. Sophie had been up twice. Once at eleven, then again at three. But he was managing pretty well on six hours of broken sleep.

Plus, while he'd fed his daughter in the middle of the night, he'd decided this was the day he was going back to work. And Sophie was going with him.

He met his Wednesday morning lecture from 9:00 to 10:30, and at first Sophie was a definite distraction. "My daughter, Sophie," he said, after everyone had drifted in and settled down. "The sound of my voice seems to have the same effect on her that it has on many of you." He looked at his watch. "She should be sound asleep within ten minutes."

Which she was, and as word went through the hall with pointed fingers and a few smiles, there was a quiet but on-going *awww*, that gave him a ridiculous puff of pride. As if the fact that she could fall asleep was something he had a hand in.

He took care of her in his office until noon, with about ten visits from various members of the department and a lot of oohing and ahhing. Ken stopped by, as well.

"Just for a while, Ken. Doesn't seem to be a problem, so far. And I need to keep too busy, if you know what I mean. It keeps the thoughts at bay."

"Up to you," Ken said. "Whatever works. Sandy's been telling everyone what a shame you didn't start on this a long time ago. She thinks you're father of the year."

Sophie caused a greater stir in the seminar. Far fewer people, and she was always more wakeful during the early afternoon.

"She's very girly looking," said one of the members, who introduced herself as Maureen. "And very pretty." That last part with a tinge of surprise.

"That's my wife's contribution," Chris said. "What I gave her is her sense of gravitas."

People chuckled. Maureen looked at him, then smiled and sat down.

Maybe it was just his imagination, but they seemed to pay a good deal more attention then he was used to. And when Sophie let out a squawk with twenty minutes still to go, he patted her, said something comforting, and then told the group, "She and I tend to have this ongoing disagreement over Dreiser's use of pathos in this book." Then made a mental note to put that as a discussion point on the first exam.

After that, it was back to his office for another feeding, and then to the hospital.

The doctor would be there at two-thirty, give or take a half-hour, and Chris needed questions answered.

Max and Anna must have been there already, because the video was changed, and there was now a photo album on the bedside table. Chris paged through. Dozens of pictures. All that he'd taken. All that Max had taken. All with dates and descriptions. Some in Anna's writing, some in Max's. It was one hell of a good family he'd married into.

There was an envelope inside the album with his name on the front. Inside was a note from Anna. *My dad and I talked last night. If you think it will help, he'll send in an expert he knows at Johns Hopkins. Here's my dad's number. He said call him any time. P.S. He left a request for Mom to get better at the Chapel of Our Lady of the Miraculous Medal on the rue de Bac. He said he didn't know what else to do. Love, Anna*

Chris folded the note and put it in his pocket. "You have everyone pulling for you, Lily," he said. "All that good energy has to be worth something."

He sat with her until the doctor arrived at two-forty-five, and then asked if they could speak outside the room.

"We're into the second week," Chris said, Sophie bobbing at his shoulder. "What do we expect if nothing changes."

She was stable, the doctor told him. Her autonomic nervous system was functioning normally. "We can give it another week," he said, "and if things are unchanged, we have to make the assumption she may remain in this state indefinitely. She'll be transferred to a nursing home—you have several to choose from. And then all you can do is continue to wait and hope."

"Maintenance," Chris said.

The doctor nodded.

Lily in a nursing home. For a split-second, he wanted to knock the man right off his feet. But he'd developed a slot in his brain where all the unimaginable things he thought and heard and experienced were absorbed and then disappeared. And that's where this particular byte of information about a fucking nursing home was shuffled to, so he was at least able to shake the doctor's hand, thank him, and then return to Lily to tell her about Sophie and her first day of college. How she'd started hiccoughing half-way through his lecture.

"A girl near the front raised her hand," he told Lily. "She wondered if Sophie might need some water. So I said, 'Is that what you do? Give your baby water?' And she said, 'oh, I don't have a baby. I just figured if it works for me when I have the hiccoughs, it might work for her.' Frankly, the thought that babies might need water had never occurred to me, Lily. But then Sophie started sucking on her fist—did I tell you she does that now? Suck on her fist? And the hiccoughs stopped. So when I got home I looked it up—giving babies water, and wouldn't you know you're not supposed to. They don't need it. It can even be harmful. You'd have known that. But don't worry, I'm researching everything, and so far, so good. Also, so much for unsolicited advice from college students."

He stared at her for a minute. "What do you think about a screened porch? Off the back of the house where the deck is. I thought it would be a great place for Sophie. Outside, but protected, you know?" He chewed his bottom lip. "We'll have to talk about it."

After her bottle, Sophie fell asleep in her carrier, and then Chris fell asleep, too, in the chair. Something was after him. Bodiless, amorphous, evil. He ran, but it was on him, and he woke himself up with a start. He looked at Lily, leaned toward the bed and put his hand over hers. Every once in a while he had a crazy impulse to shake her. *Lily*, he wanted to say, *for christ's sake, Lily, you can't do this any more. You have to wake up. You have to wake up!*

***

The next few days rolled by in a fog of classes, feedings, and Lily. The only time he felt anything like himself was in the classroom, doing what he'd been doing for thirty years. It had a way of taking him over, and sometimes he would glance down at Sophie, asleep or kicking her legs or looking back at him or sucking on her fist, and wonder for just a split second where this baby had come from.

Gradually, he began to notice that the students listening to his lectures had grown. Usually, the opposite occurred. A lecture with fifty students morphed to forty-two. But when the office sent him a new class list, fifty-three had become seventy-one.

Instead of rushing out after class, his students formed a plug around Sophie. *Oooh, she's getting big. Look at her eyes, they're so blue. Bye, Sophie. Getting any sleep, Professor? If you need a babysitter, here's my number.*

And Sophie seemed to eat it up. Looking from face to face, kicking her legs harder and harder, until the stimulation overwhelmed or her stomach told her it had been too long since lunch. Then she went from a source of intense interest to clearing the room.

"Fair weather friends, huh Sophie?" Chris would say. "It's okay. I'm sticking around."

"Sophie's quite a hit," he told Lily. "Admin is thinking of making it school policy to have an infant in every classroom. Seems to bring out the best in people."

A gray-haired nurse came in with some papers. "Dr. Bavier left these for you," she said. "You'll have to designate a destination by tomorrow since your wife is being transferred on Monday."

Today was Saturday. They'd given him the same papers on Wednesday and Friday. They'd ended up in the wastebasket, exactly where these were going to end up.

"Curtis-Hill," she said. "That's where my daughter was in a similar situation. They gave her excellent care." She looked at him, and he thought she was going to say more. But then she pressed her lips together, gave him a sympathetic smile and left.

Fuck Curtis-Hill.

∗∗∗

And now, throwing back the covers and sitting up on the edge of the bed, having gone through all those days and weeks and months yet one more time in his mind, he says it again, under his breath so he won't wake Sophie. "Fuck Curtis-Hill fuck Curtis-Hill fuck Curtis-Hill."

CHAPTER TWENTY - EIGHT

At seven A.M., Anna texts him to come for a picnic in Lily's room at two o'clock. Sophie has a fussy morning, or maybe it's his fault. Online Nanny says, *Your baby is highly sensitive to your mood. Even on a bad day, try to be as relaxed and upbeat as possible. Remember, every moment with your baby is precious.*

Sometimes Online Nanny makes him sick.

"Even on a bad day, huh?" he says to Sophie. "I'd like to show that goddamn woman a bad day." Upon which, Sophie screws up her face and begins to scream. "Okay, okay," he says, finishing the snaps on her onesie, picking her up, jiggling her. "I'm sorry. I'm sorry. I'm sorry I swore. I'm sorry I'm being an idiot. I'm upset. You're going to have to bear with me, mysh. Can you do that? Can you bear with your old man?"

It takes her a while to calm down. At least until Chris begins to whistle, and that's something new. He hasn't whistled at all since she was born, and it seems to have a strange effect. First, she goes silent. He holds her away from his chest so she can see where it's coming from, and so he can see her reaction. Which is to frown so hard, little lines appear above her nose. Which makes him instantly stop. Because that's Lily's frown. Those are Lily's lines.

Sophie's frown disappears. She looks up at the ceiling, back at him, then away. Not as if she's searching for the noise, but as if the noise never happened.

"I wish I could forget like that," he tells her, watching the way her face constantly changes, the way her eyes search, study, then search again until they find a new focus. "Don't worry, Sophie," he tells her, "you'll learn to whistle some day. Though you'll have to get it from me. Because your mom can't whistle worth a damn."

Then he whistles two tunes for her. *Mary Had a Little Lamb* and *Three Blind Mice,* and her eyes come rushing back to him, Lily's frown in place through his entire performance.

He's late for the picnic, but they haven't started. Everything is laid out on a card table. Checkered tablecloth, bright red napkins, plastic plates, forks, spoons. Bright green plastic cups. Even a bottle of wine. And as soon as he walks in, Anna starts opening plastic tubs. There's potato salad, pickles, tuna sandwiches, ham sandwiches, potato chips. And for dessert, something Anna calls *Clafoutis.* "Very French," Anna tells them. "A cherry custard pie."

Anna and Max, who are making it their mission to be pointedly positive, keep up a constant banter. Which, after a while, works itself into Chris' mood and manages to lighten it from the dead black it had been all morning to a shade of gray that at least lets some light in.

Anna's the one who takes Sophie from her carrier when she wakes up. Anna is definitely Sophie's second favorite person. Although she wants no one but Chris when she's unhappy and miserable, she gives Anna all her attention when she's in a state of tranquility. Stares at her so hard and long, seemingly transfixed by this completely different creature, that it always makes Anna laugh, the look of intense concentration on that little face. It's clear she's trying very hard to understand who this person is. This person who talks to her in a high, singing voice, the way most women talk to babies; who bobs her head around and has an assortment of noises and expressions that Chris can't possibly match.

"You are the goofiest little person in the world," Anna says, lowering her face until she and Sophie are nose to nose. "Yes you are, yes you are."

"Almost as goofy as her big sister," Max says.

And how, Chris wonders, would Lily be talking to Sophie? With playfulness, he guesses. Affection. Surprise. Intimacy. With a range and nuance, he simply doesn't have. So thank god for Anna.

He discovers he's hungrier than he imagined, everything delicious. Simple and fresh. Not that he rues the frozen meals Sandy keeps piling into his freezer.

"I'm thinking of quitting the convenience store and getting a different job," Max says, creating a Dagwood by combining a ham and a tuna and layering the tuna with pickles and mustard.

"Sick of working nights?" Chris asks.

Max shakes his head. "It's not the hours so much. I've been getting up at four o'clock pretty much all my life. I don't really seem to need a lot of sleep. It's just a crazy place to work and I think I'd like something a little less stressful."

"You mean a place where people don't show up waving guns and yelling *give me your cash!*" Anna says.

Max takes a big bite of his sandwich, nods. "Exactly. And someplace where people don't drive into the building or where skunks don't show up at three in the morning."

"Whoa," Chris says. "Someone drove into the building? With you inside?"

"What skunk?" Anna frowns at him. "You never said anything about a skunk."

"It happened Friday night," he says, "the skunk." Then he looks at Chris. "The person who hit the building, that happened last week." He takes a big bite of his sandwich, chews, swallows. There's a blotch of mustard on the side of his mouth and Anna tosses him a napkin. "So," he says, wiping at the mustard, "this guy came in around two A.M. and bought cigarettes and ten lottery tickets. He was all fidgety, like I couldn't do anything fast enough for him. Didn't even wait for his change. Just ran outside, jumped in his car, started the engine, hit the gas, and rammed right into the side of the building."

"His own fault, of course," Anna tells Chris. "And yet after he did it, he was furious at everybody else."

"Yeah," Max says, "do you believe that? *He* was the one who got mad. At the police, at me, at his car. He actually got out and kicked his car! Put a big dent in the fender, as if the flattened front end wasn't enough." He takes another bite.

"I mean, I had to close the store, call and report what had happened, had to wait for a structural engineer to come and inspect the building. Which turned out to be fine. But no one could be in the store until he okayed it, so I essentially sat in my car for four hours until I could open up again, and then I had to deal with all the people who couldn't buy their candy bar or their milk in the middle of the night." He shakes his head, finishes his sandwich, and takes another.

"But what about the skunk?" Anna asks.

"Oh *that*. Well, I looked up and saw this guy waving his arms at me from the parking lot and pointing to the door. So I came out from behind the counter, walked over to the door, and there's a skunk hunkered down right outside. Pretty skunk, mostly white with a black stripe down its back, and it was very concentrated on licking the cement." He takes a bite of his sandwich. "So I remembered that a kid had spilled a Slurpy there earlier that night, and the skunk was after the syrup that had soaked into the cement. Skunks like sweet things just like us. But the thing is there wasn't much I could do to make it move. And then, all of a sudden, the police were there. *Again*. This is like the third time this month."

"They came about the skunk?" Anna asks.

"Someone had called them. So the police and I are outside at the back of the building looking around the corner at the skunk, and they want to shoot it!"

"*Shoot* it?" Anna says. "Why did they want to shoot it?"

"Because they didn't know what else to do. But I told them that was crazy because first of all, there's no reason to kill it, and second, it's too far away to hit it for sure with a pistol, so there's a good chance they'll miss, and the bullet will ricochet into the building or off somewhere else, and then the skunk will direct-spray everything within ten feet. Plus, that smell will go a mile and stick around for a couple of days."

"You should major in wildlife biology," Chris says. "Or maybe you already did."

"So?" Anna says, "what happened??"

"I talked them into not shooting it, went inside, got a bag of caramel popcorn. Then I tossed a few pieces from the corner of the building, and of course it ate them, and I just kept tossing pieces of popcorn across the parking lot, walking toward the woods, and pretty soon, Voila!"

"Voila is right," Chris says. "That was masterful."

Max shakes his head. "I'd rather deal with a whole herd of cows for a month than one guy in too much of a hurry or one cop who wants to shoot a skunk or one customer like Mrs. Gubellini, who comes in five nights a week to tell me all about the space aliens who moved in next door."

Suddenly, they're all laughing. It doesn't last long. Lightness drains away quickly in that room, but for the moments it lasts, the laughter is a beautiful thing.

Chris looks across the room at Lily, gets up, walks over to the bed.

Anna," he says, "come here."

Anna stands up with Sophie still in her arms and comes around the other side of the bed. Max comes, too, and stands beside Chris.

"What?" Anna says.

"Look at the color in her face."

"Her cheeks are pink," Max says.

Anna hands Sophie across the bed to Chris. "Mom?" she says. "Mom, can you hear me?"

Chris lays his hand on Lily's forehead. Her skin's warm, but not hot. It isn't a fever. They stare at her for a minute, then Chris goes out and comes back with a nurse.

"She has color in her face," he says, "for the first time since the aneurism."

The nurse checks her vitals. "I think her breathing may be less shallow. "I'll let the doctor know."

A little pink in Lily's cheek. It's such a small thing. But at the same time it feels huge.

They stay with her through the rest of the afternoon and into the evening. The doctor comes in around seven and examines her.

"It's hard to say, but she does seem to have increased responsiveness in some ways. It's a good sign. We'll monitor her closely. But it's unlikely her coming out of the coma will be precipitous. It's almost always a gradual process. The fact that it may be starting now, within that two-week period we talked about is hopeful. So I'd go home, try and get a good night's sleep, and come back tomorrow. I doubt anything significant will happen tonight."

"But you'll let me know if it does," Chris says.

"Yes. Of course."

They stay for another hour, all Anna's attention on Lily. Max puts away the remains of the picnic. Chris feed Sophie, whose eyes never leave his face. It should be unsettling, to be studied so intently, but, in fact, it's the exact opposite.

When the bottle's empty, he tucks her into the carrier, and goes over to Lily. Anna's holding one of her hands, and he picks up the other in both of his.

"Hey beautiful," he says. "Your daughters are both here. Me and Max, too. We just had a picnic and you missed a great meal. But we'll do it again soon as you're well." He looks at Anna. "Right?"

She nods. "Right, Mom. You look pretty. Your cheeks are all pink. Remember the time I got into your makeup and when you saw me, you screamed? And even a bath and a scrub couldn't get it all off?"

"She's right, Lily," Chris says, "you're a knock-out. Even though Anna's hair is longer than yours now. I say you two have a contest and see whose hair is longer by Christmas. Winner gets a trip back to Bimini. We'll all go. All four of us. No, five! All five of us."

"Tell you what, Mom," Anna says. "When you get home, I'll cut my hair to the exact length of yours. That way we'll start even."

"Three short-haired women in my life," Chris says. "Who could have predicted that?"

He doesn't know if what he felt then was Lily —a movement of Lily's hand— or just his imagination. He looks at Anna, who has either failed to notice, or felt nothing. So he just bends down and kisses Lily lightly on the lips. "You sleep tight," he says, and we'll all be back tomorrow."

***

When he gets up at three o'clock with Sophie, there's a text from the hospital. *Increased responsiveness confirmed. Moving out of ICU tonight into general admission. Room 222.*

He lays awake the rest of the night, listening to Sophie's noises, his hand stretched out touching Lily's side of the bed. Part of his brain wants to imagine what might happen tomorrow. That he might walk into her room and find her sitting up in bed or maybe fully dressed and tapping her toe. "What took you so long," she'll say, "I've been dying to go home for hours!" But what if it's the opposite. What if he walks in and the color's gone from her cheeks and they're getting ready to ship her to that goddamn nursing home. It isn't possible to go to either place. Because one is unimaginable and the other is sheer, improbable fantasy.

But then Sophie, back in her crib, begins to cry, saving him. He knows she can't be hungry or wet. Decides she simply can't sleep either. It's in the air. So he brings her into the bed, puts her next to him, puts pillows behind him so he can sit up comfortably, checks his phone even though it's made no sound. Sophie seems content to look around. Her legs pumps, her arms swing. Every day, she has better control over her body. Sometimes, when he talks to her, or when Anna is emoting, it almost looks like she's trying to smile. That's supposed to be a few weeks off, yet, but he's pretty sure she's working on it.

"Then you'll turn yourself over," he tells her. "That'll be big, huh? Sitting, crawling, walking." He can't imagine it.

Sophie looks at him in passing, as if she's come to take his presence for granted and he isn't nearly as interesting as he used to be.

He sits forward. "Hey, mysh."

She turns her head, looks at him, then up at the ceiling, at the wall above his head, then back at him.

"I know it's early, but I can't wait. We need to get to the hospital. I'm going to take a shower and give you a bath. How's that sound?" Her arms and legs move faster. She makes a noise—half-grunt, half-sigh. She makes new noises every day.

By the time he finds Room 222, Sophie, who, as usual, fell asleep in the car and slept until he carried her into the elevator, is wide awake and kicking.

"I think dance lessons are in her future," a woman on the elevator says. And then getting off, she adds, "Good luck. Your granddaughter's adorable."

He knows he's going to have to get used to it, because he's going to hear it a lot.

Lily isn't sitting on the edge of the bed, isn't fully dressed or tapping her toe. She's as still as the day before. But her cheeks are still pink.

He takes Sophie out of the carrier and holds her so she's facing Lily. "Lily," he says, "it's a beautiful day out there. Sophie and I were up early. Four-thirty." He yawns. "She's here to have breakfast with you."

He pulls a chair up next to the bed and holds Sophie so she's sitting on the bed, her feet pushing against Lily's arm. And then Sophie lets out a squawk. Not a cry, a squawk. The loudest noise she's made yet. And Lily's eyelids move.

Chris swallows. "That's our girl," he says. "Did you hear her? No manners. No self-control." He stands up, takes Lily's hand and puts it against Sophie's cheek. Sophie turns toward it, so Lily's palm is covering her nose and mouth, Lily's fingers on her forehead, touching her hair. And that's when Lily opens her eyes. She stares at the ceiling; Sophie makes smacking noises against Lily's palm; squawks again, and Lily's eyes move toward the sound, her head turns on the pillow.

She seems to have the same trouble focusing as Sophie did in the beginning. Chris leans down, so his face is just above Sophie's. Lily looks at him. "Hi," he says, and she smiles. Then her hand moves slowly away from Sophie's face, up and over Sophie's head. The tips of her fingers touch his chin. Her lips move, but nothing comes out.

"It's okay," he tells her. "You've been out of commission for a couple of weeks, sweetheart. But you're getting better now. You're going to be fine. And we're fine, too —Sophie. Me. Anna. All you need to do right now is relax and think about getting better. Sophie and I are going to be here all morning. So if you want to sleep, you go ahead and sleep."

She looks from Chris to Sophie and back again.

"Yeah," he says, "isn't she the most beautiful thing you've ever seen?"

Lily smiles. Then her eyes close. Her hand slides down to Sophie's legs.

His throat's full, his heart's pumping, and Sophie's noises turn fussy, so he picks her up. He fishes his phone out of his pocket, texts one word to Anna: *AWAKE*, and hits send.

CHAPTER TWENTY-NINE

Within the hour, Anna's there, and as soon as she kisses Lily's cheek and says "Mom," Lily opens her eyes again. "Hi," she whispers to Anna, who immediately releases two tears, one from each eye.

"Sorry," Anna says, wiping them away, laughing a little, "but I've been sort of worried about you."

Lily raises her hand to Anna's face. "Okay," she whispers. Then, "baby?"

"Sophie's right there." Anna points to the other side of the bed, and slowly, Lily turns her head, looks up at Chris, at Sophie in his arms. "Not a dream," she says.

Chris raises the head of Lily's bed so she can watch him give Sophie the rest of her bottle. Her hands keep raising off the bed and then falling still. Her head moves back and forth on the pillow. "Can't."

"You're going to be holding her day and night pretty soon," Chris tells her. "But you have to get your strength back first. Don't worry, okay?"

She nods.

When Sophie falls asleep on his shoulder, he lays her on Lily's thighs. Lily holds Sophie's hands, watches her, looks up at Anna, smiles.

Then her eyes close, but she opens them again. "Sleep," she says, making a lifting motion in the air above Sophie.

Chris picks Sophie up. "It's okay, sweetie," he says, "go to sleep now and we'll all be here when you wake up again."

***

Chris calls Ken, who says he'll cover the two afternoon lectures himself. "Is it okay if I pass along the good news?" he asks.

"Ring it from the church bells," Chris tells him.

The rest of the day revolves around Lily's wakefulness. Each time she's awake longer, more verbal, more animated. So that by four in the afternoon, she's sitting up, Sophie propped against her with pillows, almost holding her for the first time.

Max, who arrived around two, is videotaping everything—Lily, Anna, Sophie, the nurses. The doctor, who comes in during the afternoon, waves at the camera, says hello to Lily and explains to her what happened. She's obviously overwhelmed, exhausted by the time he leaves.

Chris takes Sophie. "Maybe it would be best if we all cleared out so you can get a good rest," he tells her.

She shakes her head. "Stay," she says, looking up at him, tears in her eyes.

"We'll stay, Mom," Anna says, "it's okay."

And then Chris sees the old Lily kick in. The no-nonsense Lily. The Lily who wants to make sure *they* get a good night's sleep. She shakes her head. "No," she says. "Go." She looks at Chris. "Sophie likes crib?"

He nods. "But she's not in her own room. She's in ours."

Lily smiles at him. "Good," she says.

She watches them file out, waves, blows a kiss to Anna. When Chris looks back before he closes the door, she's already asleep.

Driving home, he feels like Superman.

"We're not completely out of the woods," the doctor had told him out in the hall. "But I think it's safe to assume she's going to be fully herself again. We'll do a CT scan before she goes home to make sure everything's looking optimal. But she seemed to take in what I told her. How does she seem to you?"

"In slow motion," Chris said, "physically and mentally. And somewhat overwhelmed."

"I'm not surprised at that. It's a big, noisy, fast world she's come back to. She's young. She'll adjust pretty rapidly."

"When can she go home?" Chris said.

"If she continues to progress ... two, three days?"

Sophie trilled in his arms at that precise moment, a kind of musical squeal that sounded like pure joy and made them both laugh.

"That's a pretty powerful incentive you're holding there," Dr. Bavier said. "Give it a little time, and your wife's going to be just fine."

Chris held out his hand. "The words don't do it justice, but thank you. You saved her life."

***

Chris wakes up with a start, knowing instantly that something's wrong. He looks at the gray light coming through the window, then at the crib. Sophie's chewing on her fist, making loud smacking sounds. She's kicked off her blanket and seems to be watching her own feet pumping in the air. Then he looks at the clock. Five. She fell asleep at midnight, and for the first time in two weeks, he's slept for five straight hours. And then he remembers. Lily's okay. He lies there letting it course through him. Lily's okay.

The phone starts ringing at six. Anna first, wondering when he's going to the hospital. Then Sandy MacDonald, who gets all choked up while she's asking if he needs her to babysit. Then Lily's sister, who he called last night. "Sorry to call so early," Heather says, but I knew you'd be up with the baby. I wanted to let you know that I can come and stay for as long as a month, if you think you'll need me, starting next week. If not, then I'd at least like to come in November. For two weeks. My vacation. Think about it and tell Lily, okay?"

Every day it seems to take longer to dress Sophie because she never seems to stop moving anymore. In the middle of a diaper change, she'll suddenly arch her back and turn her head, as if she's heard something behind her. Her arms are never still. Nor her legs. And she's starting to grab onto things, which immediately go straight into her mouth.

"Hey," he says, trying to get one of her arms into a sleeve, "a little cooperation here? Can you give your old man a break and be still for one second?"

She looks at him. And just like that she smiles. And then, just like that, it's gone. But he knows it was a smile, not just an accidental approximation, because the smile wasn't only on her lips, it was in her eyes, too.

"You have to remember what you just did," he tells Sophie. "Because you're going to have to do it again today. And when you do it? That's the one that's going to be your first smile. For your mom. And what just happened here? It never goes beyond this room. Got it?" He leans down and kisses her on the cheek. "Got it, Sophie?" Her fist comes up and catches him on the nose. "I'll take that as your sworn word."

***

Lily's sitting in a chair when he and Sophie arrive. Anna's on the bed. Max has his video camera trained on the door, ready to catch the look on Chris's face when he sees Lily.

"Look at you," Chris says. "Perpendicular at last."

"I've been waiting and waiting." She puts her arms out. "For both of you."

He makes a mental note. Language, timely. Physical response, greatly improved.

Your daughter," he says, and glances at Anna, "your *number two* daughter has decided to pursue a career in *wiggling*. She practiced the entire time her poor old man was trying to squeeze her into her clothes." He sets the carrier down, lifts Sophie out, and hands her to Lily, who takes her carefully and then, with Anna's help, proceeds to undress her.

"Do you have any idea how long it took me to put that stuff on her?" Chris says.

"Her arms," Lily says, "chubby! Her legs. She's ... so ... perfect." She looks at Chris, and it's all there in her eyes.

"I had to do a good job," he says, "or else answer to you."

"I want ... to go home," she says, "but I need a ... thing ... of my head."

He waits.

"CT," she says. "Scan."

He nods. "Don't rush it, Lily. Another day isn't going to make any difference."

She and Anna re-dress Sophie, who seems to be more cooperative for them.

Lily fades after about two hours, Sophie asleep on the bed. "Sleepy," she says, looking at Chris. "Bathroom ... help me? Then bed?"

"I have to leave," Anna says. "I have an exam."

"At home," Lily tells her. "See you ... there."

Anna nods. She and Max hug Lily goodbye.

"Anna's classes," Lily says, "all this..."

"I think she's in good shape." He helps her stand up. She walks more or less on her own to the bathroom, needs a little help sitting down and getting up again. "A little ...unsteady," she says, "but better."

"Just got to get your sea legs back," he says. "Two weeks is a long time."

She slips into bed without disturbing Sophie. "Two weeks," she says."

She grabs hold of his hand, presses it against her cheek. It's the first time they've been alone. It feels very good.

"Sandy called," she says, closing her eyes. "Said, 'just listen.' Told me ... you ... magnificent." She shakes her head slowly back and forth on the pillow. "You? A knack with babies?" Then she opens her eyes and looks at him.

"Not babies," he says. "Baby. *Our* baby. Poor Sophie had no choice but to make the best of it. She got stuck with me."

Lily smiles, her eyes close. Pretty soon she's snoring.

He sits there looking from his beautiful sleeping wife to his beautiful sleeping daughter, thinking how there aren't too many perfect moments in a lifetime, and knowing this sure as hell is one of the all-time best.

An hour later, Lily wakes, sits up, lets her feet dangle over the edge of the mattress, seems content to watch him feeding Sophie.

"I was a little slow on the burping thing," he tells her. "But I think I have it down. Agree?"

She nods. "You deserve a star."

It comes out in a piece. An entire sentence. No hesitation, no effort.

They smile at each other when Sophie burps. "I remember things," she says. "Not good things. I was drowning. And then you were there. You swam to me, and put your hand under my back. Held me up. I stopped being afraid that I was going to die." She frowns. "Funny ... you were out here. I could hear you. But you were in there with me. All the time."

"All I did was watch you and worry."

She shakes her head. "No. You were there. And I heard Anna laugh. She wasn't in there, but her laugh was ... like music. And I wanted to come back. So badly."

"I guess David had some French saints praying for you."

She laughs a little. "Anna told me. He called last night, but I was asleep. Left a message. Everything he'd wished for had just come true."

Chris tells her about Heather, and Lily opts for a November visit. "I need quiet time. Just you and me and Sophie." She looks at him. "Are you exhausted?"

"Right about now," he says, "I'm not feeling much of anything except pure joy."

He puts Sophie in the carrier and she sits there swinging her arms, kicking her legs, looking around, making an assortment of noises ... gurgles squeals grunts trills. He knows her vocalizations will gradually slow until she falls asleep. Five, maybe ten minutes.

They both watch her for a while.

"I just thought of something," he says. Lily looks at him. "You have it, the family you always wanted." He watches her frown. Then her eyes light up and he relaxes. She knows what he's talking about.

'Two girls and a boy," she says. But then she frowns again, but only for a moment until it dawns on her. "Max," she says. "Now we have Max, too."

"He's a great kid," Chris tells her. "I have this idea it comes from growing up with animals. He possesses an unusually well-developed sense of empathy. Knows what a situation calls for without anybody saying a word. He was great to have around. Total support for Anna. For all of us."

"We Shea women pick only the best men," Lily says. Then she gets a quizzical look on her face. "Did you know," she says, "that a cow will hide when she's about to have her calf?" She looks at him. "Why is that in my head? How do I know that?"

"Because you've been listening. That's a Max fact. He gave us a primer on cattle one day. And it was just what the doctor ordered. Anna and I were in the pits, but Max got us out. By talking about cattle. And that was one thing he told us. How he and his father often had to search all over the farm for a new mother cow who'd gone off and hidden her calf."

They look at each other and start to laugh at the same time.

Chris gets up and goes and sits beside her. He puts his arm around her and she feels little and big at the same time. Big because the only person he's held in the past two weeks only weighs about seven pounds. Little, because obviously she's lost weight and he can tell.

"You have to start eating again," he says. "Build yourself up."

"I am. Pancakes for breakfast. A scrambled egg. Oatmeal." Then she lays her head against his shoulder, closes her eyes.

"Tired?"

"No. I just love feeling your arm around me."

"You know," he says, "I was scared as hell most of the time."

"The thing about you," she said, "is even if you're scared on the inside, you don't show it on the outside. You're..." she squeezes his hand, "...solid. It's who you are. And it's why Sophie wants you when she's upset."

"And who told you that?"

"Sandy. She told me how Sophie wouldn't be calm ... until you held her. And Anna and Max. They said it, too. Max might have helped, but you kept everyone going. No matter what."

"Funny. But that's exactly what I'd say about you."

She shakes her head. "No. It's different." Then she says, "Remember Sugarbush?"

He doesn't say anything for a second, then, "Well, when you look back on it, that could have been one of the most reckless things I ever did in my life. Sometimes there's a fine line between being the hero and simply acting without thinking."

"Not reckless, Chris. I remember. Coming around that curve and seeing ... that little boy. How small he looked lying in the snow ... what was he, seven, eight?"

"Eight. And he should never have been on that trail in the first place."

"But he *was* there. Hurt. Everyone hysterical. The boy's father. The person who'd run into him ... and was hurt himself. And nobody *doing* anything. Until you did."

"Two years of med school helped. I could tell he was in trouble, that his breathing was difficult. There was blood coming out of his ears."

"Yes," she says, "but you didn't panic. I froze solid. Should we move him? Or not? You just picked him up. Skied off down the mountain."

"Well, the kid was getting colder by the second. His skin was turning blue. I just wanted to get him the hell out of there to someplace where he could get help."

"But that's what I mean. You *acted*. The rest of us ... fell in behind. *You* saved his life."

He looks around the room.

"What?" she says.

"Isn't this where the music comes in? You know, the kind that makes your heart swell."

She gives a very feeble punch to his leg. "Take the compliment, okay? And I had a little ... talk with Anna ... yesterday before you came. Well, mostly *she* did the talking. She told me about that first night ... when she came to dinner. You drove her back to the dorm? She said you told her ... one thing. That you sent me away once. And I had ... forgiven you for that."

He clears his throat. "I said that, huh?"

"You know you said that. So the way I see it ... you did the right thing on the mountain ... the right thing with Anna ... the right thing for Sophie. And you'll do the right thing ... always for us." And then she yawns hugely. "I just talked way too much."

Sophie sneezes, starts to cry, and Lily puts her arms out. "I want to cuddle her before I fall asleep."

Chris picks Sophie up and deposits her in Lily's arms.

"Did you sneeze so hard?" Lily says, in that same sing-song way Anna talks to Sophie. "It's not nice, is it ... that you had to wake up when you were *so* sound asleep."

Sophie opens her eyes wide, looks at Lily, and then she does it. Just like he told her to. She smiles. An unmistakable smile that's much bigger and lasts much longer than the smile she gave him that morning. A smile that makes you want to jump up and touch the ceiling.

"Oh!" Lily says. "Are you smiling? Smiling at Mommy? Oh, Sophie. The most beautiful smile I've ever seen."

He takes a mental picture of what he sees. Of a singular connection taking place. Of Lily holding Sophie, talking to her as he imagined she would, of Sophie looking back at Lily as though she's the only person in the world.

CHAPTER THIRTY

Lily comes home on a brilliant September day with a clean bill of health and an ice cream cone in her hand.

"I've been dreaming about soft-serve," she tells him, as she's wheeled out the hospital door toward the car he left parked at the curb. "Vanilla and chocolate swirl, dipped in chocolate."

So he takes a detour on the way home and she gets what she's been dreaming about.

He gets what he's been dreaming about, too. Lily in the back seat with Sophie, talking to her, crooning, laughing. "I think she has your eyes and my nose," Lily says. "And maybe my chin."

Lily's scar is invisible now; her hair, about a half-inch long; the shape of her head, perfect. Anna brought three scarves yesterday, and one, a mass of orange pink purple, is wrapped around Lily's head, its two ends hanging down her back.

"I look like a wreck," she said, before they left the hospital.

"You look fantastic," he told her. "Long hair, short hair, no hair. You're a knock-out."

She'd put her arms around him. "Keep talking like that and I just may have to marry you again."

He's taking the rest of the week off. Yesterday, he brought Sophie to campus. Two of his lectures gave him a standing ovation when he walked in. The first one made Sophie cry. The second one, she seemed to expect. If she grew up to be a performer, he'd know why. The seminar people were prepared with a bottle of champagne. The fact that Lily was okay was ringing across campus like bells.

Ken had come in with tears in his eyes and a promise of food for at least another month. They'd suffered with him and now they were celebrating with him. And, aside from the first applause,

Sophie had taken it all with aplomb, a few kicks, and a bout of hiccoughs.

But today is just for the three of them. No plan, no problems, no worries.

The banner Max and Anna hung from the front porch ceiling last night comes into view half-way up the driveway. WELCOME HOME LILY, MOM, MOMMY.

"Did you help do that?" Lily asks Sophie.

Inside, there are flowers everywhere. A bunch of vari-colored helium balloons is tied to the stair railing, some reading IT'S A GIRL! others, CONGRATULATONS! The dining room table is heaped with gifts; baby gifts, judging from the riot of pink wrapping paper. And Chris notices that the kitchen has gone through a transformation — no dishes in the sink, the counters cleared and spotless, and the heaping basket of dirty baby clothes he'd left in the mud room is gone.

The refrigerator is full of food —orange juice, eggs, butter, yogurt, fruit, cheese— all the things he'd been meaning to pick up before Lily came home, but hadn't.

Not to mention a plastic-wrapped plate of sandwiches and a freshly-made pitcher of lemonade.

"Tell me you didn't do all this yourself," Lily says, stopping to read the cards attached to each vase, deciding to save the gifts for later.

"I think," he says, "the place was a shambles when I left this morning."

"Oh good," she says. "A Chris with no short-comings at all would be a little too impossible."

"I'm totally possible," he says. "As I recall, the diaper genie had been over-filled since Sunday and there were no more clean glasses or bowls in the cupboards. I was going to run the dishwasher before I left but I forgot."

"Who?" she says, looking around.

"I have no idea. But to do it all in less than three hours took a crew."

"Leprechauns," she says.

"At this point, nothing would surprise me." He looks at Lily. "You should sit down. It's been a big morning."

She shakes her head. "No. I feel wonderful." Then she sweeps through the house because she says she needs to see all over again how absolutely marvelous it is. He leaves Sophie asleep in her carrier and follows Lily. Every room is in perfect order. Sophie's clothes all folded nicely in her bureau drawers, extra packages of diapers stacked beneath the changing table. Their bed is made, and, he guesses, the sheets changed for the first time in two weeks.

"It's a little embarrassing," he says. "I'd guess I'd gotten used to the chaos."

"You took care of the important stuff," she says, putting her arms around him.

Sophie dictates the rest of the day. Lily takes one feeding, Chris the next. Chris gives Sophie a bath. Lily dries her off and dresses her. When she sleeps, they lay down on the bed together, Lily dozing, Chris looking at his sleeping wife and his sleeping daughter.

That night in bed, they lie pressed together, shoulders, arms, hips, legs. He takes her hand and they intertwine fingers and hold on tight.

"I guess I'm going to owe you for at least the rest of my life," she says.

"And that will be for...?"

"Oh ... for making you worry about me, for making you very sad, for forcing you to become a single father overnight. For all the poopy diapers and the burping and the bottles and no sleep. For making you take care of everyone all by yourself." She stops. "Is that enough?"

"There's the endless hours of walking and jiggling, the smelling like sour milk. But then on the other hand there's the fact that I have a daughter named Sophie, who seems to think I'm okay. And a wife who talks and walks and holds my hand under the covers. I'd say maybe we're even."

"Were you really scared, Chris?"

"Terrified."

"Of Sophie?"

"Yes. At first. Though she was pretty good at teaching me what to do. And I was beyond terrified at the thought of losing you. Don't ever do that again, okay?"

"Okay."

"But … say you *did* owe me. Even though you don't. But if you *did* … exactly how would you pay that debt? If there *were* a debt, which there isn't, of course, but just saying there were."

She laughs. "We'd just have to use our imaginations."

"Indefinitely?"

"For as long as the debt remained."

"It would be a gargantuan debt. If it existed."

"I know."

He turns his head on the pillow. "You have no idea how much I've missed you."

"Tell me how much."

"Achingly. Endlessly. Incessantly. Continually. Longingly.

"That's a lot of adverbs."

"You're a lot of Lily. And there's more. With all my heart. My soul. My brain. My lungs. My…"

She starts to laugh. "That's enough. I get it. I get it."

Sophie makes a noise and they go still. "I think it wasn't a wake-up noise," he says, "just a *dreaming about waking up later noise*."

"I have to learn all those noises. I have to learn who Sophie is."

"If it took me two weeks; it should take you less than a day. And once you've got it, maybe I can leave for a couple of hours?"

"You're already tiring of us?"

"I have to get back to the gym. I think I'll add an extra day."

"Four days a week?"

"Anything that will help. I mean, do you realize how long I have to live now?"

She turns, pats him on the shoulder, snuggles against him. "It's okay, gramps," she says. "We'll just take it one day at a time." Then she sighs and her breath is warm on his skin. "Tell me a story, Chris."

"After that remark, you expect a story?"

"Mmm-hmm," she says.

He thinks about it for a second. "Remember the queen and the king?"

She nods against his chest.

"And that rift that separated them for a long time?"

She nods again.

"Well, they couldn't believe it, but it happened a second time. Not for as long as that first separation, but it took them completely by surprise. And the king, at least, almost abandoned hope, thinking everything was lost. But the queen was very wise, and before they were separated, she gave the king the most precious thing she had. It was his job to guard it, and because of that, even though he was devastated over losing his queen, he couldn't give up. The queen had no magic, and she had to fight her way home all by herself, but because she was so special, so strong and determined, she began to find her way home little by little, while all the king could do was wait. That magnificent queen fought until she was reunited with the king and the precious thing she'd left in his care. And this time they really did live happily ever after."

"Mmmm," she sighs.

He's still awake long after she's asleep. He decides he's going to ask Max to take a photo of Lily and Anna and Sophie together. Lily will resist, she'll want to wait until her hair has grown to some reasonable length. And he supposes it could wait until December.

But if he can talk her into doing it now, he will. He wants another photo to balance out the one already on the mantel. Proof of what's possible.

He thinks if the angels ask him to remember the most perfect moment in his life, he'll have a hard time choosing among some of the moments of the last three days, but this may well be it. Lily beside him again, the relaxed, even motion of her breathing, the warmth of her hand still in his. Sophie in her crib just a few feet away.

He knows life is fragile; happiness, like quicksilver; love, too often misunderstood and unreliable. He learned that early. Learned to live on the outside of those things. To only trust himself and take nothing more than he was willing to give. And it had worked. Kept the mistake from happening again. Kept life simple. Until this woman lying beside him came along.

Before Lily, he realizes now, he'd given up. But she wouldn't stand for that. And now he knows that despite losing Lily once and almost losing her again, he's the luckiest man in the world. Because five minutes with this woman lying beside him makes up for everything else. Five minutes with Lily makes everything worthwhile.

So no matter what happens ahead, he's already on the plus side.

Lily sighs in her sleep, and he turns his head, presses his lips against her temple. "*ya zdes', lyubov moya,*" he whispers. *I'm here, my love.*

BOOKS BY THE AUTHOR

SHORT STORY COLLECTIONS
AFTERNOON DELIGHT BOOK I
AFTERNOON DELIGHT BOOK II
AFTERNOON DELIGHT BOOK III
AFTERNOON DELIGHT BOOK IV
AFTERNOON DELIGHT BOOK V
COW HORMONES

NOVELS
CLICK
DON'T LOOK DOWN
A DANCE WITH THE DEVIL
PAYBACK
LOVE CANAL
RIDDLE
STINKBUG
50 ACRES MORE OR LESS
MOON OF THE DARK RED CALVES

www.ingramcontent.com/pod-product-compliance
Lightning Source LLC
Chambersburg PA
CBHW022001170626
46808CB00001B/252